## Praise for the novels of Michelle Major

"A dynamic start to a series
with a refreshingly original premise."
—*Kirkus Reviews* on *The Magnolia Sisters*

"A sweet start to a promising series,
perfect for fans of Debbie Macomber."
—*Publishers Weekly* (starred review)
on *The Magnolia Sisters*

"*The Magnolia Sisters* is sheer delight,
filled with humor, warmth and heart....
I loved everything about it."
—*New York Times* bestselling author RaeAnne Thayne

"This enjoyable romance is perfect for voracious
readers who want to dive into a new small-town series."
—*Library Journal* on *The Magnolia Sisters*

# MICHELLE MAJOR

# Wedding Season

HQN

Recycling programs
for this product may
not exist in your area.

ISBN-13: 978-1-335-48000-2

Wedding Season
Copyright © 2022 by Michelle Major

Springtime in Carolina
Copyright © 2022 by Michelle Major

For questions and comments about the quality of this book,
please contact us at CustomerService@Harlequin.com.

HQN
22 Adelaide St. West, 41st Floor
Toronto, Ontario M5H 4E3, Canada
www.Harlequin.com

Printed and bound in Barcelona, Spain by CPI Black Print

# CONTENTS

# WEDDING SEASON

To my sister and all the amazing educators out there.
Thank you for the difference you make—
I appreciate you.

# CHAPTER ONE

Runaway bride alert. Spotted at Sunnyside. R u downtown?

MARIELLA JACOB MUTTERED a single swear word then thumbed in a response to the 911 text she'd just received from her business partner, Emma Cantrell.

On it.

She gripped her phone and moved toward the front door of A Second Chance, the retail boutique she owned in Magnolia, North Carolina, population just enough to make things interesting.

"I've got to do a quick errand," she called to Jasmin Augustine, the young woman who worked for her.

"Everything okay?" the petite brunette asked.

"Right as rain," Mariella confirmed. At least she was going to do her best to make sure today's scheduled wedding stayed that way.

Luckily, she'd worn espadrilles instead of her usual heels to work, so she practically jogged down Main Street toward the town's popular Sunnyside Bakery.

If someone had told Mariella when she'd moved to Magnolia three years earlier that she'd end up back in the wedding business, she would have laughed in that person's face. Then punched them in the throat.

At one time, weddings had been her life. She'd built a career as a dress designer, creating gowns for everyone from uptown socialites to Hollywood A-listers to various daughters of royal families throughout both Europe and Asia. At the height of her popularity, a custom Belle Vie gown could go for upwards of six figures. Brides—and their wealthy parents—lined up to pay that kind of money for the privilege of wearing one of Mariella's creations.

One monumentally bad decision made after half a bottle of top-shelf vodka plus a few glasses of red wine thrown in for good measure had wrecked Mariella's world, not to mention her heart.

She preferred not to think about her heart.

The irony that she was the last person who had any business counseling a bride with cold feet wasn't lost on her, but she didn't break stride.

Her life was different than it used to be, and most of the changes suited Mariella just fine. The biggest difference was that in Magnolia she had real friends, her two partners at the Wildflower Inn, Emma Cantrell and Angi Guilardi, being the best of them.

Emma hadn't necessarily set out to make the inn one of the premier wedding destination spots in North Carolina, but thanks to a high-profile event the three of them had planned last year, the Wildflower Inn was quickly gaining that reputation. Mariella understood better than most the importance of the right image, and word getting out that one of their brides had jumped ship on the way to the altar wasn't the vision any of them wanted to project.

She took several deep inhales to control her breathing as she approached the bakery and then walked into the cheery shop with a serene smile plastered across her face.

Mary Ellen, the bakery's longtime owner, made eye contact from behind the counter and inclined her head toward one of the café tables.

As if Mariella could have missed the woman chowing down on what looked to be a baker's dozen donuts while wearing an elaborate wedding gown, complete with a bejeweled bodice and a ridiculously long train.

She approached the table slowly, trying not to cringe as a dollop of strawberry jelly dribbled off the woman's chin to land smack dab in the middle of her lap. A white wedding dress and jelly did not mix well.

"Hi," Mariella said as she slid into the chair across from the woman. "Suzette, right?"

The bride's green eyes narrowed. "You're from the inn."

"I'm Mariella. We met when we were planning the decorations. The tree branch centerpieces were my idea."

"The centerpieces are beautiful." The bride, who'd remain dry-eyed up until this point based on her impeccably done makeup, sniffed. "I love the little fairy lights wrapped around them. When James proposed, it was on the balcony of one of our favorite restaurants in Raleigh. They had the same sort of twinkle lights. It was supposed to remind us of how far we'd come. And now..."

"You've made it as far as the bakery." Mariella reached across the table and plucked the half-eaten donut from the woman's manicured fingers. "There's still time for you to enjoy those fairy lights."

The bride, Suzette, shook her head. "I can't go back." She looked miserable and heartbroken, which Mariella figured was better than angry and bitter. When she'd hurled the three-carat engagement ring at her fiancé's cheating head, she'd been all fiery temper. The heartbreak had truly set in later, along with a healthy dose of humiliation.

"Tell me why. I remember you and your fiancé. Emma

has been on a wedding roll, but the two of you stood out. Trust me, I've seen a lot of brides. I have a good sense for who's going to go the distance. I'd bet on the two of you."

The woman gave a watery smile. "Me, too," she agreed. "James is a great guy. I'm lucky. That's why I can't go through with it."

"Maybe all the carbs are messing with your brain cells." Mariella picked up a napkin from the table and dabbed at the corner of Suzette's mouth, which was caked with powdered sugar. "I understand a bride who hits the dusty trail before the wedding because their husband-to-be is a jerk, not someone who's snagged a great guy."

"I'm the jerk, and I don't deserve him. I don't deserve to be this happy."

"What makes you think that, honey?" Mariella's phone buzzed, but she ignored it. Out of the corner of her eye, she could see Emma at the window of the bakery. The Wildflower Inn wasn't far from downtown. She gave an almost imperceptible shake of her head. There was something this bride needed to tell her. If Emma burst in now, Suzette might clam up again and take off before they could salvage her day.

Once again, Mariella marveled at the fact that she was the one trying to save a wedding as opposed to wrecking it.

Suzette's mouth pinched into a thin line. "There's something he doesn't know about me. About my past."

"I saw the way that man looks at you. I can't imagine there's anything you could tell him that would make a difference."

"I'm not who he thinks I am."

Mariella had seen and heard a lot in her day, but she might be in over her head on this one. Then she thought about Emma as well as Angi, who had given up the security of working in her family's Italian restaurant to manage catering for the inn. How much every event meant to each of them. She would not let down her friends. She'd let down too many people in her life already.

"Are you a spy? Or a serial killer? Because I can see how that would be a deal breaker for some people."

"I'm adopted," Suzette whispered as if she were sharing something way worse than body parts in the freezer.

Mariella's heart gave a little thud, but she reminded herself that this was about the troubled bride and not her own regrettable past. "Is your biological father a serial killer?" she asked quietly.

Suzette huffed out a humorless laugh. "I don't know my biological father, and I've only met my mother once. I tried to track them down when James and I got engaged. It's only fair that he knows where I come from. I wanted to know, too."

"What happened?" Mariella's heart was accelerating at an alarming clip. "What did you find?"

"Nothing about my father. But I tracked down the woman who gave birth to me. I refuse to call her my mother because she wants nothing to do with me even now. She wouldn't even talk to me."

"I'm sorry."

Suzette gave a shaky nod. "I couldn't tell James. What would he think of me? Why would he want to be with a woman who is so unwanted even after twenty-seven years?"

"Your birth mother's actions have nothing to do with you." It was easy for Mariella to say those words with complete conviction. "I met your parents the day you toured the inn. Your mom was thrilled to see you so happy. You have a family who loves you. You have a fiancé who loves you."

"I'm not worthy of that love. If he knew—"

"It doesn't change a thing."

Mariella looked up as her runaway bride gasped. The groom in his black tux and white cummerbund stood at the side of the table.

"There's nothing that could make me not love you, Suzie-Q. Even you running away on our wedding day."

A soft sob escaped Suzette. "I'm doing it for your benefit. You should be with somebody amazing."

"I am."

Mariella glanced around and realized everyone in the bakery was staring at them. But James was oblivious to anyone except Suzette.

He dropped to his knee in front of her. "You are the love of my life. You are the woman I want to grow old with. I wish you would have told me sooner since it was important to you, but it doesn't make a difference. I love the person you are. I love you. I don't care about what happened in the past. Just please don't give up on our future."

Mariella wasn't a crier, but even she dabbed at the corner of one eye as Suzette threw herself into her beloved's arms.

"I'm sorry I didn't tell you. I'm sorry I didn't have more faith in us. I just felt so worthless when she rejected me again."

"That woman doesn't deserve to have you in her life, sweetheart. Your real parents are waiting back at the inn along with our family and friends. We love you. I love you."

Emma stepped forward, offering Mariella a grateful nod.

"I think this love story deserves a true happily-ever-after in the form of the most amazing wedding and reception you can imagine. Shall we all head back to the Wildflower?"

Suzette smiled, then her face crumpled as she glanced down at her dress. "I've ruined it," she said with a sniff.

Mariella stood. "I can fix this." She untied the fabric that wound around the bride's waist and then covered the jelly stain before making a bow out of the excess tulle. "You're perfect. The most perfect bride who ever was."

She didn't mention the slightly smudged makeup or the bits of powdered sugar still clinging to Suzette's chin. Emma would handle that. Mary Ellen led the bakery patrons in a round of applause. Emma walked the couple out of the shop amid supportive cheers and loaded them into the inn's bright white van.

"I think you deserve a congratulatory muffin for that," Mary Ellen said from behind the counter. "You did an amazing job helping that sweet girl. They're probably going to name their firstborn daughter after you."

"That was better than bingeing a whole season of *90 Day Fiancé*," one of the customers nearest Mariella agreed.

She blew out an unsteady breath and pressed a hand to her stomach. Suzette's revelations might not have made a difference to her fiancé, but they'd rocked Mariella's world.

*Leave the past where it belongs*, she told herself. *You made the best decision you could at the time.*

"Any blueberry muffins left?" she asked Mary Ellen, forcing her voice to remain steady.

"I have a fresh batch in the back," the bakery owner answered and disappeared into the shop's kitchen.

Mariella began to clean up the remains of Suzette's donut massacre then stopped when the little hairs on the back of her neck stood on end.

"You really have this town fooled."

The deep, rumbly voice scratched across her nerves like sandpaper. It was the last voice on the planet she wanted to hear right now, or ever for that matter.

She glanced up into the piercing hazel eyes of Alex Ralsten, the only Magnolia resident who'd known her in her former life. The man who'd seen her at her worst and would never let her forget it.

ALEX RALSTEN STARED into Mariella's summer-sky-blue eyes and tried to let the wave of anger that typically consumed him in her presence overtake him. Anger he could manage. Maybe his reaction to her wouldn't be so intense if his body wasn't painfully attuned to her beauty. From her delicate bone structure to her fair complexion to those blue eyes surrounded by dark lashes. She had shoulder-length blond hair that looked like it would be perfect spread across his pillow.

At the moment her normally lush mouth pursed into a stern line. It was the same look of consternation she always gave him.

When Alex first arrived in Magnolia, he'd enjoyed her reaction. In truth, he hadn't been built for holding a grudge no matter how much he wanted to. No matter how much she deserved it. Even that motivation was fading.

Yes, she'd made a scene at his wedding when she'd revealed his fiancée's infidelity as they stood at the altar with most of Manhattan's social elite watching. The proverbial kick in the pants was the fact that his life being turned upside down had in some ways been a blessing.

Without Mariella's interference, he never would have realized how unhappy he'd been. Not until it was too late anyway. But he wasn't going to give her credit. Somehow he knew deep inside that finally forgiving Mariella and letting his guard down around her could do more damage than any sort of public humiliation.

"I'm doing my job," she said through clenched teeth.

"Spreading your particular brand of pre-wedding joy

and generosity to unsuspecting brides at the Wildflower Inn?" He raised a brow in challenge.

"I've never denied my past." Her chin hitched ever so slightly, and he couldn't help but admire her gumption. She'd lost as much as he had in the aftermath of his wedding day. Maybe more.

Although he wasn't going to let her off the hook. Not now. Not ever.

"The inn is getting a lot of press these days," he continued. "Emma is becoming known as a wedding planner expert. I noticed you've tried to keep your name out of the articles."

If looks could kill, Alex would have been a dead man based on the death glare Mariella leveled at him. But after a moment, her gaze shifted away and he saw her breath hitch.

Damn.

It should have felt like a victory, getting a reaction out of her. Instead, he had the bothersome urge to apologize.

"I've had my share of fame." Her tone was reed-thin and sharp as the crack of a whip. "I have no desire to be front-page news for any reason. But if you're giving some kind of veiled threat that you would try to make me the story, I'd think again. Emma and Angi are well-loved in this community. People aren't going to appreciate my past dragging them down."

She didn't give herself enough credit, and Alex had to admit it made him curious. Had it always been this way, even when she was one of the world's most sought-after bridal gown designers? Did she make herself small as a rule or had that started after the public spectacle of his wedding and her subsequent blacklisting in the fashion and society communities?

"I don't need anyone else to know what you're capable

of, Mariella. As long as you remember the lives you ruined."

She opened her mouth, but before she could answer, the
bakery owner joined them. "A blueberry muffin plus one of
my new coconut and almond butter energy bars for later."

Mary Ellen smiled at Alex. "This one works too many
hours without a break."

He offered Mary Ellen a genuine smile, one that turned
his features from handsome to drop-dead gorgeous. "I
could never forget to stop for lunch."

"I appreciate you taking care of me," Mariella told the
bakery owner as she took the bag.

"Actually, you two have a work ethic in common." Mary
Ellen's gentle, maternal gaze switched between Mariella
and Alex. "I drove by the old mill last night on my way
home from book club. It was after ten, and I saw your car
in the parking lot. It had been there on my way to work as
well. Either you've moved in or you're burning the candle
at both ends."

Alex blinked. He'd been in Magnolia for several months
now but still wasn't used to the way everyone in town
seemed to know each other's business or how people cared
about their neighbors.

"Maybe you need a couple of energy bars as well," Mary
Ellen suggested.

"I'm fine," Alex said automatically. As if fine was the
best he could expect. "There's a lot to take care of with
the company's move to Magnolia. I don't mind the hours."

"You still need to rest." Mary Ellen patted his shoulder.
"I'm glad you've hired Heather. She deserves a chance,
and I think she'll be able to make sure you don't burn out."

"Yeah, she's great." Alex flicked a glance at the door.
"I should go."

"Me, too," Mariella said. "Not with you," she quickly amended with another glare at Alex, earning a chuckle from Mary Ellen.

"I'm going to be watching out for both of you," Mary Ellen said before heading back to the counter.

Alex followed Mariella out onto the sidewalk, where a gentle breeze blew her blond hair away from her face. The scent of citrus and whatever lotion or soap she used curled around him, nearly making his knees go weak.

He needed to get a handle on his reaction to her and remember that they were enemies.

"Who's Heather?" she asked as she turned to face him, looking angrier than ever.

He forced his lips not to curve into a smile. Mariella clearly hated her curiosity when it came to him as much as he detested his own in relation to her. He liked having an effect on her. "My new assistant. She moved to town a few weeks ago and worked at the bakery but has an interest in fashion so was looking for a foot in the door at the Fit Collective. Mary Ellen asked if I'd do her a favor and hire the kid. She's young—just starting college in the fall—but really sharp."

"Some small-town version of *The Devil Wears Prada*?" She gave him a dismissive once-over. "Or Levi's, in this case."

Alex didn't bother to hide his grin. "I'm plenty happy to have traded Brooks Brothers for clothes I can buy at the local hardware store." He let his gaze wander from her cashmere sweater to the leather capris she wore. "Nice shoes, by the way."

"You still don't belong here." She crossed her arms over her chest, and he commanded himself not to notice her body, perfect as it was.

"That makes two of us, and yet here we are."

"I was here first," she muttered. He'd heard the argument before, but it didn't sway him.

"You're not running me off, Mariella. I needed a fresh start, and this is the place I've picked for my home."

"My plan was to leave the past behind me. You are a physical reminder of so many mistakes I've made."

"I can't say that upsets me too much," he lied. It didn't make sense, but he hated that he made her so uncomfortable. Hated even more that sometimes he'd purposely drive by her shop to get a glimpse of her through the picture window. Talk about a glutton for punishment.

She let out a low growl. "You are an infuriating man. Stubborn and callous. I don't even know if you have a heart."

"Funny." He kept his voice steady even as memories flooded him, making his head pound. "That's the rationale Amber gave me for why she cheated with your fiancé. My lack of emotions pushed her into his arms. What was his excuse?"

She looked out at the street for nearly a minute, and Alex wondered if she was even going to answer. He followed her gaze to the park across the street, situated in the center of the town. There were kids at the playground and several families walking dogs on the path that circled the perimeter. Magnolia was the perfect place to raise a family.

If a person had the heart to be that kind of a man—the type who married the woman he loved and set out to be a good husband and father. Alex wasn't cut out for a family, but he liked it in the small coastal town just the same.

"I was too committed to my job," she said suddenly and so quietly he almost missed it.

"Ironic since it was your job that introduced him to Amber."

"Yeah." She made a face. "This is what I'm talking about, Alex. A past I don't want to revisit."

"Then stay away from me, Mariella," he advised. "Because I'm not going anywhere."

"Then maybe I will," she said and walked away.

# CHAPTER TWO

"YOU'RE NOT LEAVING."

"No way."

"You belong in Magnolia. Who is Alex Ralsten to suggest you don't?"

Mariella tried to smile at Emma and Angi as they stood in the Wildflower Inn's bright kitchen later that night but her face wouldn't cooperate.

She appreciated the solidarity of her two best friends, even though it still surprised her that they would feel any loyalty.

Growing up on the south side of Philadelphia, the only daughter of a single mom who was rarely sober, Mariella hadn't made friends easily. She learned early on not to trust anyone but herself, and eventually her demons had gotten bad enough that even she wasn't reliable.

The one thing she'd had was an intense desire to get out of her life and the poverty that she knew. She'd spent hours in her local library poring over fashion and specifically bridal magazines. It was a different world than the one she knew. Clean and white and brimming with possibilities. That's what she wanted.

One of the older women in the cramped apartment complex where she lived had given her a sewing machine and taught her how to use it. She'd put together a portfolio that, thanks to her socioeconomic situation, landed her a scholarship to Parsons School of Design once she got her GED.

Her mom hadn't believed she had it in her to make something of herself or escape the nightmare of their life until Mariella had walked out the door and not returned.

For a while, it had been touch and go whether she would actually survive given where she came from and her riotous self-destructive streak. There had been some near misses thanks to her penchant for partying with the wrong crowd. Plus, a string of loser boyfriends and their callous treatment had almost convinced her to give up.

But she kept pushing forward with her eye on the prize and her heart locked up tight. She stopped partying and worked harder than anybody in her class and channeled her dream of a romantic fantasy into dresses that made women believe their perfect lives were attainable.

She was like some modern version of Rumpelstiltskin, spinning hay into gold. The blackness that had been planted in her soul and the shame she felt at what she'd had to do and give up to make her dreams come true had poisoned her from the inside out.

In some ways, she didn't blame her former fiancé. Yes, he was a cheating jerk-wad, but she was at her core unlovable and it had been her folly to believe she could be anything else.

Her friends in Magnolia saw her as someone different. They didn't seem to care about her rough edges but saw the person she desperately wanted to be without knowing how to embody it. They believed she was already that person and who was she to tell them any different?

"He didn't specifically suggest it, more of an implication that this town isn't big enough for the two of us. I just wish he would go away." She shook her head. "I don't want to leave Magnolia."

"You're. Not. Leaving." Angi Guilardi wagged a finger in Mariella's direction. "I'll have words with hoity-toity Alex if I have to."

Angi was an Italian spitfire, and she and Mariella had butted heads over and over when they'd first met. The two of them were like twin sides of the same coin, Emma would have said.

Emma was the glue that held their unlikely trio together. She came from a prominent, wealthy family, the kind of old-money people Mariella's business had catered to for years. Old or new money hadn't mattered when they were ordering a custom gown from Belle Vie.

But Emma had wanted something different, and she'd created a new life for herself in Magnolia. She'd taken a dilapidated mansion and with the help of her contractor fiancé, Cam Arlinghaus, she'd turned the Wildflower Inn into something amazing.

Mariella had practically forced Emma to partner with her. There was something about the restoration of the old house and the new life it was gaining that spoke to Mariella. She'd walked by late one night and immediately felt a deep desire to be a part of it.

She hadn't actually wanted to work with Angi but now she couldn't imagine her life without the creative chef. Without either of these women.

"You're right," she agreed. "I'm not leaving, but Alex is going to be a big part of this community. The Fit Collective has already brought dozens of new residents into town, and I know how it goes with corporations when they pick a headquarters. He's going to sponsor events and add value in ways that I can't. Besides, other than to me, he's a really nice person."

Emma inclined her head. "Are you worried that he's going to be more popular than you?"

"I'm worried that he's going to find a way to belong in Magnolia in a way I'm simply not capable of. People are bound to be reminded that I share a history with him. One where I ruined his life."

"His fiancée was cheating on him," Angi said. "She's the one who ruined his life."

"I publicly humiliated him."

Mariella still couldn't specifically call to mind the details of her tirade, although the images were stamped across her mind like a tattoo. One of the wedding guests had filmed the whole thing and uploaded it to YouTube. Alex's ex-fiancée was an A-list Hollywood actress. America's sweetheart, Amber Turner. Their wedding was to be the thing of fairy tales and probably would have made the cover of *People* magazine. Instead, grainy photos of an angry Mariella had been splashed across both mainstream magazines and the seedier gossip sites.

Yes, Amber had been the villain, but she'd used her powerful PR machine and her public image to turn the tables and make Mariella the bad guy.

It had been a hard lesson. But Mariella understood she was never meant to be the heroine of anyone's story, even her own.

"Seeing him makes me reconsider all the reasons I chose Magnolia for my new start. I don't want the past to poison my current life."

"We won't let that happen," Emma promised. She reached across the counter to squeeze Mariella's fingers.

"That's right." Angi nodded. "We've got your back. You

are part of this town now. Don't let anybody chase you away."

"Maybe I need to be a silent partner for this wedding season?" Mariella could see the disappointment in both of her friends' faces, but she wouldn't back down on this point. "The Wildflower is getting more and more press, and I don't want to taint the narrative. My reputation is going to drag you down."

"That's not true," Emma insisted. "I can name at least three brides who partially chose the inn as a destination because it meant they'd get to work with you on their wedding dresses. You have a gift, Mariella. Both for designing fashion and for creating perfect days."

Mariella chuckled at that. "Nothing about me is perfect."

Angi picked up her phone from the counter, hit a few buttons and then pushed the device in front of Mariella's face. "You're wrong. This is the photo from last week's wedding."

Mariella smiled. "She looks happy."

"And confident and beautiful," Emma added. "I think some of that confidence comes from the fact that she feels beautiful in the dress you designed for her."

Mariella's return to design had started with the first wedding they'd hosted and Holly Adams, the bride. She was a Magnolia native who married into a political family akin to the Kennedys in their power and reputation. She'd been so nervous and worried about presenting the right image.

Mariella hadn't planned to have anything to do with bridal fashion when she was fired from her own company. Walking away from what she'd built had left a hole in her soul and barely a shred of creativity, not to mention dignity. But she hadn't been able to resist helping sweet and guileless Holly. Because that wedding had gotten national attention, Mariella had also received notice. She'd ignored the reporters who'd reached out for interviews asking if she was trying to make a comeback in the fashion world.

In the age of online oversharing, there was no rock she could truly hide under. A number of the direct messages she'd received had been from prospective brides who told her how much it meant to them that she cared about making an ordinary woman feel beautiful on her wedding day.

Several of the missives had touched her deeply. The desire to make women feel their best as they started a new chapter in their lives had been one of the things that had driven her in her career.

She'd selectively agreed to work with a few brides, but that didn't mean she wanted the same kind of big career she'd had before.

"I love working with the Wildflower brides to create their perfect gowns." She took the phone from Angi's hand and placed it screen side down on the counter. "But I can't handle more publicity or press right now. I want to live a quiet life. It's all I can manage at the moment."

She hated admitting that but would not lie to her friends. She'd told more lies and half-truths during her downward spiral than she cared to admit. Too many people had been hurt, and she wouldn't take the chance of doing that again.

She winced as Emma and Angi shared a concerned look. "Is it your sobriety?" Emma asked after a moment. "If you're worried about losing control—"

"I'm not going to drink again," Mariella promised. It was a promise she made every day. A vow she'd taken at the rehab center where she'd landed after her life imploded. "Or do anything else. I just don't like what Alex makes me feel."

Another shared look between her friends.

"What?" She held up her hands. "You two understand that I see you making faces, right?"

"You and Alex," Emma murmured. "What's the deal there?"

"Nothing is going on with Alex. We've had nothing to do with each other since the moment I ruined his wedding day." She pointed a finger at each of her friends. "And if the two of you make eye contact with each other one more time we're going to have issues."

"No eye contact," Emma promised.

Angi wiggled the feathery brows that framed her espresso-colored eyes. "But you can't deny the sparks between the two of you."

Mariella felt her mouth drop open. "He might wish he could shoot fire out of his eyes toward me, but no sparks. None."

"Definitely sparks." Emma nodded. "I'm an expert on sparks."

"I agree," Angi said. "He looks at you in a certain way."

"Like I make his stomach upset." Mariella rolled her shoulders as she glanced toward the gleaming tile backsplash when she couldn't quite meet Emma and Angi's speculative gazes. She didn't like the direction this conversation was going and had no intention of admitting, even to her two best friends, the way butterflies flitted through her chest every time she looked at Alex. At least when he wasn't outwardly glaring at her. The angry stares kind of put a damper on the butterfly wings.

He was a handsome man. Thick chestnut-hued hair stylishly cut with a lock that had a tendency to flop into his face, and gorgeous hazel eyes. Tall and solid with just the right amount of muscles and an air of confidence that pulled people to him like a magnet. Her reaction was nothing more than having a pulse.

"Remember Gabe and I didn't have the greatest history when we started." Angi looked down at the sapphire ring that adorned her left hand with a dreamy expression almost comically out of character for her.

Mariella knew that was what love could do to a person, but she and Alex certainly weren't headed in that direction. "You and Gabe had a falling-out as teenagers. Alex had to leave his life behind because of the scene I made at his wedding. It's hardly the same thing."

"It's a connection, and that's a start." Angi clearly wasn't convinced that Mariella and Alex were akin to oil and water. "I can't help but wonder if that's what has you so riled up over him."

"I'm not riled up."

Emma made a face. "I hate to be the one to point this out but your eyebrow is twitching."

Mariella lifted two fingers to the offending brow and willed her face to cooperate. "I'm leaving now because you two annoy the snot out of me."

Angi grinned. "Can I offer you a tissue?"

"Can I offer you my foot up your—"

"Enough you two." Emma choked out a laugh. "Mariella, if you don't want your name mentioned during the spring bridal events, we'll respect that. I'll even take your bio off the events page of the website, although I'm proud to have you as a partner."

Mariella's snit of temper disappeared. She loved her little retail boutique and had enough in savings from her former career that money wasn't a driving factor in her job. But working with Emma and Angi at the inn was one of her proudest accomplishments. They'd built it together, and she didn't want to give it up.

"I think it's a good idea, but I'm still committed to doing my part. Once Alex gets bored running his little athleisure operation or realizes he misses the big city or his stepfather calls him back to take over the family business, things will get back to normal around here."

"What if he doesn't leave?" Angi asked. "And don't start that nonsense about you being the one to walk away."

"I won't for now." Mariella shrugged and fought the urge to nibble on her fingernails. She'd given up nail-biting as a nervous habit years ago and wouldn't give any man the satisfaction of making her feel weak and anxious. "I'm just going to lay low and do everything I can to make sure Alex Ralsten and I don't cross paths."

ALEX SAT AT his desk the following afternoon as Fit Collective employees filed out on the way home or to wherever they were headed at the end of the day.

The company's new headquarters was situated on the east side of Magnolia. The surrounding area was mostly rural, and Alex had plans to develop a series of walking paths in the forest that bordered the property. He'd worked with a designer to create a space that would promote both productivity and a sense of community.

There were common work spaces for each of the departments as well as comfortable seating and nooks for employees who wanted a relaxed atmosphere.

To be honest, he knew very little about women's fashion, particularly high-end athletic garb, but he'd been waiting years for the chance to run a company the way he believed would lead to long-term success and productivity.

As the stepson of a successful hotelier, Alex had been

expected to join the ranks of his mom's husband's company. She wanted him to prove his loyalty to the man who'd married a divorced, disgraced aging socialite.

Although Peter Stark hadn't been as much of a jackass as Alex's real father, he'd only been interested in his wife's son from her first marriage until their own son had been born.

Sure, Alex could have continued to work as part of the hotel chain's upper management staff with the implicit understanding the power and control would always belong to either his father or his younger brother, Jonathan. Alex could develop as many plans for innovation and improvements as he wanted, but none of it would truly make a difference. His place in the world had been mapped out for him the moment his half brother drew a first breath.

He'd fallen in love with starlet Amber Turner when they'd met at a fundraiser at the New York City Opera. She'd been wild, untamed and enough of a rebellion from his mother's expectations to pique his interest. They'd had their goals for a family and future in common—a solid foundation to build on, or at least that's what he'd thought. At that point, he'd still believed that if he proved himself often enough, his stepdad might give him a real chance at contributing to the business.

Amber was often away on movie sets, but at the start of their second year of dating, she'd been hired for a series filmed in New York City. Suddenly, they were together like a regular couple, which was both good and bad as far as Alex was concerned. Also both positive and negative in that his mother had accepted Amber into the family. In the age of social media, her worldwide popularity trumped pedigree, even for Genevieve Ralsten Stark, the snobbiest of the Upper East Side snobs once her second marriage had reinstalled her on her well-heeled pedestal.

Alex had caved to the pressure of putting a ring on Amber's finger despite a few lingering doubts, figuring that in his early thirties, he was due for his trip to the altar with the woman he loved. Maybe he'd also been due to have his life turned upside down.

"I'm heading out unless you need anything else."

He blinked away his familiar ruminations on life as Heather Garrison, the young assistant he'd hired at the recommendation of Mary Ellen from the bakery, appeared in the doorway.

"All fine here," he answered although he hadn't truly felt fine in a long time. "It's supposed to be a gorgeous weekend. Don't spend too much time studying."

"I have a huge project to turn in next week for statistics." Heather mock cringed then tucked a strand of long blond hair behind one ear. "Gosh, I hate statistics."

He smiled. "Understandable."

"But I'm going to work on my laptop outside. That counts, right?"

He liked Heather and appreciated her drive and determination. She was only eighteen but already halfway through her undergraduate degree. Something about a combination of homeschooling and taking college-level classes for the past couple of years. He couldn't imagine being so focused and mature at such a young age. Was it weird to be jealous of a teenager because she had her life more figured out than he did?

"If it works for you. Good luck. I'll see you on Monday."

"Have a nice weekend." She waved then disappeared as he turned his attention back to his computer.

A knock at the door had him lifting his head.

"You know that hanging around the office doesn't count as a nice weekend?"

"I'm trying to impress the boss," he said, one side of his mouth quirking, as Luann Bowman entered his office.

The sixtysomething founder of the Fit Collective chuckled, her voice low and throaty. "We're partners, Alex. Equals and you well know it. In fact, you're the CEO. You have the power. You could push me out if you wanted to."

Her gray hair was pulled back into a low knot and she wore what Alex had come to think of as her uniform—Fit Collective leggings and a drapey blouse. She looked every inch the aging supermodel she was, although her delicate beauty masked a randy sense of humor and will of steel.

"If you really wanted to impress me, you'd take off your shirt, but I can't say that even as a joke."

Alex gripped his skull with both hands and tried to resist the urge to pull out his hair. "Luann, you just said it."

She shrugged. "Yeah but it's only you and me here. You don't count."

"I do count. I'm an employee."

"You're the CEO. I handpicked you myself. Don't tell me I'm offending your delicate sensibilities. Remember, I've known both your father and stepfather for years, Alex. I know the things I say can't be the most shocking you've ever heard."

"That might be true, but it's not the point. We are putting together a new company and leaving behind your former mistakes. We can't take another scandal. You've got to rein in your comments."

She rolled her eyes. "With the way my hormones have fallen off the face of the earth, I don't care about seeing any man-chest. Although I'm sure yours is worthy."

"Luann," he all but shouted.

"I know." She held up her hands as she walked forward and then plopped into the chair in front of his desk. "I'll control myself. I have been controlling myself. It's just you and me right now."

"You can't say those things to me. Do you understand what's at stake?"

Her kohl-lined eyes narrowed. "Trust me, Alex. I am well aware of what's at stake. As well as how much I've already lost. I like you. I like your ideas for the company. Our company. Maybe I'm still bitter about losing control of what I built."

He knew her heart was in the right place, and he wanted to feel sympathetic and supportive. Luann had been at the forefront of turning basic workout gear into something fashionable. She'd started her first company fifteen years earlier after a painful divorce from her fashion designer husband when she was trying to reinvent herself as well as support her daughter.

Her talent for creating styles that made women feel beautiful every day while taking care of business or working out had propelled her company to the forefront of the growing casual fashion market. But two years ago she'd nearly lost everything after a series of cringeworthy and inappropriate social media comments coupled with interviews where she trashed the women who made up the bulk of her clientele. Her company had recently gone public and the board had voted her out unanimously.

But she'd still had a majority percentage of ownership in the company so had remained on staff in a consulting capacity. The board had hired a series of people to step in and run things but no one had been able to overcome the bad press, and other companies had caught up to their niche market, eating away at their brand dominance. They'd eventually pushed her out of the business she'd created.

Alex had run into Luann about eight months after his

wedding day fiasco in a bar in midtown Manhattan. It just so happened that he'd been working with an engineering friend from his days at Wharton to start a company with the other man's design for a new type of workout fabric. One that was lightweight, breathable and also remarkably forgiving and flattering for all body types. He'd mentioned it to Luann and her eyes had lit with possibility.

She might have an unfortunate inability to hold her tongue, but she also truly had a passion for making quality clothes. They'd talked long into the night and she'd convinced him that she realized how damaging her previous comments had been and how much it meant to her to prove to her client base that she appreciated them in all their various shapes and sizes. Together with his engineering friend, they'd decided to launch the Fit Collective.

It had been Alex's idea to headquarter the company in Magnolia. After visiting the town for a friend's wedding he'd become convinced that the move to a small town would attract the kind of employees they needed to build a company with the positive and affirming culture he envisioned. He also thought it was important to get Luann out of the city where her past was always lurking. To say nothing of his own.

He knew it was a risk to partner with her. He'd invested everything he had into this company—time, money and his reputation. She was a creative genius, but despite the fact that he believed she deserved another chance, he wasn't going to let her ruin this for him before it even really started.

"You know the deal," he reminded her. "If there's even a whiff of inappropriate behavior, you're out of this partnership."

Her glossy mouth turned into a pout. "You can't do it without me."

"I'll find a way if I have to." If the past few years had taught him anything, it was that he would manage to move forward no matter what obstacles life threw at him.

# CHAPTER THREE

MARIELLA WAS IN the storeroom of A Second Chance the following week when the insistent knocking started. She ignored it, but whoever was at the shop's front door wasn't going to be deterred.

She glanced at her watch as she made her way to the front of the darkened store. It was 9:00 a.m. so she still had an hour until her official opening for the day and couldn't imagine someone in such desperate need of any of the items she carried in her retail boutique.

The middle-aged woman who stood on the other side of the door looked vaguely familiar although Mariella couldn't place the connection. A gust of wind blew through the open door, making the chimes on a nearby display tinkle in the silence that stretched between Mariella and the stranger. The air was cool, which would change soon as spring gave way to the oppressive heat of summer, but a disconcerting line of sweat pooled at her hairline. There was something about the woman…

"May I help you?" she asked, not bothering to keep the edge from her voice. She treasured her quiet mornings listening to old Joni Mitchell albums and immersing herself in the business side of running her small store.

"It really is you," the woman said with a faint sense of awe. "I'd heard talk around town and even saw your name in the local paper for some wedding you planned, but I didn't believe it."

Mariella froze. She still didn't think she knew the stranger but recognized the stink of wealth and big-city polish written all over the woman despite her casual attire. She had to be someone from Mariella's past. This was the reason she didn't want her name in the public eye anymore. She'd had her brush with fame and had the scars to prove it. They'd mostly mended but sometimes the whisper of a phantom ache felt like legitimate physical pain.

"I'm Luann Bowman," the woman told her. Recognition dawned swift and sudden.

"From the Fit Collective." Alex Ralsten's new business partner and a woman whose fall from fashion grace was as legendary as Mariella's own.

"I wanted to meet you," Luann said. "May I come in?"

Mariella's first reaction was to slam the door in the woman's face. The way Luann studied her was troublesome. Like she knew the guilt and shame Mariella carried deep inside, not just for her outburst at Alex's wedding but the other mistakes she'd made in her life. The ones that were even more shameful.

She didn't want to have anything in common with Luann. They weren't military veterans who could compare war stories like heroes returned from conflict. They were women who had made terrible choices, but Mariella had done her best to bury her feelings about the past within the secret recesses of her soul.

Luann raised a sharp brow as if in challenge. Mariella had the simultaneous realization that this woman was a fighter and that she probably didn't play fair.

There was no way for Luann to know that Mariella could never resist a challenge, but she'd thrown down the gauntlet just the same. With the bone-deep suspicion that she'd regret it, Mariella stepped back to allow the other disgraced fashion designer into her shop. She watched as Luann studied the store and couldn't decide if she took in the space with a discerning or dismissive eye. Either way, the perceived judgment rankled.

"So this is how you've reinvented yourself?"

"Don't worry," Mariella said, proud of the condemnation that dripped from her tone. "I'm not going to start carrying competing athleisurewear lines and giving you and Alex a run for your money in the local community."

"Oh, sweetheart." Luann breathed out a shrill laugh. "Alex has way bigger plans for the Fit Collective than coastal North Carolina. But you know his history so you must understand his pedigree and the expectations he places on himself."

Mariella bit down on the inside of her cheek to keep from answering. She knew enough about Alex and his estranged father, domineering stepfather and brittle mother, as well as the contentious relationship the different factions of that powerful family had with each other. It was the stuff of society rags, but Alex's reputation had always remained golden-boy pure as far as she could tell. At least until his wedding day.

"Are you looking for a particular outfit?" It felt safer to switch into sales mode. "I can make some recommendations although I'd prefer if you came back during business hours."

"I like you," Leann said quietly.

"I'm not sure the feeling is mutual." Mariella didn't bother with niceties. Luann exuded a familiarity that grated on her nerves, and she didn't want to admit that she recognized an unwanted kinship with the woman.

Luann flashed a wide grin. "Your honesty makes me like you even more. I want to hire you."

Mariella lifted her hands. "As you can see, I have a job."

"A couple of them," Luann clarified. "I've seen photos from the weddings you've helped plan. You have an eye for design. Not just fashion, although I think a few of the wedding dresses you've created recently have been far more interesting than anything you did with Belle Vie."

That pricked. "I was extremely successful with Belle Vie," Mariella countered. "There were brides all over the world who wanted to wear my gowns on their wedding day."

"No doubt," Luann agreed easily. "But we both know that a large portion of success in the fashion world is good branding and perception. I became a millionaire many times over on that principle."

"There's a difference between us." Mariella crossed her arms over her chest. She'd thrown a thick flannel shirt over the silk blouse she wore because it was often cold in the back of the store in the early morning.

She shouldn't care what this woman thought about her style or her current choices in life, but she couldn't resist engaging, never one to turn away from a fight. "Even at the height of my fame, I respected the women who hired me. I never would have publicly shamed them."

Luann's breath hitched, and Mariella knew she'd hit a nerve with the seemingly unflappable woman.

"That's exactly why I'm here."

"To tell me about how you disrespect your customers?" Mariella raised a brow. "I'm not sure I'm the best person to take your confession on that front."

Luann shook her head. "I love my customers."

"At least the ones with thigh gap," Mariella quipped. She remembered one of Luann's infamous interview answers—

that the clothes she designed were more suited to women in the best shape of their lives. Mariella didn't understand it even then. It wasn't just whip-thin women or those with lots of muscle who wanted to be active.

One of the things she hated from the bridal industry was how women felt pressure to diet and exercise themselves into a specific-size wedding gown just so that they could spend years—sometimes the rest of their lives—looking back to those photographs of the one day when they felt beautiful. She wanted women to feel beautiful all of the time, which is what she was trying to achieve by being more selective in choosing which brides to work with.

"You need to understand how I grew up."

Mariella noticed a vein had popped out on the edge of Luann's temple.

"My mother was extremely thin. She was a model when she first came to this country from Eastern Europe. I took after my dad, and he was from a long line of Hungarian farmers. Working-class with sturdy bodies to match. My mother could not understand why I wasn't naturally thin. I was taught from a young age to tame my body using whatever measures necessary. Diet, obsessive exercise, pills—whatever it took. And I did that during my modeling career, quite successfully I might add. I started my first company because I saw an opportunity in the exercise industry. But I had a skewed version of what women should look like. Mostly from my own skewed body image. I wanted a way to make women feel beautiful and comfortable, but I did the opposite. I felt the opposite."

"So now you know better. And Alex is giving you another chance. I don't understand why you're here."

"Because I'm not good at being politically correct," Luann admitted. "I believe my heart is in the right place." She shook her head. "I know it is. Still, I'm terrified that I'm going to screw things up when Alex is building an amazing company with a positive, affirming corporate culture."

"Follow his lead," Mariella suggested. She still didn't understand why Luann had come to her, but she was reluctantly moved by the other woman's show of emotion. It was clear Luann did care. Mariella understood the fear of disappointing the people who were relying on you. That was why she'd asked Emma to remove her name from the Wildflower Inn marketing materials.

"I asked him to take his shirt off the other day."

Mariella blinked, certain she'd heard the older woman wrong. "You asked who to take off his shirt?"

"Alex. It was a joke. It was supposed to be a joke."

"Did he take it as a joke?"

"No. Although he wasn't offended. He should have been. He was mostly annoyed and told me I need to watch what I say in the office."

"Can I assume he didn't take off his shirt?"

"He did not, more's the pity." Luann covered her face with her hands for a moment. "See, there I go again. I'm all inappropriate humor. It's my defense mechanism. Now that I've worked through a lot of my eating disorder issues and obsession with exercise, sometimes I feel like I'm the one walking around naked. People see me for who I am without the walls I've put up."

"Is that such a bad thing?" Mariella asked although she knew the answer. At least she knew how she would feel. How she felt much of the time.

"It's the worst." Luann didn't pull any punches. "I don't want to sabotage or do anything that would hurt the Fit Collective's chance of success. Alex has invested too much in this. I owe him for giving me a second chance when no one else would."

Mariella drew in a deep breath. "As much as I appreciate everything you're saying, I can't figure out what any of it has to do with me. You must know my history with Alex. I'm the last person he would want helping."

"You are the person I want," Luann answered simply.

"Why?" Mariella couldn't fathom a world where she would have something to offer Luann.

"Because you honor women's bodies in your designs. We both know that's a rare thing in the fashion world. A lot of designers want women to conform to some unattainable ideal. You make them feel beautiful just the way they are."

"What do you want me to do—coach you on how not to offend people? I'm pretty new at that myself." Mariella shouldn't get involved in any way but she appreciated the compliment from Luann. Helping women feel beautiful gave her a great amount of personal satisfaction. Not that she was under any illusion that she could transform the fashion world, but it would be powerful for a company with the potential of the Fit Collective to embrace that idea in design. They couldn't do that if the press they received was from Luann being unable to control her mouth.

"I highly recommend counting to ten in your head before you speak," Mariella continued. "That's a good start. Or make sure Alex does all the interviews and stay off social media. Whatever you do, don't get on Twitter and start a late-night rant."

"I want to hire you as the new creative director for the Fit Collective." Luann flashed a smile that bordered on a grimace. "I want you to take over my job."

ALEX HEARD THE commotion outside his office as he finished up a call with one of the company's investors. He'd been at the computer since before sunrise and his back protested as he stood. He didn't care that he worked long hours, had very little social life since he'd arrived in Magnolia, and spent most of his time out of the office working on his laptop at home.

This company was his chance. His opportunity to make a difference in the corporate world the way he knew he could. If he was being completely honest, his chance to prove to his stepdad that he should have been given a chance within the family business.

At this point in his life, he wanted to show everyone that he didn't need his family. He didn't need anyone but himself to find success. Disconnecting the call, he was halfway around his desk when his office door burst open to reveal Mariella Jacob standing at the threshold.

He couldn't help glancing at her hands, which to his great relief held nothing but a cell phone and a leather purse. Not that he thought she'd barge into his office armed, but the look in her eyes was pure warrior princess. So much so that he wouldn't have been surprised to see her wielding a sword and shield, although he reminded himself again that he was the injured party between the two of them.

Yes, her life had been ruined—possibly even more than his—after that video went viral and Amber's PR people stepped in to take care of the rest. But it had been Mariella's choice to down the liquor or wine or whatever substances she'd had on board that had given her the courage to interrupt a wedding mid-vow.

Her gaze found his. "Did you put her up to it?"

Glenna, the receptionist his assistant had hired last week, charged in after her. "I'm sorry," the woman said on a rush of breath, tugging at one of her long braids. "Heather is running an errand, but I told this woman that without an appointment she couldn't talk to you. She didn't listen."

Alex felt one side of his mouth twitch.

"It's okay, Glenna. Mariella and I go way back."

The normally sweet-natured millennial gave Mariella a wicked side-eye. "I know. I've seen the video. We all have. Everyone has."

Something in the air crackled as he felt an unwanted pang of sympathy for Mariella. Would she ever live those few minutes down? Alex certainly wanted to forget them.

"Yes, well… I'm sure this won't take long," he said and walked forward, closing the door as Glenna took an automatic step back. It was clear she would have liked to stay, whether as a pseudo-guard for him or so that she could report back to the rest of the staff he didn't know.

"For someone who wants to stay out of the public eye, storming into my company headquarters in the middle of the workweek isn't the smartest choice."

"Did you send Luann to me?"

He turned from the door, nonplussed, and that's when he realized his mistake. He shouldn't have moved toward her. He should have instructed Glenna to shut the door because now he was standing next to Mariella. Close enough that he could smell her shampoo and see the flecks of gold in her blue eyes. And the pain she was trying to mask with anger. Anger was definitely her go-to emotion, but he knew without a doubt that it barely scratched the surface of what she was feeling.

"First, I know nothing about Luann coming to you. I have no control over how she spends her time outside of work hours."

"You're her boss." Mariella flung the words at him like an accusation and then stalked toward the window that looked out to the woods behind the building. She'd been smart to move away from him. At least one of them had a decent self-preservation instinct.

"Only because I'm the CEO," he conceded. "It's only for the org chart. In most ways, we're partners. And in all ways, she does what she wants."

"She wants to hire me." Mariella didn't turn around as she dropped that bombshell, which was a blessing. Alex needed a moment to school his features.

"Why in the hell would she give you that impression?" he asked when he was certain he could speak without emotion.

"It's no impression. She wants me to take over her role as the chief designer and creative director for the Fit Collective."

"That's the most ridiculous thing I've ever heard."

"At least there's one thing we agree on," Mariella said with a soft laugh. That laugh did dangerous things to Alex's body.

"I don't understand what you're talking about or why she would say that."

Mariella finally turned and he noticed he wasn't the only one who'd gotten control of his emotions in the past few seconds. "She's worried about messing things up with her candid comments. She told me about suggesting you take off your shirt. From what I know about Luann, that kind of PG-rated comment is going to be the least of your concerns."

"We can handle it."

She gave him a long once-over. "Who knows? It could be a morale booster. Replace casual Friday with shirtless Thursday?"

He knew she was trying to rattle him and damned if he didn't feel heat steal up his neck.

"You would be less of a wild card of impulsivity how?"

"I made that point." Mariella nodded. "Forcefully with many swear words. Luann is convinced, and if you didn't know about it—"

"Of course not."

"Then you have to help me unconvince her."

"Have you heard of the word *no*?"

"I tried, but I'm not sure she'll give up." Mariella glanced at the floor for a moment. "I wanted to make sure it wasn't something you'd come up with as a way to lure me in and then publicly humiliate me."

"It's been three years since my wedding day," he reminded her. "I don't care what they say about revenge being served cold, Mariella. You don't matter enough to me to work that hard."

He expected her to call him out on his lie. He thought about her far too much, especially in the quiet, lonely hours of the night. But something that looked like pain flashed in her crystal-blue eyes, and he realized he'd hurt her with his callous comment. He shouldn't feel guilty for that and yet...

They both glanced at the door as Heather entered with a knock.

"Alex, I'm so sorry." His assistant flicked a hostile glance toward Mariella. "Glenna told me what happened. If I would have been here, I could have stopped her."

"I'm not some kind of assassin," Mariella muttered.

"You're worse," Heather said, her voice fraught with more emotion than the situation warranted.

"It's okay." Alex repeated the words he'd said to Glenna. Damn, he must have really looked like a sad sack in that wedding video—and possibly even now—for his employees to be so overprotective.

"It's not." Heather took a step forward, her gaze now

fixed on Mariella. "She has no right to be here. The damage she's done—"

"You don't even know me," Mariella argued, moving toward the young assistant. "This is none of your business."

"Heather, it's really fine. There was a misunderstanding with Luann and—"

"I know you," Heather whispered, and something close to panic snaked along Alex's spine as the girl continued to stare at Mariella with an explained fury.

He didn't know what was happening at this moment but had a feeling it didn't have anything to do with designing workout apparel.

Mariella drew in a shaky breath as her eyes widened, abject panic in their depths. "You can't."

"I do, and I think you know me, too." Heather tucked a lock of hair behind her ear and it was then Alex noticed that her blond hair was the same pale honey shade as Mariella's. In fact, the two women could be related now that he looked more closely. They could be—

"You know me." Heather's voice quivered with emotion. "Because you were the woman who put me up for adoption less than twenty-four hours after I was born."

# CHAPTER FOUR

MARIELLA PICKED UP the glass of water from the counter of
the Wildflower Inn's kitchen later that night then placed
it back down when it was obvious her hand continued to
tremble.

After driving nearly an hour out of town, Mariella had
turned her car around and come to the inn. She was afraid
to go home. Afraid her...the girl with the wounded blue
eyes and hair the color of her own would have been waiting for her.

How could she ever truly face the child she'd given up
eighteen years ago?

That decision had been the most difficult one she'd ever
made but also the easiest. She'd been a naive, ignorant teenager who'd made a huge mistake believing the whispered
lies and promises a boy had made to her in the shadows of
his dingy bedroom at a late-night party.

At that point, she'd known she wanted to get away from
the life she'd grown up in but had no clue how she was
going to manage it. She'd had no idea if she would truly
make it out. There was a better than average chance she
wouldn't and no way she would risk another girl growing
up with those kinds of obstacles.

A friend of her mother's had told her about the adoption
attorney who would make sure her baby had a good life.

Mariella had always assumed her child had grown up

with a family who loved her. With vacations to Disney World and summer camps and a mom who baked cookies and kissed boo-boos instead of opening their home to a revolving door of men.

But she didn't know for sure. Nothing was certain in life, and it felt like the curiosity that stabbed at her as though she were lying on a bed of tacks would never be fully satisfied.

"Tell me again. You really just walked away from her today?" Emma asked from the other side of the island. It was nearly eleven, and the guests who were in town for the weekend's wedding had all gone up to bed. This kitchen had become a refuge of sorts and Mariella gripped the edge of the granite like that piece of driftwood at the end of the *Titanic* movie.

"Well, I made it as far as the lobby, and then I puked into the garbage can next to the receptionist desk. But I kept moving. I picked up that trash receptacle and didn't slow down. No way was I going to let Alex or…that girl catch up to me." She sighed. "I'll have to return the trash can at some point, once I hose it down."

Emma shuddered. "I'm guessing they won't want it back."

"Alex seemed as shocked as I was," Mariella said softly. "But he had to know about Heather. That was her name. Heather. How else would she have ended up in Magnolia? He hired her. Maybe the whole start with Mary Ellen at the bakery was a ruse."

"I only met him the two weekends he spent at the inn as the best man in Brett and Holly's wedding." Emma tapped an elegant finger to her chin. "He didn't strike me as cruel. Why would he have done something like that?"

"To punish me. Isn't it obvious?" She knew the accusation was far-fetched, but she wanted to blame someone. To share the blame for the pain in her daughter's eyes. "I'm not saying I don't deserve it."

"I'm saying you don't deserve it," Emma told her. "I don't believe Alex had anything to do with it. Even if he wanted to hurt you, do you really think he would have brought an innocent girl into it?"

Mariella's mind and heart were too pulverized to think or feel with any sort of clarity. As far as she was aware, no one from her current life had even known about the baby she'd given up for adoption when she was sixteen.

"Why didn't you tell us?" Emma asked as if reading her thoughts.

"It was part of my past," she told her friend. When she'd shown up at the inn knowing she must look like a woman well beyond the verge of a nervous breakdown, Emma had bundled her into a back bedroom then called Angi. The two of them had taken turns sitting with her until Angi left to go home only a few minutes earlier. Mariella knew she needed to do the same. She couldn't hide out at the Wildflower indefinitely, pretending like her world wasn't imploding.

"You probably thought that ruining my life in a viral YouTube video was my low point. In fact, that was nothing. My life doesn't mean a thing compared to the life of the daughter I gave up. And now she's here."

"Don't you think it would be a good idea to figure out why?"

Mariella met her friend's concerned gaze. "Well, sure," she said, not bothering to mask her sarcasm. "I should invite her for tea and she can tell me how my decision when she was an infant ruined her life."

"You don't know that it did."

"Of course I do. My mom didn't give me up, but I know what it's like to not be wanted by a parent. Why else would she be here? Hell, she and Alex have probably compared notes. She works for him. Maybe Luann Bowman knows her, too. Maybe this is all just one big giant joke on me."

"You won't know unless you talk to her."

"That is not going to happen. Heather is better off without me, and nothing good can come from it. Plus, I'm not giving Alex a chance to see me weak and broken. I've worked hard to rebuild my life. I succeeded in making something of myself when I went to New York and I found a way to remake my life in Magnolia when that one blew up in my face."

She gave a harsh chuckle. "You might call me the queen of second chances. Or maybe I'm on my third or fourth chance by now. Who's really counting?"

"It sounds like you are." Emma reached for Mariella's hand, but Mariella jerked it away. She couldn't be touched right now. She couldn't allow herself to be comforted even though that's exactly what she'd come here for. She loved her friends. She loved her store and the business they were building at the inn in their tiny little corner of the wedding industry. It was different than the company she'd created in New York City. It felt real and right but that wouldn't stop her from leaving.

"Do you think I can rent my house fully furnished? I don't need much from there. You and Ang can pack up—"

"No one is packing up anything." For all of Emma's sweetness, she had a backbone of steel and that was on full display with the way she was staring at Mariella.

"You can't possibly think I'm going to stay here."

"You bet I do. You and Angi and I have been through

this. Magnolia is your home. We are your people. The family you chose."

"I didn't say I was moving to Antarctica," Mariella countered. "I'll have Wi-Fi and phone service. We can text and talk and I'll do long-distance consultations for gowns. I've always wanted to spend more time on the west coast. Maybe San Francisco. I bet I could work at a clothing store there."

"You own a clothing store here," Emma reminded her.

"I can still own the store here. I'll just give Jasmin a raise so that she can manage it. A single mom would appreciate the extra income."

"That's why you're so good to her," Emma murmured. "You take care of that girl the way someone should have stepped in to take care of you."

"She's a great employee. She works twice as hard as anyone I'd hired before her. As long as she can manage the baby and her hours, it doesn't matter to me what's going on in her personal life. Don't make me out to be some sort of Mother Teresa."

Emma's smile widened. "No one would ever do that. Although I did think it was strange that you hired a girl to help you in the shop when she was eight months pregnant."

"She told me she didn't want to take maternity leave. And she's not like me. Jasmin is twenty. I was barely sixteen. She's taking college courses in the evening. I was lucky to scratch out my GED."

"You're helping her."

"I need to go home." Mariella took a step toward the door then stopped. "What if she knows where I live?"

"She's the daughter you gave up for adoption, not an ax murderer."

"I think I'd rather take my chances with the ax," Mariella said. It was impossible to think about facing Heather again.

"I doubt she's going to be waiting for you in the bushes. Yeah, she's in Magnolia, but she didn't specifically seek you out."

"She knew I was here. I still think Alex has something to do with this."

"Just promise you won't do anything rash and certainly nothing that could be recorded."

"I learned my lesson."

"It's going to be okay," Emma said in her bride whisperer voice, the one she used to calm frantic nerves and make people believe in happy endings.

Mariella wished she could believe.

After promising Emma she wouldn't do anything foolish, Mariella drove home on the dark streets of Magnolia, so different than the never-ending lights and bustle of the city. When her career was in full swing, she would have never guessed she'd be happy in a small Southern town that rolled up the sidewalks at the time when she and her friends used to be getting ready to head out for the night. Depending on her mood, she would have laughed or possibly kicked someone in the shin for even suggesting it.

Small-town life suited her more than she could have guessed. It gave her a sense of peace she hadn't even realized she wanted from life. Still, as she drove slowly down the quiet street, she glanced around like she was in some low-budget thriller and a villain could be lurking just as she and Emma had joked about.

Her street remained peaceful, and by the time she'd pulled into her garage and made her way to the cozy kitchen, she at least felt confident that she was safe from the past for one night. Tomorrow she could deal with whatever came next, even if what was next meant starting over once more.

Mariella washed her face and changed into a cotton nightgown, letting the familiar routine calm her even more. She was just slipping between the sheets when she heard the knock at the door.

She could have ignored it. It was late and, for all anyone knew, she was fast asleep. But as much as she might consider moving on and relinquishing her life, at her heart, Mariella was a fighter. She rarely shied away from a confrontation, and tonight was no different. If the daughter she'd given up wanted to scream or yell or even do her own shin-kicking, Mariella would take it.

She deserved anything this stranger her heart recognized wanted to dish out. She padded to the door and opened it, inwardly ready for whatever Heather had to offer, only to find Alex Ralsten standing on the other side.

ALEX WASN'T SURE why he'd come to Mariella's cute brick rancher near the center of town. He hadn't known his assistant, Heather Garrison, had any relation to Mariella, let alone one so fraught with turbulent emotions.

Mary Ellen Winkler had been the one to suggest he hire Heather. According to the motherly bakery owner, Heather would be of more help to him than she was to her making fancy coffee drinks and serving up pastries. The girl was young but extremely capable with the ability to keep track of everything.

Of course he hadn't known she was Mariella's biological daughter. Even though he had no reason to care about Mariella and it shouldn't matter to him that she'd been hurt, the look of pure devastation that had morphed into betrayal when she looked at him felt like a knife to the gut.

He'd followed her out of his office but stopped as he

came around the corner to see her retching into a garbage can as she hurried out the company's front entrance.

"I made her puke," a small voice had said behind him, and he'd turned to find Heather staring toward the parking lot with tears streaming down her face.

"She's in shock," he'd told the girl then ushered her back toward his office.

He'd had so many questions—how had Heather found out about Mariella being her birth mother, did she want a relationship or just to get a closer look at the woman who'd given her up, did her parents have any idea about any of this—but he hadn't asked any of them. The girl had been too upset and Alex wasn't even sure what was appropriate in the situation.

Things were even more complicated because of his history with Mariella, but he'd sent Heather home for the day—she was staying in a rented guesthouse outside of town—and done his best to diffuse the avalanche of rumors already hurtling through the company's staff. He hated gossip and didn't want Heather to have to deal with it.

Selfishly, he also didn't want his name or the company tied to Mariella and stirring up old memories of his past with her. Easier said than done if Luann had truly offered her a position. Could Luann even make that offer without his approval? Not really, but he knew better than to believe he could stop the talented and temperamental designer from doing anything she set her mind to.

He had a complete nightmare on his hands and he had no idea how to begin dealing with any of it. A late-night visit to Mariella's house probably wasn't his best bet, but he told himself he needed an idea of where her head was at to stave off any more potentially damaging public scenes.

"I'm checking on you," he said lamely, watching as her blue eyes narrowed.

"Is this your idea of revenge? Because I know you gave me that line about not wanting it served cold or whatever but this pain feels white-hot. It feels more than personal, Alex. It feels like you're trying to destroy me."

The words were spoken softly but the anger in them nearly knocked him off his feet. "I didn't know."

He concentrated on her anger because that was easier than seeing the pain and vulnerability in her summer-sky-blue gaze. Once again he reminded himself that it shouldn't matter. Mariella Jacob was nothing to him. "I'm not gloating. I wanted to check on you, Mariella. To explain—"

"What? That now you've truly exposed me for the person I am? Not only a ranting drunk who would make a spectacle at a wedding but the kind of weak, cowardly person who would give up a child because that was easier than dealing with the challenges of being a single mother?"

"Is that why you gave her up?" He didn't believe for a minute that was the reason. He couldn't imagine Mariella ever backing away from a fight or a challenge.

"What is she doing here?" she whispered, looking past him out into the inky night.

He could hear crickets chirping from the surrounding trees and a cool breeze rippled behind him, offering some respite from the increasing heat and humidity of the North Carolina spring.

People told him that the heat wasn't quite as bad in Magnolia because of the town's proximity to the beach. If the temperatures continued to rise on the trajectory they seem to be headed, it was going to be one hot summer.

"I don't know," he answered honestly. Maybe he should

have pressed Heather more, but the girl had been too distraught. Besides, what would he have shared with Mariella? If he was going to take sides, it wouldn't be with her. "Like I told you, I had nothing to do with this. You have to believe me."

"Why?" The question was spoken on a soft puff of air. He didn't know how to answer it. He didn't know why it mattered what this woman thought of him. He hadn't chosen Magnolia because of Mariella but had to admit that getting under her skin was an unintended benefit of being there.

He knew it probably wasn't fair. His fiancée had been the one to cheat. Mariella had revealed it. But he hated the way she'd done it so publicly and the way Amber's PR team had spun things to make it look like the star had no choice given the dull and loveless relationship she'd found herself in with him.

It was difficult to separate everything that had happened in the weeks and months after the ruined wedding and assign blame to the appropriate parties. Alex found it challenging to think about that time and not become consumed by the anger and bitterness he'd felt toward Mariella.

"Because I wouldn't hurt that girl. Hell, I didn't even know her before Mary Ellen suggested her for the position. It doesn't matter either way. Heather is innocent in all of this even if she did come to Magnolia to find you. People go looking for their birth parents all the time. She has a right to know you and to get her questions answered. I wouldn't deny her that, but I'd also never use her to hurt you. Not because of your feelings. Because of hers."

He hadn't exactly meant the words to land like verbal bullets, but it was clear they pinged into Mariella with that kind of force. Once again, Alex wasn't sure why that bothered him. He didn't owe this woman anything.

"She's really upset. Your reaction was over the top—no surprise—and it bothered her a lot."

"I throw up when I'm stressed. Maybe you remember that from the wedding. My reaction had nothing to do with the girl."

"I do remember. At the time, everyone thought you were just wasted."

"I was wasted," she agreed without hesitation. "I never threw up after too much wine or whatever else I had going. More's the pity. There were plenty of nights I would have liked to purge my system. Unfortunately, I just had to ride it out."

He admired her blunt honesty—reluctantly—but admired it just the same. The fact that she didn't shy away from the truth. If Alex hadn't spent so much of his life avoiding harsh truths then maybe that ill-fated day, and the relationship with Amber in general, wouldn't have gone so far.

"Even if she's seen the video, Heather was apparently unaware of the emotional destruction that can ensue when you're pushed to the brink."

Her mouth tightened, but she didn't deny it. He wasn't sure whether that was good or bad at this point.

"You don't have a dog in this fight," she reminded him. "That girl—"

"Heather," he clarified. "Your daughter's name is Heather."

Mariella winced. "What do you care at this point? She's your employee. Whatever happens with her and me is none of your business."

"It's my business because she works for me. This is a small town and it's a close-knit company culture."

"So this is all about covering your assets?" She lifted a hand when he would have argued. "Forget it. I know that's not what it is. I'm angry and knocked off my game. I didn't expect any of this. I came here to make a fresh start because I was a stranger in Magnolia. Because other than that stupid viral video, these people didn't know me and half of them don't even have internet. Then you show up and she... I just never expected any of it. This wasn't how it was supposed to be."

Amen to that, Alex thought. None of this was how it was supposed to be, especially not the part where he felt something other than anger and bitterness toward Mariella. The part where he couldn't seem to stop himself from wanting to comfort her.

So much so that when a strand of hair blew across her face, he reached forward and brushed it away. The warmth and softness of her skin shouldn't have surprised him. Hell, she looked like she could be some sort of beauty company model with her creamy complexion, luminous eyes and rosy lips.

It was the shock of awareness that got to him. The bone-deep understanding that he felt a connection to this woman who had publicly humiliated him. The knowledge that if he pulled her close and pressed his mouth to hers the connection would flame like lighter fluid on a campfire. Despite the fact that he should think of her as an enemy, it didn't stop him from wanting her.

Her eyes dilated and her lips parted, and the urge to trace his thumb over the cupid's bow of her mouth nearly undid him. She could be his undoing even after he'd worked so hard to rebuild his life and the walls around his heart.

He pulled back and rolled his shoulders. Shuttered his gaze so that at least he wouldn't reveal himself at this moment. He wasn't the same gullible, trusting person he'd been before the end of his relationship with Amber. Physical attraction was one thing, but he could handle that.

He could handle all of it with a little breathing room. He just needed space to help him remember that Mariella wasn't his. She could take care of herself, and he needed to let her do just that. "I'm also here to tell you not to go after Heather. If you don't want a relationship with her or to listen to what she has to say, that's your business. Don't try to take her down to protect yourself."

He didn't really believe Mariella would do that and it wasn't at all the reason he'd sought her out tonight. This wasn't the same situation as when she'd ruined his life and a lot of that disastrous day had been fueled by drugs and alcohol.

All evidence pointed to the fact that she'd cleaned up her act and remained sober to this day, but he wasn't taking any chances. He needed to keep his distance from her. They might be in the same small town, but it didn't mean they had to be part of each other's lives. "One more thing. I don't know what Luann told you or offered, but there is no place for you at my company."

Her mouth thinned again. "Understood," she said with a sneer. "Your inclination to play the rescuing hero is admirable in a knight errant kind of way. But I was never much for heroes, Alex. Or having somebody tell me what I can and can't do. That girl came here because she wants something. Maybe an apology, maybe an explanation. I don't owe her either one. Just like I don't owe you any promises. Things haven't changed."

"No, they haven't," he agreed because it was easier than calling her out on the lie. Just like the day of his wedding had changed both of their lives, he knew that Heather's announcement would do the same.

He took a step back. "Don't worry. I'm not looking to be anyone's hero, Mariella, especially not yours." He turned and walked in the direction of his car parked at the curb in front of her house. When the door slammed behind him, he told himself it was for the best.

# CHAPTER FIVE

MARIELLA WENT TO the beach on Sunday. She'd lived in Magnolia for two years but could count on one hand the number of times she'd visited the ocean since her arrival. Sometimes she would drive to the parking lot in front of the public boardwalk, roll down her windows and listen to the sound of the surf hitting the sand. Close her eyes and let the roar of the waves move through her.

She was afraid of water, and although she couldn't remember the specific incident in her childhood that had precipitated the fear, it was ever-present and all-consuming. Strange that she'd chosen to move to a coastal town where the ocean was weaved into the fabric of life like the change of seasons or the rise and fall of the sun each day.

It was possible to visit the beach without getting more than her toes wet—if she chose that—yet she still didn't venture to the shore. Plenty of people learned to swim as adults, but she didn't like admitting weakness. Her inability to even tread water counted as a weakness in her mind. And some long-buried part of her still feared that the lure of the dreamy, creeping sea might prove to be too much to resist.

Shortly after she'd left her old life behind, she'd gone to Mexico to be alone and lick her wounds away from the spotlight and the city. Her future had seemed hopeless, a dark void she couldn't imagine navigating when her light had been so fully snuffed out.

The thought of what might happen if she didn't face her future had curled around the edges of her consciousness like smoke from one of her mother's Marlboro Lights whispering through the kitchen late at night. She'd been fragile—only a few weeks sober—and she'd walked out to the ocean late one night and entered the cold waves.

Goose bumps had erupted across her skin, more from the understanding of what she was doing than the bite of the salt water.

A wave had crashed over her and she'd gone down for a moment, sputtering and choking as she tried to catch her breath. Tried not to drag in salt water along with the air.

The moment has been a wake-up call. The ocean communicating its power made her aware of the lack of hers. But instead of feeling less, Mariella's appreciation of her place as nothing more than a fleck of humanity had been a comfort. She'd spent so long trying to convince herself and everyone around her that she was big and important and something other than the small girl with the strung-out mom from the seedy side of Philadelphia.

She'd managed to drag herself from the dark water, which had been the start of her reinvention. Even though she understood and respected the power of the ocean, she hadn't gone back in. Not even after moving to this town. A part of her respect came with the need to stay away. Not to get sucked back into the temptation of taking care of her problems in a way that was final.

She was different, of course. Stronger and more resilient. At least she hoped so. So why did she come here now after her run-in with Heather and then Alex?

It was a sunny spring day although a blessed cool front had come through town. The beach was dotted with families flying kites and a few intrepid kids splashing in the frigid water of the Atlantic. Once summer came, this stretch of sand would be a canopy of color with bright umbrellas and families in all varieties of swimwear enjoying a break from the heat.

Maybe Mariella would come back then but not for the same purpose that she'd entered the dark ocean in Mexico. She wasn't that person any longer—or so she told herself— even though she still feared the water might reveal something different about her.

Would she want to confront her weakness again? Would she be driven so low to feel that she was out of options other than the pull of the waves?

She approached the shoreline, shaking off those difficult thoughts.

Emma had been right. She'd built a life here, a good one. She'd be a fool to run away, although foolhardy felt like it was part of her inner makeup. She sucked in a breath as the cold water splashed over her feet and receded again.

She continued to stand in that spot until her body acclimated to the temperature. The tide streamed in and out with its endless rhythm. Sometimes a wave crashed closer to the edge and hit her harder, water splashing against her shins and soaking the edges of the long shorts she wore.

Sometimes the force of it would peter out before it got to her and she'd be left almost yearning for that cold punch of water. She wasn't sure how long she stood there. Long enough that the sun heated the shadowy places inside her. While her lower body still felt the cold from the water, her upper body was warm and languid.

She'd brought a towel with her. Maybe she would sunbathe for a little bit although she knew better. A woman in her thirties couldn't afford to spend time under the bright sun for the damage it would do to her skin. At this point,

Mariella couldn't bring herself to care. She returned the wave of a boy who ran past splashing through the water and then turned and came face-to-face with Heather.

It seemed strange suddenly that she didn't know the girl's last name. Her daughter's last name.

"Are you stalking me now?" she demanded as heat infused her cheeks. Rudeness was a comfortable defense mechanism for her, and she needed all the fortification she could get to combat the emotions rushing through her. How was she supposed to survive living in the same town as the child she'd given up?

The girl wore a sports bra and athletic shorts, her blond hair pulled back into a high ponytail, sweat glistening on her arms.

"In your dreams," she answered with a sneer.

Pride bloomed in Mariella's chest. She took no credit for this young woman but appreciated her badass attitude nonetheless. And the truth was she had dreamed about her daughter many times over the years. The child was always a faceless, shadowy entity running at the edges of Mariella's mind as if determined to stay just out of reach.

Even in her wildest imaginings, she couldn't have conjured a moment like this. A wave pooled around her ankles at the same time Heather lifted a hand with ragged nails to her mouth and then dropped it again, her fist clenching. Mariella gasped, more from the familiarity of that gesture than the shock of the cold water. Biting her nails was a habit she'd had to work hard to overcome, and she'd spent most of her childhood and teenage years with her nails chewed to the quick.

"Are you going to run away and then puke your guts out?" The girl lifted a brow.

Oh, yes. Mariella's heart knew this young woman.

"That had nothing to do with you," she said instead of hissing out the snide remark that was on the tip of her tongue. "It's just something that happens to me."

"Right," Heather agreed. "Sort of like an unwanted pregnancy and giving away your daughter to strangers. Also just something that happened."

A bead of sweat dripped between Mariella's shoulder blades. She couldn't blame Heather for thinking that. Of course she would. No one could know what that decision had cost Mariella.

There was no explaining how the moments after the nurse gently lifted her baby from her arms had broken her in ways that could never be patched together.

She wasn't going to share that. Chances were Heather wouldn't care either way. And it would only make Mariella more vulnerable to the girl's animosity when it already felt as though her heart was on full display. The solid walls she'd built around it were no deterrent for her guilt and the regrets from the past.

"Have you had a good life?" she asked. When Heather continued to stare at her, Mariella wondered if the question had been lost on the wind that seemed so ever-present along the shore. But it was the one thing she wanted to know most of all. Truly, it was the only thing that mattered.

"My parents," Heather answered finally, "are amazing. They gave me everything, and I'm so lucky to have them." She was practically shouting now, and it seemed like it had less to do with being heard over the wind than some sort of tide of emotion that was also tugging on her the same way it did Mariella.

"You don't even matter to me." Heather practically spat the words in Mariella's face.

They didn't land with the pain that the young woman obviously expected.

Mariella was long past believing she mattered, so the daughter she'd hurt by trying to do the right thing didn't need to remind her.

"Then what are you doing here?"

Heather started to lift her hand to her mouth once again then crossed her arms over her chest instead. "It's a public beach. I'm allowed to be here."

"In Magnolia," Mariella clarified, although she had trouble believing the girl didn't understand what she meant by the question.

Heather glanced away for a brief moment before shifting her glare back to Mariella. "Also a free country. I can live wherever I want."

"What about school? Shouldn't you still be in high school with graduation around the corner?"

The girl snorted. "Like you care. I graduated early and I was taking concurrent college classes. I'm really smart, you know. Like I test off the charts and whatever."

The information floored Mariella. "That's amazing. You truly must take after your adoptive parents."

"Definitely not you." Heather wrinkled her nose. "I would never be so stupid as to wreck my life the way you did."

"I'm glad to hear it."

"Maybe I take after my biological father?"

Did Mariella sense a modicum of vulnerability in the girl's question?

Suddenly she felt like she was in the dark ocean once again. As many times as she wondered what happened to the baby she gave up, she'd purposely hollowed from her mind thoughts of the boy she'd been with for her first time.

The memories came rushing back in a tumultuous mix of pain and regret. His whispered words. The cheap beer he'd plied her with all night. The cigarette smell on his breath and the way his hands felt clammy against her skin. The way he wasn't gentle with her, not because he was cruel or violent but because he was a kid, too. Neither of them had known better.

"You do not," she said with complete certainty. "I don't know what you want me to tell you, Heather. If you want to yell at me or scream, go right ahead. But I did you a favor by giving you up. I gave you a better life than you ever could have had with me. I gave you a future, and I won't apologize for that."

Across the board, Mariella wasn't great at apologies. Alex Ralsten was the perfect example of that.

"I don't want anything from you," the girl said. She sounded like she meant the words, but Mariella knew they couldn't be true. Why else would she be here?

"Is it money? I don't have as much as I once did, but if you need financial help—"

"I don't want anything," Heather repeated. When her voice broke on the last word, she turned and ran down the beach, leaving Mariella standing alone, the way it always had been.

ALEX SAT IN Sunnyside Bakery staring at the perfect glazed donut in front of him. He loved donuts, and Mary Ellen made the best he'd ever tasted, but he couldn't force himself to take a bite, not with his mind spinning in a million different directions.

Heather Garrison had called in sick yesterday, and he sent up a silent prayer that she'd show up at the office this morning. He worried he'd been too forceful with the young woman after the confrontation with Mariella.

Heather hadn't wanted anyone at the company to know about their connection, and while he respected that—or at least wanted to respect her right to decide—he wasn't sure what to do with her obvious upset over this situation.

"You can stare at it all you want, but that pastry isn't going to reveal the secrets of life."

He forced a smile as he glanced up into Mary Ellen's jovial face.

"I could use some insight, even if it comes from a donut."

"Typically," she said, patting him on the shoulder, "the sugar rush helps with any problem."

He nodded. "And it's a more appropriate coping mechanism than getting drunk enough to forget the real world at seven in the morning."

"You don't seem like the type to drown your sorrows in alcohol."

"Sometimes I wish I were," he admitted.

"Would it help to talk? You know bakers can serve the same role as bartenders. I'm a pretty good listener."

Alex felt his smile turn sincere. He appreciated the offer. One of the things he liked best about this little town was the way everybody seemed to care about everyone else.

His mother, who was cynical when he espoused the virtues of small-town life during their weekly phone calls, told him that people were simply being nosy. But Alex knew what it was like to have people in his business who didn't care.

He believed his neighbors in Magnolia considered him more than a juicy topic of gossip.

"How well did you get to know Heather while she was working at the bakery?" he asked.

A frown puckered Mary Ellen's forehead. "Well, I know she's a sweet girl, a hard worker and is partial to fruit-filled pastries. She grew up in Pennsylvania and moved down here to experience life before she starts full-time at UNC in the fall. She's nearly halfway through her undergrad degree already because of the college classes she took in high school and those she tested out of. But I'm guessing you know all of that since you hired her."

He inclined his head. "Not the fruit-filled pastry part, but I'll remember it when I'm buying Friday breakfast for the team."

"So you're not thinking of firing her?"

"No. Not at all. She's great. It's a bit scary that some-one so young can have such maturity and a great mind for business. I think she's going through some personal stuff, and I'm not sure I'm the right person to handle it. I don't know if she has anybody in her life who is the right person."

"Is this boy trouble? Because that Manning kid was sniffing around her a while back. He's fine and comes from a decent family but Heather seemed freaked out by the at-tention."

"Good God, no." Alex ran a hand through his hair then pushed the plate to the other side of the table. "I don't want to know about boy trouble with one of my employees."

He didn't want to get involved at all. He felt like that was part of the reason he had so much success early in his corporate career in hotel management despite his stepfa-ther not being willing to give him a meaningful role. Alex got in and got the job done. He took care of his employees without becoming overly involved in their lives. He always found that a bit of personal distance made the job easier.

Now he had to admit his mom had a point. It was easier

to have distance with the anonymity of a big city available when he needed it.

Damn, he needed it right now.

"I can't help you if you won't tell me what's going on." Mary Ellen used one finger to push the plate back in front of him. "But I will at least keep you well fed."

He nodded. "I appreciate that. I can't share any details with you so…"

"Just know that I'm here to support you and Heather if she needs it."

"Thank you."

"How did you know I loved glazed donuts?" Luann Bowman slid into the seat across from Alex. She picked up the donut with elegant fingers and took a dainty bite then moaned out loud. "This is amazing." She patted Mary Ellen on the arm. "Have you ever thought about franchising?"

"No," the other woman said.

"Well, you should," Luann insisted.

"Enjoy your morning." Mary Ellen squeezed Alex's shoulder then turned to walk away.

"I'll enjoy it more with a dirty chai," Luann called out. The bracelets on her right arm jangled as she lifted a hand in what looked like a royal wave.

"Coming up."

"She doesn't like you," Alex said when they were alone.

Luann let out a small laugh. "As if I care."

"You should care. The company you founded is now based in this town. Mary Ellen holds a lot of sway here. You don't want to get on her bad side."

"We are bringing jobs to the community. People who are going to come and buy her overpriced coffee and donuts. She should be thanking me,"

Sometimes Luann reminded Alex of his own mother and not in a good way.

"I appreciate you meeting me. I know mornings aren't your favorite time of day, but this is important and you weren't returning my calls yesterday."

She shrugged. "I was busy."

Right. Busy avoiding him, Alex suspected. "Did you offer Mariella Jacob a job at the Fit Collective?"

He narrowed his eyes as Luann placed the uneaten portion of donut on the plate. She used a napkin to wipe the tips of her fingers, and he had a feeling she was drawing out the moment on purpose. She liked drama, but he'd believed she cared more about the company than any sort of personal theatrics. Maybe he'd been wrong in his judgment—hell, wouldn't his stepdad enjoy that fact.

"Not just any job. I offered her my position as creative partner. You should be on your knees praying that she accepts it. She's exactly what the company needs. Maybe what you need."

## CHAPTER SIX

ALEX TRIED TO control the flash of hot temper that flamed through him at his business partner's flagrant disregard for any sort of hiring best practices or business etiquette.

"Why would I do that? Why would you do that? There is no way in hell I'd work with Mariella Jacob, and I can't believe you'd suggest it."

"Don't let your ego get in the way." Luann glanced up at the young barista, maybe Heather's replacement, who brought her drink to the table. "Thanks, sweetheart," Luann said as she gave the girl a wide smile. "This is exactly what I need right now."

"You're welcome."

"You are lovely," Luann continued. "Have you ever thought about modeling?"

The teenager giggled. "No, but one of my life goals is to be a social media influencer."

"Even better," Luann agreed. "Follow us at hashtag fit collective and we'll see if we can't get something going."

"Okay."

As the girl walked away with a huge grin on her face, Alex shook his head. "Why would we give up any of what you just did there? You're a natural with the brand."

Luann took a sip of her drink. "It was on the tip of my tongue to tell that girl she needed to show less of her horse-toothed grin and more bosom if she wanted any sort of meaningful social media following."

Alex went stock-still.

"That's right. I held back." Luann nodded. "Showed some self-restraint. That's not going to last, Alex. I'm well past the age of giving a rat's patoot about doing or saying the right thing and the current culture isn't going to tolerate my brand of humor or the way I do business. You have to see that. I certainly do."

"I don't believe you can't control it," Alex countered. "You're smart and creative, Luann. A visionary. This is your chance for reinvention. This is the chance both of us need and want. This is what you told me you wanted. Why the sudden change of heart?"

"That's the thing, kid. I'm not so sure I do want it and I know it's crap timing that I'm realizing that only now. This has been a fun little interlude, but I don't feel the desire to censure myself. The company's success is important. I want you to be a success. Hell, I want the money. But I don't care about being politically correct. I'm going to say the wrong thing to the wrong person, especially in this Mayberry bubble you've chosen as our home. We both know it."

"You don't have to be in Magnolia." Alex wasn't sure if any of his arguments would hold weight. He didn't know what to say to convince her. But he had to try. "You can design from anywhere. We'll keep it behind the scenes."

Luann laughed out loud at that, a raucous sound that had heads in the small coffee shop turning in their direction. "Can you imagine me taking a behind-the-scenes role?"

"We had an agreement. I went out on a limb for you. With the investors. With the employees. I put everything I have into this company."

"I know." Her smile faded and she looked almost tender,

as out of character for Luann as it would be for a shark in the open ocean. "That's part of why I'm suggesting this. I know how much you have riding on the success of the rebrand. I appreciate your faith in me, Alex. I do. I don't want to let you down."

"What do you call this conversation?" He looked at the donut in front of him because it was too hard to meet her gaze. There was a faint hint of pink around the place where she'd taken her bite. Lipstick smeared on the flaky outside of the pastry. Luann was simply another person who couldn't stick it out with him. Alex wasn't much for paranoia, but he was definitely getting to the point where he considered taking it personally. He simply wasn't enough. He hadn't been for his mom once his father left them or for Amber and now...

"I'm not going to leave right away. Not until I have somebody amazing to take my place."

"Mariella is not that somebody."

"Don't be so sure. Have you seen the dresses she's been designing recently?"

Alex started to shake his head then paused. "One of them. The woman my best friend married at the Wildflower Inn wore one of her designs. It was fine."

"The dresses I've seen have been more than fine. They've been works of art and different than her previous designs when she ran Belle Vie. Those dresses were about the event and the spectacle of a wedding. What she's doing now is personal. It's about each individual bride and making her feel beautiful. Exactly what you want and need at the Fit Collective. You want someone who can design clothes that make all women feel beautiful. No matter their shape or size or if they're doing CrossFit or yoga or pushing their kids around the mall in strollers." She frowned. "Do people still go to the mall or has the mall been canceled along with so many other things in the age of the online life dominating everything else?"

Alex felt a muscle tick in his jaw. "I don't know about the mall, Luann. I'm kind of hung up on the thought of my business partner and the lead designer for my company ditching me."

"Don't be dramatic. When we get down to it, I'm doing you a favor."

"This doesn't feel like a favor, and Mariella is not going to be a part of my life." He gave the older woman a pointed look. "A part of the life of anyone at the company. There are things you don't know that I'm dealing with that involve Mariella. Complications."

"Like her making your assistant cry and puking in the lobby?"

"In a manner of speaking."

Luann lifted the donut halfway to her mouth then dropped it on the plate again. "Damn carbs," she muttered. "You could probably eat these sugar bombs all day long and still have those washboard abs that I'd like to see more of."

Alex suppressed a groan. But Luann wasn't finished. "Once your hormones start going haywire, that's the end of bread and pastries and pasta and cake and most everything else that's worth eating. If my trainer tries to hand me one more protein shake or kale salad I'm going to shove them up his perfect backside."

"This is what I'm talking about." Alex rubbed two fingers against his temples. "Somehow we went from talking about the business to a scene with Mariella to your trainer's butt."

"It's such a good butt," she said on a sigh.

"Will you stay focused?"

"Focus isn't part of my creative process," Luann told him.

"Can you pretend?"

"I used to be more into role-playing but that's not my deal anymore either. I had some great costumes back in the day. My favorite was the milkmaid—"

"Are you doing this on purpose?"

She gave him a subtle smile. "A little. I talked to Mariella about the position before the scene at the office. I don't know why she was puking but if you think she's drinking again, that's another issue."

"I don't think she's drinking. That business in the lobby had nothing to do with you."

"But something is going on?"

So much. Alex wanted to confide in Luann. In someone. He wanted the responsibility of being privy to Mariella's connection with Heather taken off his shoulders. He wanted to give it to someone who might know how to handle the whole situation with grace and insight.

As Luann continued to stare at him with a look of abject curiosity, he knew he couldn't tell her. Not that he thought she'd specifically try to hurt Mariella with the information or do anything malicious, but she was a loose cannon. And although Alex was well aware he didn't owe Mariella anything, he wasn't going to share this piece of information without her consent. He went as far as to tell himself he was doing it for Heather's benefit and certainly that played a part but not the biggest part.

"I've got it under control," he lied, fairly confident Luann knew he wasn't telling the truth. But she didn't call him out on it. He appreciated that.

"At least consider Mariella."

"I'd rather you consider finding a way to make this work.

We just got things up and running. The new collection debuts in a few weeks."

"Which is exactly why I want to bring her on now. Introduce her as the face of the rebrand."

"Mariella is never going to be the face of my company," Alex said with unequivocal conviction.

"Our company," Luann reminded him. "Yes, you're technically my boss but we're also partners. That was the agreement. You wouldn't have to offer her the same autonomy I demanded. You'd be in charge of her, Alex. That must appeal to you on some level." She picked up the last bite of donut and popped it into her mouth as she stood and picked up her chai. "Consider it. Mariella is the right thing to do for everyone."

He never thought he'd entertain the words *right* and *Mariella Jacob* in the same sentence. Even more so when seeing her under the cover of night had felt far too enjoyable.

"Not for me, Luann." He stood and cleared the plate, waving to Mary Ellen as he walked out.

He'd come to Magnolia to simplify his life. What a fool he'd been to think that living in the same town as Mariella would be simple. But he wasn't leaving so maybe the only choice was to make sure she did.

MARIELLA STOOD WITH Jasmin in front of the cash register the following Saturday morning. "You have such a way with babies," the young mom said as she watched her daughter offer Mariella a gummy grin.

Mariella bounced the tiny girl in her arms and smiled down into the baby's cherubic face. "Do you hear your mommy talking nonsense? I've never had a way with a baby in my life. It just so happens that you are such a sweet baby."

"I'm sorry about bringing her here." Jasmin checked her watch for what felt like the millionth time in the past half hour. "The new babysitter I hired should be here any minute. I never guessed how difficult it would be to find reliable child care."

"I told you it's fine." Mariella turned as a mother-daughter duo approached a row of wide-brim summer hats. "Try the one with the peach ribbon," she told the preteen girl. "It's perfect for your face shape."

The girl nodded and took the hat Mariella had indicated from the display. "Oh, my gosh," she breathed. "I love it. It makes me look like Grace Kelly."

The mom smiled and winked at her daughter. "I wasn't even aware you knew who Grace Kelly was."

"I saw a TikTok about her," the girl said, and Mariella stifled a laugh.

She understood the power of social media. She'd started the online accounts for Belle Vie immediately upon launching the company.

Some of Belle Vie's early success had been due to her savvy marketing in positioning herself and her brand of wedding couture in the social media sphere. Of course, she lost access to her social media accounts when she left the company.

The vitriol she'd received online in response to Amber's smear campaign after the wedding had been enough to make Mariella never want to put herself out there for judgment or public consumption again. Only recently had she created accounts for A Second Chance.

However, she was also proud of what she was building in the Magnolia community. She provided more than just a convenient spot for locals to buy and sell clothes. She did her best to also source gifts from local artists, particularly women of varying backgrounds. Every time she posted, she tried to remind herself that it wasn't about her anymore. It was about the people who benefited from her store and the community she served. She was a conduit for helping to get merchandise into the hands of people who would appreciate the work that went into crafting it.

She'd arrived in Magnolia at the start of the revival of the town championed by three half sisters who'd discovered their relationship and then used it to create a deep connection.

She benefited from the work Avery, Carrie and Meredith had put into making Magnolia a desirable destination for vacationers and visitors from around the region.

The Grace Kelly-inspired girl's mother bought the hat with the peach sash along with one for herself, as well as several bath products made by a local goat farmer. As Jasmin rang up the sale, Meredith carried little Isabella around the store talking to other customers.

To her surprise, people didn't seem put off by the baby the way she would have been while shopping back in the day. In fact, holding Isabella had the opposite effect. Customers smiled and talked to her, asking questions about the merchandise as well as her opinion on specific items.

Mariella knew she could be intimidating and didn't exactly try to fight that image. She was creative and cared about her store as well as the brides she designed for now, even it was on a much smaller scale than what she'd done in her past life. But she didn't want anyone asking questions or getting too personal.

She was just finishing up with a customer near the far end of the store when Jasmin called her name. She felt a little pulse of something go through the baby as if she was reacting to the sound of her mother's voice. That was impossible, Mariella thought. At two months, the child had to be too young for that sort of recognition. She placed a gentle hand on the back of Isabella's tiny head as she walked toward the counter then stopped dead in her tracks when she noticed Heather standing next to her employee.

Jasmin reached for Isabella. "Your new sitter is here," she said as if the girl could understand her words.

Heather smiled at the baby then glanced at Mariella with a look of utter disdain and a bit of challenge mixed in, like she was daring her to reveal their connection.

Mariella stood stock-still but didn't release the baby to her mother. She didn't know what to do. Why was Heather doing this? What did any of it mean?

"I don't mind if you keep Isabella at the store," she said, wrapping a protective hand around the baby. "Customers seem to like her. Maybe I should put her on the payroll." She gave a laugh that sounded terrible and phony even to her own ears.

"That's fine during the week when we're not as busy." Jasmin stepped around the counter and took the baby from Mariella. "But it's too much of a distraction for me on weekends. Besides, Heather comes highly recommended by Mary Ellen. She has lots of experience babysitting, right?"

Heather nodded. "My twin sisters are eight years younger than me. They were a surprise. My mom needed a lot of help when they were little."

"Sounds like a great fit," Mariella agreed. What else could she say? What was she supposed to do with this new piece of information about the daughter she'd given up?

Heather had sisters. She didn't sound resentful about having to help with them but had she turned into some kind of glorified nanny for her family once the babies arrived? Mariella had so many questions. She was curious about this daughter she didn't know even though she had no right to be.

"You'll just be upstairs with her?" She directed the question as much to Jasmin as to Heather.

"That's the plan," Heather said.

"This is my sweet Isabella." Jasmin held the baby toward Heather who took her with a smile. At least this didn't seem like the start of one of those cable-television movies where somebody got their revenge by stealing a baby.

Oh, lord, what was the world coming to when Mariella would even entertain the thought that Heather might do something so nefarious?

"Definitely just upstairs," Mariella repeated. "I've heard there's some sort of summer cold going around town and we wouldn't want to expose Isabella to anything that could make her sick."

Jasmin gave her a funny look then laughed. "Mariella is like the doting aunt," she told Heather. "She took such good care of me during my pregnancy and now Isabella, too. I don't know what we'd do without her."

Heather nodded, and Mariella doubted that Jasmin noticed the tightness around the edges of the teen's smile.

"Lucky," Heather murmured. "You sure are lucky."

A customer approached the register at that moment, and Mariella moved around to start the process of ringing them up while Heather followed Jasmin toward the staircase that led to the upstairs apartment. They could access the one-bedroom flat from the alley between the two buildings or from inside the store.

Should she have said something more than she had? Explained the connection she and Heather shared or claimed the girl as her daughter in front of Jasmin. She hated this feeling of uncertainty that grasped her every time Heather was around or she thought about the girl. Mariella had never dealt with so much uncertainty.

Even at her lowest in the depths of grieving the company she'd built and lost along with the man she'd given her heart to, she hadn't been this insecure. She kept moving forward. At least after that night in the ocean.

Resilience was her superpower, honed by years of dealing with obstacles and challenges in her childhood. She had nothing to rely on but backbone and so she made it strong. Nothing could truly get to her or shake her confidence. Not until she got to Magnolia anyway. Between Alex and Heather, Mariella was rattled to her core.

She thought she could deal with him. She could avoid him. She could tell herself he didn't matter. There was no fooling herself with Heather. The girl was a part of her whether either of them liked it or not.

Jasmin was back ten minutes later. "Heather is so sweet. I owe Mary Ellen a huge thanks. I guess she's working at that new fashion company as well, but that's Monday through Friday and she wants to earn a little extra money because she's starting college full-time this fall."

"Makes sense," Mariella agreed. "Although are you sure you know enough about her to trust her with Isabella?"

"Oh, yes." Jasmin straightened a display near the cash register. "She had a crazy amount of references. Way more than I gave to you when you hired me."

"But I was only hiring you for this store. Not to take care of a baby."

Jasmin laughed and patted Mariella on the shoulder. "Seriously, your protective instinct is adorable, but I feel confident with Heather. I even talked to her mom."

Mariella startled. "Her mom?"

"Don't worry, Auntie Mama Bear, I did my due diligence."

"What's her mom like?" Mariella hadn't realized she said the words out loud until Jasmin answered.

"Sweet woman. Sounded a bit frazzled and she misses her oldest daughter. She said the sisters miss her, too. That they are super close. I can't imagine a moment when Isabella goes to live off on her own. Especially if she's just seventeen about to turn eighteen. Heather must be so smart to have graduated high school early."

"Mmm-hmm." Mariella was unable to say more around the ball of emotion lodged in her throat. Her child was so smart, even if she'd had nothing to do with it. Heather was intelligent, beautiful and people loved her. Her baby was loved. She did her best to ignore the tangle of curiosity and regret knotting inside her belly. How could Mariella feel anything but joy at this moment?

# CHAPTER SEVEN

MARIELLA LET HERSELF into the apartment above the store just before noon, not bothering to knock. She repositioned the takeout bag she held in her arms, making sure the plastic crinkled enough that her arrival wouldn't be a secret.

Not that the apartment was large enough for someone to sneak in.

Heather looked up from where she sat on the couch. Isabella was cradled in her arms, wide awake from what Mariella could see. Heather placed the phone she'd been holding with her other hand on the cushion next to her.

"You should keep the door locked," Mariella said, glancing over her shoulder. "It's safer that way."

Heather gave her a dubious look. "Because of the high crime rate in Magnolia?"

Mariella stepped forward. "It's good practice. A smart habit to get into for a young woman living on her own or taking care of a baby."

"Smarter than certain habits," Heather acknowledged with a nod. "Like drinking or drugs? Those are habits single women can get into as well, right?"

Mariella didn't bother to respond. She was well aware of her past mistakes. Every single one of them. "I brought lunch for you." They'd ordered carryout, and Mariella had offered to bring the sandwich to Heather.

Jasmin had already been up to check on the baby once

during a lull in customers so seemed fine with Mariella delivering the food. The young mom thought Mariella's preoccupation with Isabella and her babysitter was cute because she didn't know about the shadows that lurked in the dark corners of Mariella's heart and the very good reasons Heather had to hate her.

"I can hold her while you eat," Mariella offered as she took a plate from the cabinet above the counter. This tiny apartment had been her first home in Magnolia, so different than the airy loft she'd had in Manhattan.

Plenty of people lived in way smaller apartments in the city. She certainly had when she'd first arrived. Buying that pricey piece of real estate had been a big moment for her. There'd been hours spent hours walking the streets of New York City during her first year there, imagining the lives of the wealthy and powerful people who lived in those historic brownstones and swanky high-rises with doormen guarding the entrances against people like her.

She hadn't minded downsizing when she came to Magnolia, but after a few months she found herself craving a yard. She'd never had a garden to tend. The thought of adopting a dog from Meredith Ventner's animal rescue had even crossed her mind, although she hadn't yet taken the plunge. She had her goldfish, Millie, and that seemed like plenty of responsibility for the moment.

"You seem fairly adept at multitasking," Mariella observed as she unwrapped the sandwich.

"Not really."

"You weren't struggling to manage your phone and your nanny duties at the same time." Why had she made the stupid little dig? What did it matter with a baby that young if Heather was on the phone at the same time she was holding her? At least she was holding her and hadn't left her alone and deserted in her crib for hours.

"I'm reading to her," the girl said. "I have an eBook downloaded on my phone." She held up the device as she joined Mariella at the counter. "It's what I used to do with my sisters. I would read to them from my English class required reading. I could entertain them and get my homework done at the same time. My mom says she thinks part of the reason I'm so smart is because of how much she read to me as a kid. She loves to read."

Heather transferred the baby to Mariella's arms and moved the plate to the scuffed table. "She also likes to bake, and she volunteered as the room mom when I was little. She's a good mom. I'm lucky."

"Jasmin is a good mom, too," Mariella said then wanted to kick herself in the shin for her insensitivity.

It was a relief that Heather's adoptive parents were good to her. For years, she'd wished and hoped and prayed for just that. She had no right to the sudden pang of jealousy.

"That makes me happy," she said, purposely gentling her voice.

"I wasn't trying to make you happy." Heather's sharp tone cut like a knife. "I don't care about your feelings."

"I wouldn't expect you to. What are you reading? One of the great classics or some treatise on philosophy?"

Heather rolled her eyes.

"What?" Mariella shifted her hold on Isabella when the baby started to fuss. "I know you're really smart. I just figured you'd read the kind of stuff smart people read."

"I like mysteries," Heather said quietly. "I read plenty of classics and important books in high school and I'm sure I will again when I get to UNC. When it's just me, I like commercial fiction. I read pretty much anything. But cozy mysteries are my favorite."

"Have you ever tried Brenda James?" The popular cozy mystery author kept Mariella enthralled for hours each time she released a new book.

Heather paused in the act of taking a bite of sandwich. "Her Darby Kelleher series was my favorite. I actually cried when I finished the last book. I didn't want it to end."

"Did you know they're making a movie of it?" Mariella asked.

"I heard that. Books are almost always better than movies. Amber Turner is starring in it, right?"

The few moments of joy Mariella had felt sharing something in common with her daughter seemed to fade away as quickly as they'd started thanks to the reminder of Amber.

She worked to keep her face features neutral. "I introduced her to those books."

"Along with your fiancé?"

"Something like that."

"Sorry," Heather said. "That must have sucked."

"Yep," Mariella agreed, unsure what else to say. What else could she say? Her past wasn't a secret. She should have expected that Heather would have seen the video.

Isabella had settled again and was contentedly sucking on her fingers. It was a recent trick she'd learned much to Jasmin's delight. Apparently a purposeful awareness of her own hands was a developmental milestone around two months and the fact that Isabella had discovered them a few weeks early made her mother certain she was destined to be a genius.

Mariella's daughter was a genius, or close to it as far as Mariella was concerned. The whole nature versus nurture argument was a load of crap. Heather might have gotten her sun-kissed highlights from her mom and her soulful smile from her biological father, but Mariella gave credit for every bit of her intelligence, caring and any other good traits she possessed to the people who'd raised her.

Just as Mariella had wanted.

She was so much more than Mariella could have imagined, and her dreams about her daughter left pretty big shoes to fill.

An awkward silence filled the apartment for several long moments. The only sound was the soft noises Isabella made sucking on her fingers.

What were the little habits Heather had as a baby? Mariella brushed aside the question she wouldn't give voice to. What was the point of thinking of her child as a baby when she didn't even know her now?

For the first time since she'd met the girl, Mariella admitted to herself how much she wanted to know her daughter and how curious she felt about every aspect of Heather's life. The realization whispered through her like a night breeze, making promises in the darkness that the light of day might not be willing or able to deliver.

She was about to suggest they set up a date for coffee or even a meal. The thought of putting herself out there in that way terrified her, but it was what she wanted. She wished she had more of an idea what Heather wanted, but the girl kept her motivations private.

Then Mariella's phone started going wild both with incoming calls and texts. The noise startled Isabella, and the baby began to cry. Heather immediately reached for her, and Mariella handed over the baby as she pulled her phone out of her back pocket.

"Damn it," she whispered and then grimaced. "Sorry, Isabella."

"I don't think she's old enough to repeat or even understand swear words," Heather said.

"Good point." Mariella typed in a reply to the urgent text from Emma.

"Everything okay?"

"Not exactly. There was a wedding scheduled at the Wildflower Inn today, and the bride didn't show for it. It's our second runaway this month, although we found the first one. According to the note today's bride left, she took off with the best man so somehow I doubt she's returning. My business partner texted that thing are getting chaotic with the guests. I need to get over there and help with damage control."

She started for the door. "Could you run down to the store and tell Jasmin what happened? I'll do my best to get back but not sure how long it's going to take to deal with the situation over there."

"Yeah, sure," Heather agreed although Mariella knew the girl could be lying. But she didn't have time to worry about that.

"Thanks." She should say something else. Something insightful and generous. The words just wouldn't come, and she doubted they'd make a difference where Heather was concerned. She'd left behind any enthusiasm she had for the fake-it-till-you-make-it school of thought a long time ago. Why bother when she had her hands full just surviving?

ALEX STOOD ON the front porch of his house a few blocks away from the Wildflower Inn later that evening. Night hadn't completely fallen over his neighborhood filled with stately older homes that spoke of the town's bygone era.

Shadows crept along the edges of the front porch, and the sky had taken on a muted mix of purples and pinks. This time of day had quickly become his favorite, when the world quieted and he could feel the shift from day to night.

The house Alex had purchased was on the smaller side compared to mansions like the Wildflower Inn, but he thought it was perfect. It had a brick facade that had been painted a pale yellow with crisp white trim around the windows and black sashes for each of the panes.

"I don't understand what you think I can do to help," he said to the man in front of him.

Cam Arlinghaus had arrived ten minutes earlier to make a case for Alex's assistance that he still found hard to believe. "You can talk to him. Emma can't have a guest locked away in an upstairs bedroom for much longer. She's not going for the *Flowers-In-The-Attic* aesthetic."

Alex snorted. "What the hell is up with the book reference?"

"I heard Angi say it and it sounded legit," Cam admitted with a shrug. "What can I tell you? I'm desperate for whatever argument will work. The wedding guests have all left so the only people still waiting are his parents."

"Why don't you send them up to talk to him?" Alex ran a hand through his hair and then cocked his head to listen to a nearby sprinkler. He let the rhythmic hiss calm his nerves and imagined the mist giving a refreshing relief to a parched lawn.

He'd been working in his own yard earlier, hauling flagstone and sand as he prepared to build a patio off the back porch.

He hadn't grown up doing household or yard projects. Living in the city, his mom and stepfather had hired out anything that needed to be done around the apartment.

His real dad traveled so much he normally lived out of a suitcase.

Since coming to Magnolia, Alex had gotten his DIY vibe on. He was only a little embarrassed to admit that much of his motivation for that came from the home improvement shows he'd compulsively watched after his breakup with Amber.

He hadn't been very good at construction work at first, but he was getting better. His friendship with Cam had started in the local hardware store when the talented contractor and furniture builder had given Alex some pro tips on the cordless drill he was buying. Cam had even shared that part of Emma's desire to remake famous artist Niall Reed's old house into an inn after her divorce had come from binge-watching too many home improvement shows.

It seemed funny to Alex that Emma would create a business that specialized in weddings when her background included a similar heartbreak to his. He wanted nothing to do with love or romance or any of the crap that the wedding industry fed people. To him, it was all noise and marketing. Not the authentic type of change he was trying to create with the branding of the Fit Collective. He was all about helping people reinvent themselves and feel proud of their bodies no matter the shape or size. The wedding industry was a different story.

"We've tried to get him to open the door. His parents, me, Emma, Angi. Mariella came the closest. You could hear him messing with the lock and then he decided against opening it. The next step is calling the local fire department to help us, but Emma doesn't want any more publicity than she's already getting."

"What in the world would Mariella have said to convince him?" Alex refused to allow the curiosity he felt toward the

woman to color his tone. "It seems like she would be better at stopping a wedding than comforting a jilted groom."

"I get why you feel the way you do about her." Cam nodded. "But she's not the same as she was back then. At least
I don't think she is. Because she's pretty awesome now and
from what Emma said, she didn't exactly have that reputation back in the day."

"Not exactly," Alex agreed. "What did she say to the
groom?" he repeated, not sure where his curiosity came from.
He didn't—or at least shouldn't—care about anything that
involved Mariella.

"That if the woman who was supposed to love him would
cheat then she didn't deserve him in the first place and that
he would be better without her. It was her idea to get you
involved."

"Excuse me?"

Cam shrugged. "From what the groom said, he was most
concerned with moving on after being publicly humiliated.
I think she thought you could relate."

Alex could relate on several different levels, but it bothered him to no end that Mariella would have picked up on
that. He didn't like the thought that she had any insight into
his personality. And certainly not when it came to something as personal as how he felt about getting on with his
life. He hated that he was destined to be defined by that embarrassing moment in time. But it certainly felt as though
he'd never live it down.

One easy way was not to get involved. To send Cam back
to the inn alone and hope for the best with that jilted groom.

There was no chance of denying he understood what the
guy was going through. And based on just the little Cam
had told him, he also thought he might be able to offer some

words of encouragement, potentially enough to entice the man to open the door and face the world. It was bound to happen sooner or later because the alternative was too bleak to consider.

"Fine," he agreed and Cam blew out an obvious sigh of relief. "But I have a condition."

"Name it. The ladies will do anything."

"It's not for the ladies. I could use help with the back patio project. I'm hoping you'll be my manpower tomorrow."

Cam laughed softly. "The ladies will do anything for your help and I'll do anything for Emma. If you get this guy to open the door, I'll be here at seven tomorrow and as many weekends as you need."

"Deal." Alex stepped forward to shake hands then followed Cam toward the truck parked at the curb. "We could walk to the inn, you know."

"Every minute this situation isn't resolved makes Emma more upset," Cam told him. "So every moment counts."

Alex nodded. He appreciated Cam's devotion to Emma. It was the kind of devotion he'd planned on offering Amber for the rest of their lives. Turned out coming from him she hadn't wanted it.

It seemed to only make him weak in her eyes. And that just left him feeling pathetic. Pathetic was no way for a man to live his life.

Within minutes, Cam had parked around back at the inn. Several pairs of eyes looked up as they entered the kitchen, and Alex saw Emma let out a sigh that matched her fiancé's. He wasn't sure he could live up to her expectations of making things better with the groom, but he was committed to trying.

Emma introduced him to the groom's parents. The father

pumped his hand while the mom gave him a tight hug. "We saw your video back when it happened. Although we're grateful Arthur wasn't publicly humiliated the way you were, this is still awful for him."

"Not many people were made a public spectacle the way I was," Alex told her with a tight smile.

She hugged him even tighter. "I won't watch that Amber Turner any longer."

"You rented one of her movies the other night in the hotel," the dad reminded her.

"From this moment forward she is dead to me," the woman assured Alex with a sheepish grin.

"I appreciate that," he said. "However, she's a talented actress—I should know better than anyone—so there's no need for you to boycott her."

"Such a nice young man," the mom said. "Just like my Arthur."

"Why don't I head on up?"

Alex was grateful when Emma stepped forward. "I'll show you where he is."

They climbed the back staircase and Alex felt like the whole place was shrouded in silence, as if even the walls knew something damaging had happened here tonight. Something that wasn't a part of the eternal love and vows normally spoken within these walls or in the backyard.

"We appreciate you coming over," Emma said. She reached the top of the stairs and turned to face Alex. "When Mariella suggested it—"

"I don't want to talk about Mariella. She's not the reason I'm here."

"Oh, right." Emma nodded. "It's just that she seemed so sure you could help. I know you guys aren't exactly the best of friends, but she has a lot of faith in you."

Alex wasn't sure how to react to that and didn't particularly care for the way his heart pinched at Emma's words.

He didn't want to think about Mariella in any way, but as they headed down the hall he realized that was going to be impossible tonight because she was sitting along with the third business partner in the inn, Angi Guilardi, outside one of the doors at the far end of the hallway.

"You came." She scrambled to her feet.

"As a favor to Cam," he clarified immediately. "And because I hate to hear about another poor schmuck being played by a woman. Did you have a hand in this guy's heartbreak as well?"

Her mouth thinned and he could have gut-punched himself for being an ass. What was it about this woman that brought his emotions so quickly to the surface?

"I didn't even arrive until after most of the guests had left."

Angi shifted closer to Mariella and Emma moved to stand at her other side. Alex had noticed this occurrence before with these women. The way they had each other's backs.

Despite his personal feelings, he was glad Mariella had that kind of loyalty from her friends.

He wished he had friends like that.

Maybe he could find them in Magnolia if he allowed himself to open up to people. Trusting didn't come easy to Alex. Not anymore. "The guy's name is Arthur?"

"Who wants to know?" a voice called from the guest room.

Alex tried to ignore the scent of lavender that tickled his senses as he stepped past Mariella. It was a strange juxtaposition the way she seemed so tough but smelled so sweet and soft.

"My name is Alex Ralsten," he said to the closed door. "I have an idea what you're feeling right now."

"Really?" There was a sharp rap on the wall next to the door. "You know what it's like to want the ground to swallow you whole?"

"Yeah, I do." Embarrassment pricked against the back of Alex's neck. He could feel the weight of Emma, Angi and mostly Mariella's gazes as they watched him stare at the door.

He didn't want this. He didn't want the reminder of his past. He didn't want to rip open that old wound, the one that he thought had healed. He wasn't the man he'd been before. He'd left that person behind. This wasn't his business or responsibility, but he couldn't walk away. Not when he heard the thread of humiliation in the groom's tone. Alex recognized the sound like it was coming from his own soul.

He turned to the women. He wasn't going to do this with an audience. "Do you mind giving Arthur and me some privacy?"

"Of course," Emma answered for all three of them. She flashed a grateful smile. "If there's anything you need... or if there's anything you need, Arthur, just let us know." Silence greeted her offer.

"He'll be fine," Alex assured her. He had no business making that statement but had to believe it was true.

Emma and Angi started down the hall, but Mariella continued to stare at him. He met her gaze, surprised because he would have expected to find pity. Instead he saw a level of understanding that shook him to his core.

"Let's go," Emma called to her friend. "Mariella, come on."

With a subtle nod at Alex, she turned—almost reluctantly—and followed her friends down the hall.

"It's just you and me, buddy," Alex said to the door as he took a seat in front of it. He hoped he could live up to the expectations of Mariella and her friends. More than that, he hoped he could help Arthur deal with his circumstances better than Alex had.

# CHAPTER EIGHT

ALEX MADE IT back to his house close to midnight.

Cam had offered to drive him, but Alex chose to walk. He needed a few minutes of quiet to settle himself enough so he might be able to get some sleep.

It had taken nearly an hour of talking to the closed door before Arthur opened it. The poor guy had looked like absolute hell. His face was ashen but his eyes were puffy and red-rimmed from obvious crying. In his position a few years removed from his own heartbreak, Alex couldn't imagine that the woman who'd run off with Arthur's supposed best friend was worth all the tears and upset, but the groom was nearly inconsolable.

According to Arthur, his bride had been his dream woman and, like a fool, he'd thought they'd found their perfect love story.

Alex could have told the man that perfect didn't exist and love was something made up by people in Hollywood or card companies to sell boxes of chocolates and bouquets of flowers on Valentine's Day.

He didn't say either of those things, though. Despite his heartache, Arthur clearly still believed in love.

To the point that it sounded as if he would have welcomed his cheating fiancée's return.

The guy was delusional. At least Alex could say that once he'd been made a fool of by love and had his heart ripped out, he knew enough to shut the door on any future need for attachment. He barely dated and was clear about keeping his heart out of the equation.

Maybe Arthur would get there, too. Or maybe he'd stay convinced that love was a possibility for him. More power to the guy, Alex supposed. It was none of his business. He was glad he'd been able to help by sharing his story without much of the lingering bitterness. He'd actually begun to question why he was still holding so hard to that anger.

He was so lost in thought that he didn't see the unfamiliar car parked in front of his house until Mariella climbed out.

"Crisis averted," he said, keeping his voice casual and purposely not noticing how ethereal her beauty appeared with nothing but the moon and the glow of a streetlight illuminating her features.

The houses around them were dark, and he imagined his neighbors tucked into their comfy beds with no awareness of Alex standing on the sidewalk trying to remind himself of all the reasons he wanted nothing to do with Mariella. His body refused to toe the line on that count.

"I heard." She nodded. "I just talked to Emma, and she said you were a huge help."

"What are you doing here, Mariella? Emma said you'd gone home a while ago."

"I left the inn. I figured you wouldn't want me hovering."

"So you decided to camp out in front of my house instead? That's showing a lot of restraint. Great boundaries. Give yourself a gold star."

He waited for her snarky comeback. She had a retort for every single thing. But if one was banging around in that beautiful head of hers, she didn't speak the words out loud.

She continued to study him with only half her face illuminated by the streetlight. Clouds rolled across the night sky causing the moon's glow to emerge at regular intervals like a toddler playing peekaboo.

It wasn't as if Alex needed light to know Mariella. He would have recognized her anywhere, in a pitch-black room or a driving snowstorm with zero visibility. Her scent was one aspect but even more, he knew her energy. When she was this close, he felt as though his whole body vibrated with awareness.

He didn't choose the connection between them. He wasn't that big of a fool. But he couldn't deny it. It was always there.

"I'm sorry." She shook her head. "No, let me start with thank you. Thank you for your help tonight although I know you didn't do it for me. It meant the world to Emma, and we all appreciate it. I appreciate it."

He shrugged away the satisfaction her words gave him. Reminded himself that her opinion didn't mean anything.

"Sure," he agreed. "No big deal." Although it had been a big deal to relive the grief he'd felt after the breakup with Amber. The process he'd gone through to deal with the fallout of her betrayal and how he'd managed to overcome it.

In some respects, he didn't feel like he had much wisdom to offer. But the knowledge that he wasn't alone seemed to help Arthur. Alex wished the guy nothing but the best.

"And I'm sorry," she continued, her voice barely above a whisper.

"For what? You said yourself that you didn't have anything to do with today. You didn't even show up until—"

"For what I did to you."

Alex blinked. "You're giving me a sincere apology now? For what exactly?" He didn't like sounding so flabbergasted by her apology but couldn't hide it.

"For the scene I caused at your wedding and the way that hurt you. I should have handled it better. If I hadn't been drunk and high, maybe I would have been able to choose something different. There's no guarantee. I was angry. I didn't know how to deal with my emotions so I wanted to hurt everybody. I didn't care that you had nothing to do with it. I didn't care that you were innocent—even more of a victim than me."

"Even more?" Something about that bothered him. "We were both betrayed by the people we love."

"You didn't deserve it, though."

"You did?" He took a step closer to her and gazed down into her crystal-blue eyes. He sounded like an imbecile questioning every statement she made, but that was the only way he could think of to figure out where that gorgeous mind was going. He was used to animosity from her, but her vulnerability had the power to break down his walls in a way that terrified him.

"I was kind of a train wreck back then. I'm a little better now, at least. I don't blame Jacques for not wanting to saddle himself with me for the rest of his life. I would have run in the other direction."

"Again, the situation with our exes wasn't your fault, although you're responsible for the scene at my wedding. Nothing more than that, aside from your horrible choice in dating a man named Jacques."

She sniffed. "He was French."

"Also a total cliché. I saw pictures of him and Amber on vacation after the wedding. The guy wore a literal raspberry beret."

"He liked hats," Mariella said with the hint of a smile. "And scarves."

"Not to mention those little wire-rimmed glasses worn by men who fancy themselves as intellectuals."

"He didn't even have a prescription. Jacques had 20-20 vision."

"I think that says it all."

Although in truth she had said it all.

"Why now? It's been three years. You've made it very clear that you don't think much of me. You certainly were adamant about that at the wedding. Lots of details about my deficiencies, all caught on camera."

"That was the alcohol talking." She glanced away then back at him. "Or maybe the drugs. Sometimes it was hard to tell. You didn't deserve the things I said about you or that public humiliation. Just like your new friend Arthur didn't deserve what his fiancée did to him today. I should have apologized a long time ago, but humility isn't exactly one of my strong suits. I'm working on being a better person."

He felt his lips twitch. "Since when?"

She glanced at her watch. "Since the clock turned midnight. It's a new day. Maybe it's a new me, too."

"Your friends seem to like the old you."

"They're too nice for their own good. I don't deserve them either."

"That's a theme with you. What you do or don't deserve. Have you ever considered that you're too hard on yourself?"

Maneuvering through this strange conversation in the dark, they'd shifted closer to each other. So close now that he could appreciate the warmth radiating from her skin and feel her soft breath whispering against his jaw. Mariella was taller than most women. He liked that about her. She had a presence that couldn't be ignored. At least not by him.

"I know who I am and what I've done in life. The mistakes have piled up like dirty snow on the curb in the dead of winter. You know better than almost anyone that I've made terrible choices, long before your wedding day."

He knew she was referring to Heather. The girl had seemed to recover from her initial upset and was back to running his life and company with the maturity of someone far older. But she would not talk about Mariella or even allow him to broach the subject of her motivations for being in Magnolia.

And her personal life belonged to her so Alex didn't push the subject. He wasn't going to push Mariella either. Not when she seemed so fragile.

"Everybody makes mistakes," he told her.

She breathed out a laugh. "Do you know you're quoting a Hannah Montana song?"

"I did not," he admitted. "But she's right, although somehow I don't think Hannah Montana was the first person to utter those words."

"Maybe the first person to put them to music," she conceded. "It's late and I have no business being here anyway. I wanted you to know I'm sorry. You don't need to accept the apology or anything. I know this doesn't change your feelings about me."

Yet his feelings were changing. She wasn't the entitled fashion maven or heartless wrecker of lives he'd thought back in New York City. It was easier when he could believe that about her, but he also understood it simply wasn't true. Maybe it was the cover of darkness or the feeling of being emotionally wrung out after so long revisiting the past, but his defenses were down.

He didn't want to be alone or to feel alone right now. Maybe he no longer believed in love or wanted for himself what Cam had with Emma, but he was sick of the loneliness. And Mariella was so close and so intriguing that Alex put aside all of his good sense, at least for the moment. He bent his head and brushed his lips across hers. He should have known nothing would be simple or straightforward with this woman.

A kiss should be easy. He'd kissed plenty of women both before and after Amber. Yet nothing with Mariella went according to plan. Because the moment their lips touched, it was like a tornado of feeling swirling through him.

Yes, his body seemed to say.

This. Her. *Mine.*

None of those things could be true, but he couldn't stop the swell of emotion any more than he could stop a tornado's destructive funnel. Need tore through him, ripping away his moorings and good sense in one tremendous surge. Mariella moaned against him and pressed her body into his. At least he wasn't the only one lost to desire.

He cupped his hand on either side of her face, smoothing his fingertips over the delicate strands of her blond hair. He had to anchor himself somehow. Otherwise, he'd be tempted to take this moment further than was smart for either of them. Her soft skin and the curves of her body tempted him more than he could have guessed.

Her lips parted and their tongues mingled, the kiss quickly moving from an exploratory spark to a full-on blaze of need and desire. So much for scratching an itch. This was more than he bargained for, which shouldn't have surprised him.

Because Mariella surprised him at every turn.

She pulled away suddenly, her eyes hazy and unfocused, her mouth swollen and her cheeks flushed. He'd done that to her, made her lose control if only for a few seconds, and the satisfaction made him inordinately pleased.

"I didn't come here for that," she said quietly.

"I know. I didn't mean for it to happen. It shouldn't have happened."

"It can't happen again," she agreed.

"No."

Her eyes, which were already comic-book princess large, widened even further. "No?"

"Or yes," he amended. "I agree with you. Not again. Ever."

"Ever," she repeated.

"You should go, Mariella. It's late and if this—" he gestured between the two of them "—isn't going to happen again, you should go."

"I'm sorry," she repeated then hurried to her car and drove off, leaving him wondering exactly what she was apologizing for and if he'd end up the one who was truly sorry.

MARIELLA WAS STILL thinking about the kiss three days later as she hit the streets for an early-morning run.

The more she tried to put it out of her mind, the more it seemed to be embedded there like a tattoo across her senses. Anything could remind her of it—the brush of a soft piece of fabric over her skin or a minty stick of gum that reminded her of Alex's spicy taste on her tongue.

Sigh.

Why had he kissed her? The man was infuriating on so many levels, the deepest of which was his general kindness of spirit. She'd been a part of ruining the life of a good person.

Not that she believed in any way Alex and Amber would have ended up happy.

Her former A-list celebrity client was a consummate actress, making her adoring fans—as well as the people in her life—believe she was a kind and caring person. Without a doubt, Amber didn't deserve Alex but he didn't deserve the misery Mariella had put him through.

Going to his house and waiting for him hadn't been her smartest move but it felt necessary. She wanted him to know that she was truly sorry for what she'd done. She'd apologized and told herself she didn't owe him anything more.

That would have been the end. Except then he'd kissed her. And she kissed him back. Her body just about put on a ticker-tape parade when his tongue slid against hers. It hadn't been need and desire, although both had been there in spades.

She felt the warmth of his embrace like a revelation. It made her seem not so alone.

She was so sick of being alone. She'd become accustomed to it and figured that was her lot in life.

It shouldn't bother her. In Magnolia, she had more people who truly cared about her than ever.

She tried to put Alex out of her mind as she finished up the run then turned the corner to Sunnyside Bakery. Although it was early, not quite 7:00 a.m., Mariella had been hitting the pavement before the sun came up each day.

It was important to beat the heat but mostly because she woke early every morning from dreams of Alex and working up a good sweat was the least complicated way to move through her frustrations.

Plus, being one of the first customers into the bakery during the week meant she had time to visit with the gregarious owner. Mary Ellen was usually finishing up whatever baking she'd done for the day and always in the mood to talk.

The older woman was nurturing and gentle. Mariella

wondered what it would have been like to grow up with a mother like her instead of the one she'd had with a temper and alcohol-induced narcissism. Today there was a young girl behind the counter and disappointment swirled through Mariella. Silly to think that the bakery owner had enjoyed their dawn visits as much as she did. Maybe she'd paid the young barista extra to come in and run the front of the shop so she wouldn't have to bother talking with Mariella.

Stupid insecurities. Mariella worked to settle her panting as she walked to the counter to place her order.

"Yoo-hoo," a familiar voice called out. "I have your muffin over here, dear."

Mariella turned, shocked to see the bakery owner sitting with Luann and Heather, the only three people in the store other than the barista and Mariella.

She glanced between the trio and the front counter.

"She'll bring your coffee," Mary Ellen said, turning her attention to the young woman. "She's the sugar-free chai latte with an extra pump."

"I can't…" Mariella began.

"Of course you can," Luann said before taking a big swig of coffee. "If I got up at this untenable hour for a meeting, you will at least deign to join us."

Heather didn't speak but her glare communicated volumes. She flicked a glance at the door then back to Mariella as if daring her to make an escape.

Her daughter might be a real smarty-pants, but she clearly didn't know what made Mariella tick. Mariella had never been able to resist a challenge, which had both propelled her forward in life and also gotten her into far too many unfortunate situations.

"What's this about?" she asked, approaching the table with all the caution of a trainer entering a lion's den. Had

Heather revealed their connection and now Luann and Mary Ellen were going to rake Mariella over the coals for the choice she'd made to give up her baby for adoption?

"I know you don't like meetings," Mary Ellen said, patting the chair next to her. "Or getting involved with the town on an official basis. So I thought this might be the best time to get your attention."

"Why do you need my attention?" Mariella slowly sat next to the bakery owner.

"To talk about the Magnolia Blossom Festival."

Mariella picked up the bran muffin and methodically unwrapped it. "I'm already a sponsor. The store is paying for signage and donating a huge basket to the silent auction. Plus, I heard Emma talking about the inn offering a weekend stay as well. What more do you want and what does any of this have to do with these two?" She pointed a finger at first Luann and then Heather before tearing off a bite of muffin.

"It was my idea to meet with all three of you."

Mariella turned as Avery Keller Atwell walked toward them. "I've stopped in the store a couple of times to chat, but I know you've been busy."

The graceful blonde slipped into the chair next to Mariella, and she felt heat creep up her cheeks. Since her arrival in town, Avery had taken over marketing and community relations for Magnolia, and she was good at her job. Sometimes too good. She could convince even the most stalwart non-joiner to get involved, so Mariella had indeed avoided her during her recent pop-ins to A Second Chance. Avery wanted something, and Mariella felt like the only way to keep a distance would be to stay clear.

Mariella thanked the barista when she placed a drink

on the table in front of her and then turned to Mary Ellen. "You set me up."

"Not exactly." At least the older woman had the grace to look guilty.

"What are you doing here?" Mariella asked Luann. "I understand that Heather is here representing the company, but small-town sponsorships don't seem like they'd be your deal."

"You're my deal," Luann said, tapping a glossy nail on the table. "I told you I want things buttoned up with your agreement to take over my role sooner than later. The Fit Collective is sponsoring this little blossom festival deal, so that seemed like the perfect chance to introduce you as the new face of the brand."

"Not my idea," Heather ground out when Mariella's gaze shifted in her direction.

"Does Alex know about this?"

Heather squirmed. "He knows we're meeting about the festival. He's really into getting involved in the community."

"I love that," Avery said. She smiled at Luann. "Your reputation in the fashion world precedes you. But I'm sure you know what you're doing handing the design reins over to Mariella."

"I don't want the reins," Mariella said, choking on a bite of muffin. "I don't even like horses."

"Are you allergic?" Heather asked suddenly.

"As a matter of fact, yes."

"Me, too," the girl whispered.

"I love horses," Luann said, her tone dreamy. "My third collection was inspired by the US Olympic Equestrian Team. Ralph Lauren wasn't the only one who could get his polo club on."

Avery's smooth brow puckered. "We're getting off track."

"So far off track," Mariella muttered.

"The reason we're here today is because I need some boots on the ground as far as organizing things for the festival in these final few weeks. Our summer tourism campaign is in full swing, and I'm getting bogged down with details for that. I don't want anything about the blossom festival to fall through the cracks."

Mary Ellen beamed as she took both Mariella and Heather's hands in hers. "I suggested the two of you. The three of us will make a wonderful team."

"And I made Heather give me the meeting details because you aren't returning my calls," Luann said to Mariella across the table.

She should have gone for a ten-mile run and then headed straight home for the shower. For the past couple of years, she'd managed to be a part of the town without really getting involved in the community. It was easy with the store because she always had that to fall back on for an excuse or a topic of conversation if things got too personal.

Yes, Emma and Angi knew her well, but she kept even them at arm's length. She'd seen an opportunity to partner with Emma on the inn, and the idea of creating something new had called to Mariella. But she did it on her terms, only giving as much as she wanted to each event. The day-to-day running of the property and the care and feeding of guests she left to the other two.

"Does Emma know about this? Because I think if you're looking at the inn as a sponsor, she's the face of it."

Mary Ellen tsked. "You know very well that Emma has her hands full with the wedding season."

"Assuming she doesn't get a whole bunch more cancellations," Heather said under her breath.

"What are you talking about?" Mariella demanded.

Mary Ellen lifted her hand quickly in a lame wave and stood. "Okay, Jennifer," she said, "I hear you calling."

"Nobody was calling you," Mariella told the woman.

"Pretty sure she was. My job was to get us together. I need to check on something in the back anyway. You and Heather decide when you'd like to meet next and I'll be here."

"I'm not meeting with anybody," Mariella said as Mary Ellen bustled off toward the counter. She leveled a stare at Heather. "What are you talking about as far as alluding to cancellations at the inn?"

Heather slunk a little bit lower in her seat. "I don't know. It's just something I overheard. Forget about me. That should be easy enough for you."

"Oh, no." Mariella wagged her hand in a finger in front of the girl. "You are not distracting me this time. Do you know what she's talking about?" she asked Avery.

Avery tucked a strand of glossy hair behind one ear. "I do. Although that's part of the reason Emma isn't involved, but she didn't want you to worry. She said you had enough on your plate right now."

"Tell me."

"There was an article published in the Raleigh paper this morning. An interview with the mother of the jilted groom. She spent a lot of time badmouthing her son's former fiancée but saved a bit of vitriol for Emma and the Wildflower."

"What did the inn or Emma have to do with a cheating fiancée?"

"The mom said this isn't the first bride scheduled to get married at the inn who has gotten cold feet."

"And she talked about you." Heather pointed at Mariella, earning a glare from Avery.

"The groom's mother was angry and emotional." Avery bit down on her lower lip. "I told Emma that we can spin this from a PR standpoint. It's not going to affect the wedding business."

"But it has." Mariella didn't need to ask. She said the words as a statement rather than a question. She didn't need to ask the question when she could already tell from Avery's tight expression what the answer would be.

"She's had a couple of worried brides call."

"Have they canceled their events?"

"Why does it matter?" Luann sat back in her chair. "Love is stupid and fleeting anyway. Better to cut their losses."

"We're getting ahead of ourselves," Avery said. "This is all an unrelated misunderstanding." She gave a pointed look at Heather. "One that is going to be worked out without anybody blowing things out of proportion."

"She has a right to know," the girl said, crossing her arms over her chest. "She's part of the reason things are going bad and she has a right to know. You shouldn't keep secrets from people."

Avery blinked. "It wasn't exactly a secret. Emma wanted a chance to make things right before talking to you about it, Mariella. She didn't want you to feel responsible or guilty for—"

"Too late." Mariella grabbed her latte and stood from the table. She lobbed a glare at Luann. "I'm not taking over your role." Then she switched her gaze to Heather. "You're right about not keeping secrets. So think about what you're planning to tell people about yours."

Finally, she turned to Avery. "I'm in for your stupid

festival if it helps Emma and the inn. Parade me out with a big, fat smile and I'll charm everybody from here to Charleston."

Even though it hurt that Emma hadn't talked to her, Mariella would make it right. She had to try.

## CHAPTER NINE

MARIELLA STOOD IN the front yard of the Wildflower Inn gazing at the crisp white facade. The black shutters were like a fringe of eyebrows framing each of the gabled windows. Blossoms of riotous color filled ceramic pots on the front porch. The entire property had been given new life as a result of Emma's renovation.

Mariella had first noticed the dilapidated mansion when she'd initially moved to Magnolia. At that point, Mariella had spent hours walking the streets of the city and the trails around town.

She'd needed fresh air like a plant needed sunshine. After so many years of running herself ragged in the big city, the slower pace of small-town life was a welcome change. But she'd found it hard to quiet her mind without relying on the drinks and drugs that had become her habit. Her crutch.

At that point, she'd thought about buying the house herself. Something in it called to her. She longed to see it restored to its former glory. So when she'd heard about the stranger moving to town and converting it to an inn, Mariella had been more than a little intrigued.

So much so that she'd inserted herself into Emma's life as a partner. She didn't want to be involved in the day-to-day running of the Wildflower, but she'd loved helping to design and decorate the different bedrooms, each with a specific theme.

And when Emma had started taking on more wedding bookings, Mariella had rediscovered her passion for designing gowns and helping the Wildflower brides to create their perfect day.

Emma took care of the logistics, business and marketing. Angi handled the food and any catering needs. Which left Mariella in her happy space of creativity.

She believed she was adding something of real value to the inn, and it gave her a purpose in addition to running the store in town.

After this morning's meeting and what she'd discovered about the fallout from the inn's streak of runaway brides, she wondered if she was doing more harm than good with her involvement. The fact that Emma hadn't shared the potential issues with her had to mean her friend thought the same thing.

It was another example of why it was easier not to get involved in the first place. Every time she took the risk of giving her heart to someone or something like her work she was hurt in the end. She was bound to be rejected or spurned for simply trying, being reminded over and over that she didn't belong.

At what point would she finally get the message? She dashed a hand over her cheek when an errant tear leaked from her eye. She didn't want to cry over this. She didn't want it to matter the way it did.

It had been silly to think that she had any business in the wedding industry given her past.

The front door of the inn opened and Emma walked onto the porch. She raised a hand in greeting.

Anger rushed through Mariella and she welcomed it.

Anger was a simpler emotion than hurt or sadness. Temper she could handle.

"One of the guests told me there was somebody loitering in the front yard." Emma smiled, but Mariella didn't return it. "Do you want to come in for a cup of coffee?" her friend called, coming to stand at the edge of the front steps.

Mariella stepped forward. "I already had my caffeine for the morning. Imagine how fun it was to have three women I barely know fill me in on how my reputation is one of the things hurting your business."

Emma closed her eyes and blew out a long breath. "It's not you."

"Oh really? Because I read the interview with the jilted groom's mom on the way over here. She said I had to be asked to leave the premises in order for her son to be coaxed out of the room."

"We both know that isn't true. You chose to leave, and the groom didn't care either way. He doesn't even know you."

"But the general public does, and if they don't, I'm easy to look up. I'm bad for business, Em."

"Tell that to one of our brides who has worn a dress you've designed specifically for her on her wedding day. You make women feel beautiful."

"When I'm not making them nervous about the bad luck that follows me like a plague."

"You aren't bad luck."

"Tell that to Alex."

"He doesn't think you're bad luck, Mar. No one but you is still consumed with what happened that day."

"Stop." Mariella shook her head and tried to calm her emotions. She didn't want to reveal how much she was hurting right now. Strength and snark were what she wanted to be known for. "I was mentioned by name in the article."

"So was I," Emma said as she moved down the steps. "They painted me as a bitter divorcee trying to recapture the happiness I couldn't manage in my own life. The runaway heiress who is trying to reinvent her life by monetizing the happiness of unsuspecting couples."

"Reinventing a life shouldn't be a bad thing."

"Agreed, but you know how things go with news stories. Anything for clicks or to sell a paper. I'm working on a rebuttal now with testimonials from people who have gotten married here. I won't let this bring down what we're building."

"Yet you didn't tell me."

"Angi and I knew it would upset you. You can be sensitive when it comes to your reputation."

"Because my reputation in the wedding industry is trash. I told you I wanted to be a silent partner behind the scenes. I didn't want to have any client-facing interactions."

"Then you shouldn't be so talented. The dress you designed for Holly was a work of art. Your designs from Belle Vie are still hugely popular. You might not want a high profile, but it's hard to keep a light like yours under a bushel."

"Not really," Mariella muttered. "I was managing it just fine."

"Don't let this derail you."

"How can I not?" Mariella demanded, feeling the burn of tears gathering behind her eyes. She was not going to cry in front of her friend. "My mistakes have hurt so many people and they continue to. I was better off keeping to myself. A small life is what I need."

"Your heart and your talent are too big to play small even if you wanted to. That's obvious to anyone who gets to know you. It's why Mary Ellen requested that you help with the Magnolia Blossom Festival. You make magic out of everything you touch."

"You're delusional. There must be a gas leak inside because your mind isn't working right. Do you want me to call the utility company?"

Emma flashed a grin. "There's no gas leak."

"I'm so tired of having my mistakes damage other people." Mariella's legs suddenly felt too weak to hold her upright. Her shoulders drooped from the guilt they constantly carried. She turned and sank onto one of the porch steps. Her gaze took in the manicured lawn with its sections of colorful flowers and the winding cobblestone path that led to the street.

The inn was a happy place, but she knew that for years, the house hadn't been. She glanced around to the other stately homes that lined the street, wondering which of them held secrets.

How many people had made the same mistakes or even bigger than the ones that seemed to dominate her life? That was why she needed to stay small, not because it would undo the wrong she'd done but so that the things she wanted to remain hidden couldn't be uncovered and dissected by strangers.

She thought she'd left behind her life's penchant for attracting rumors and whispered gossip. But somewhere deep inside she knew that she deserved everything bad that came to her.

"I don't know what you're thinking about..." Emma nudged Mariella's shoulder with hers. "But I can tell it isn't good. Why don't you come inside with me and take a look at some of the testimonials that have been posted to our social media as well as travel and wedding websites?

Sometimes the best way to counteract the negative is to focus on the positive. Don't let one day define your life."

Mariella rolled her lips together. She appreciated the sentiment in her friend's advice, she needed her friend—someone—to understand.

"It's not just about that one day or even the video or even how out of control my life had gotten leading up to that. Yeah, it was terrible. I might never live it down. But it's not the worst thing I've done. Not by a long shot."

"You're a good person," Emma insisted. "What came before—"

"I told you I had a baby at sixteen and gave her up for adoption. Now she's sought me out. How can you tell me I'm a good person?"

"Oh, honey. You were a child yourself at that time." Emma tried to wrap an arm around Mariella, but she shrugged off the touch.

"No. I don't deserve your comfort. I don't regret my decision. I had nothing to give her. Less than nothing. Is this what you're talking about focusing on the positive? That the baby I loved with all my heart that I carried inside me and is a part of me had a way better life without me in it."

"Has she told you why she decided to find you? How she found you?"

Mariella picked a piece of lint from the front of her cotton pants. "I don't know the why. As far as I know, she found some papers in her father's study. The adoption was closed but her mother paid one of the nurses to slip me a piece of paper with their contact information on it."

She let out a shuddery breath. "I wrote to her—to my daughter's mother—one time. I told her everything in my heart but asked her not to contact me. It would have been too difficult to move on with my life if I had to hear about the child I let go."

"She found you from a letter?"

Mariella turned and nodded. "Heather is smart and resourceful. I didn't give a return address, but I signed my name and there was a postmark from Philadelphia, where I lived at the time. She came to Magnolia to..."

Emma leaned forward. "Does she want a relationship with you? Is that what you want?"

"Does it even matter what I want?"

"Yes, it does. You matter."

"Not to Heather."

"Of course you matter to Heather or she wouldn't have come here, Mariella."

"I don't know what she wants exactly. She's angry and curious. I think she feels bad that she even wanted to find me. She has a good life, Em. I need to believe that."

"But you can't know that her life was better without you."

"I need to believe that even more because if I gave her a better life then at least all the guilt and sleepless nights and regrets I went through were worth it." She rolled her shoulders. "You've met Heather. She's awesome. Her parents did a great job. It was worth it."

She breathed out a small sigh. "Tell me it was worth it."

"You did the best you could at the time for your child," Emma assured her. "And, yes, I've only met Heather when she was working at the bakery, but she seems great. Mary Ellen thought the world of her."

"So does Alex. He's protective of her like a big brother or something. He told me her family misses her."

"If she's here, it's because she wants to know you, Mariella."

"Or she wants to punish me or show me what I missed out on."

"Or know you," Emma repeated. "Do you want that? And don't answer that you don't matter. You do."

"I don't know. I never considered having her in my life, you know? I have a hard enough time not screwing up romantic relationships and friendships. What if I mess up things with her? She's so normal. I was never normal. I craved normal."

"Normal is cool," Emma agreed. "I didn't have normal, either, although I'm not complaining. Neither should you. Everything you went through made you into who you are right now."

"God help us all."

"I think you need to give her a chance if she wants one, or even better you can offer an olive branch. At least let her know that you're receptive to having a relationship. It might be good for both of you."

The inn's front door opened, and a moment later, Ethel, Emma's rescued dog, came barreling into the front yard. She trotted between Emma and Mariella, her tail wagging.

"One of the guests is asking about recommendations for a spa in the area," Cam said from the doorway. "Hey, Mariella."

"Hey, Cam. How's it hanging?"

Emma snorted out a laugh.

"To the right," he answered without missing a beat.

The small inside joke relaxed Mariella for a moment. It was just the reminder she needed that she had friends. She'd built a life where she could even have private jokes with people. This was her town, and she didn't want to leave it behind. Her home. As much as she wanted to right the wrongs of the past, she wouldn't relinquish it to her daughter or Alex or some disgruntled mother of the groom.

She'd more than paid her dues. If only it were so easy to remember that in the moments when she had trouble quieting her mind.

"I'll let you get back to work," she told Emma with a gentle nudge. "I need to open the store."

"I'm sorry I didn't call you right away about the article." Emma gave her a tight hug. "We are partners and that's not going to change."

Mariella nodded. "No matter."

"And you are going to help with the Magnolia Blossom Festival?" Emma smiled hopefully. "Maybe that would be an easy way to get to know Heather?"

"I don't think anything about getting to know Heather is going to be easy, but I'll help with the festival," Mariella promised.

Emma hugged her again. "Perfect."

"Nice to see you, Cam," Mariella called before scratching the dog between the ears.

"You, too. You know Meredith was here with a couple of her new rescues yesterday. We're doing a new program where guests can spend time with her animals on their vacation. Adopt a dog for a day. You should think about adopting one yourself. You'd have a running buddy."

Mariella shook her head. "No, thank you. Millie is the only buddy I need. And don't tell me that a fish doesn't count because Millie is the best."

"I wouldn't dream of arguing." Emma waved another farewell and then climbed the steps of her house.

Mariella wasn't sure the child she gave up would appreciate it but she felt a strange sense of calm, and she could use all the calm she could get in her life.

"How did the meeting go?" Alex asked Heather as she entered the office that morning. He'd just made a fresh pot of coffee in the staff lounge, wishing he'd put in an order for pastries from Sunnyside. Maybe tomorrow he'd pick some up on his way in.

The girl gave a noncommittal shrug. "To start, Luann crashed it."

"What do you mean she crashed it? Luann doesn't get out of bed before eleven most mornings."

"I mean she showed up at Sunnyside and plopped herself at the table to be part of the meeting. I think mainly she wanted to talk to Mariella."

"Is she still insisting that Mariella take over her creative role in the company?"

Heather nodded. She was the only other employee Luann had shared her plan with, and Alex was grateful to have someone who understood. "We didn't really talk about that," Heather admitted, "or the plans for the festival because everything got sidetracked."

"Sidetracked?" he repeated. He should have poured an extra cup of coffee for himself. He studied the girl more closely. "Are you okay? Did something happen to upset you?"

"Nothing upset me." The girl sounded completely unconvincing. "Other than the fact that people are such jerks."

"People like Mariella?" Alex asked the question almost reluctantly. He didn't want another reason to go at it with Mariella. Especially not after their kiss. Even thinking about it now made his blood heat. He focused his attention on Heather. "Tell me everything."

She placed her bag on her desk and sank into the chair. "There was this article about the inn and they interviewed the mom of the almost groom with the runaway bride."

"Arthur." Alex nodded. "I talked to him. He's going to be fine."

Heather sniffed. "Maybe you should have talked to his mom because she's a real piece of work. She kind of blamed the problem with the wedding on the inn or at least suggested that the Wildflower is bad luck."

"That's ridiculous. Arthur's fiancée was cheating on him with his best man and had been for six months. Long before they arrived at the inn."

"I agree. I'm telling you what the lady said and now it's affecting business."

Alex scrubbed a hand over his face. "I'm sure that doesn't make Mariella happy."

"It's not only that. The mom talked specifically about Mariella and how she has a history of ruining weddings and maybe having someone like her involved isn't the best idea."

Anger pulsed through Alex, although he might have said the same thing around the time he'd first encountered Mariella in Magnolia. He certainly hadn't been happy when he'd shown up for an engagement weekend to celebrate his best friend to find Mariella as one of the Wildflower Inn's owners.

But he'd gotten over it. He'd more than gotten over it. Even during Brett and Holly's celebration, it was clear how talented she was and what a difference her involvement made.

And now to hear this…

"Let me get this straight. You're worked up because Mariella is being unfairly targeted?"

Heather glared at him. "It's not like I came to Magnolia to ruin her life or something."

"I get that," he said gently. "I'm also a little surprised that you care."

"I don't want to care about her," Heather admitted. "It makes me mad that I do. I've got a great family. My mom is awesome. My dad, too, and my sisters love me. I shouldn't even have come here. I had plenty of other scholarship offers. I could be someplace close to home. A place where I could go back and visit them on the weekends."

"Does your family know why you chose North Carolina?"

She shook her head. "I never told them I found out who my real mom was. It would have made them feel bad. Now I'm here and I don't even know what to do. I want to hate her. It's easier to hate her."

Yeah. Alex could appreciate that sentiment.

"Trust me, kid," he said, "I agree completely. For all of Mariella's flaws and that surly 'tude, she is a hard person to hate."

"I hate that about her," Heather muttered. "She seemed so freaked out about the whole article thing and I don't know how she's going to respond. I feel like if she keeps getting pushed she's going to leave and then I will have come to Magnolia for no reason."

"Hey, now. What about this fantastic job?"

"The job is great," she agreed with a hint of a smile.

"Maybe you should spend some time figuring out what exactly it is you want from Mariella, whether it's a relationship or some resolution. You could give her a chance."

Heather didn't look convinced. "It feels like I'm being disloyal to my parents. They're the ones who put in all the time and effort to raise me. They chose me when she gave me away."

Alex thought about his mother and how she never really chose him in any way that mattered. "You could talk to them as well," he suggested. "Explain what's going on. It might help."

"I just want everything to be easy."

"Most things worth having don't come easy," he said. Damn, did he sound like as much of a fuddy-duddy to her as he did to himself? But that didn't make the words any less true. He looked around the open-concept floor plan of the company. He and Heather had been the first ones to arrive, but more employees were starting to trickle in.

He hadn't exactly fooled himself into believing that re-branding a company on the verge of collapse would be easy, but he had high hopes for simple. That had been naive or maybe willful disregard of the obvious.

When Alex had chosen Magnolia as his home and head-quarters, he'd known Mariella was here. Plus, he'd pur-posely invited Luann to return to the company in a creative role, despite his awareness that she tended to be a loose cannon.

His half brother, who loved giving Alex grief, would have told him that he surrounded himself with compli-cated women because he had mommy issues to work out.

In return, Alex would have grabbed his brother and put him in a headlock. He missed Jonathan and their weekly dinners in the city after a game of pickup basketball at the athletic club. He could even admit that his brother wasn't wrong. Alex had plenty of issues to work out, and appar-ently, he was going to get through it with the help of the women in his life.

"You're a good person, Heather, and not just because you are wicked smart. It's okay to care about people be-cause you have a big heart. Even the ones you don't want to care about."

She inclined her head, studying him in the way she had that was far more mature than her actual age. He had a feeling she knew he was giving that advice to himself as much as to her. Thankfully, she didn't mention it.

"No matter what," she said, her voice sure, "I'm not going to let you down, Alex. You can depend on me."

He wasn't sure he should have taken the comfort he did in her words, but he smiled. "I appreciate that, kid, and the feeling is mutual." He turned for his office wondering exactly what he would have to do to keep that promise.

# CHAPTER TEN

THE FOLLOWING SATURDAY MORNING, Mariella headed for the marina south of town. It was barely six, and as she parked her car, the amount of activity already taking place in the gravel parking lot shocked her.

Emma stood at the edge of the grass talking to an older man with white hair and a bushy beard. He looked like a Southern version of Ernest Hemingway if Hemingway had favored T-shirts with slogans on them. Mariella pulled her bag from the back of her car and headed toward Emma. "You weren't joking when you said they get going early around here."

"Some fish don't bite when it's hot," the old man said, "and today is going to be a steamy one. At least fifteen degrees above normal."

"Here, fishy, fishy," Mariella said in a singsong voice, pointing at his shirtfront, which had that quote scrawled across it in a bold font.

"They won't be able to resist a pretty girl like you," the redneck Hemingway said with a chuckle.

"Mariella, this is Mike Molsen. He runs the marina and tackle shop and is known far and wide as a fish whisperer. Mike, this is my friend and business partner, Mariella Jacob."

Although the fact that Emma had introduced her as both a friend and partner pleased her, Mariella inwardly cringed that the old man had heard her full name. What if he recognized her from her past? She hated that her mind went to that possibility every time she met someone new.

Mike only grinned. "Cam knows his stuff, but if you ever want to head out on the water with a real expert…" He nodded toward the ramshackle bait shop with a line out the front door. "You know where to find me."

"I appreciate the offer," Mariella answered. "And a man who knows his way around a rod."

Emma rolled her eyes, accustomed to Mariella's bawdy sense of humor.

Mike burst out laughing as his face went beet red. He leaned toward Mariella. "You're a pistol. Too much for an old geezer like me to handle. Good luck out there today. Let me know how you did when y'all get back." He headed up the gentle slope toward the shop.

"You just about gave poor Mike a heart attack," a deep voice said just behind Mariella's shoulder. "He's going to need all day to recover."

She whirled to find Alex standing directly behind her, wearing a tan T-shirt, Ray-Bans and a Knicks cap pulled low on his head.

"Did I mention Alex is coming with us?" Emma said with fake cheer.

"No." Mariella turned back to her friend. "You didn't mention it."

"Turns out I invited you, and Cam invited Alex and neither of us thought to mention it to the other." She forced out a laugh. "Quite a coincidence, right?"

"Quite." Mariella tried to stop the rapid beat of her pulse.

"I need to grab a cooler out of the back of Cam's truck." Emma continued with the forced excitement, not fooling

Mariella for a moment. "I'll meet you guys at the boat. It's going to be great."

"Seriously?" Mariella muttered to no one in particular. She couldn't help but notice that her friend refused to make eye contact with her.

"So serious," Emma chirped and then made a quick escape into the parking lot.

"Do you want me to leave?" Alex asked, his voice pitched low. "If it bothers you that much to spend the day with me…"

"It doesn't bother me. You don't bother me." Mariella gave a sharp shake of her head. "I just don't like surprises and I've had more than my fair share recently."

"Hopefully the only other surprise you get today is the amount of fish we catch."

They started toward the dock. Mariella could feel the speculative glances from the people they passed.

"They think we're tourists," she said with a small laugh.

"I wonder how long it takes to feel like you belong in a town like this."

The comment surprised her coming from Alex. "I'm sure you already feel like you belong." She cast a quick look to the side, taking in his movie-star profile with the aristocratic-looking nose and chiseled jaw. "You are being heralded as the bringer of jobs and booster of the economy. People love that."

He shrugged. "Some of them do, but I've had a couple of old-timers mention to me that they like the old mill and what it brought to town just fine. They've been hoping somebody would reopen it the way it was."

"How ridiculous. Things change. That's the way the world works."

"In mysterious ways," Alex agreed. Mariella got the

impression he was talking about more than the old mill. They reached the end of the dock, and Cam straightened from whatever he was fiddling with under the boat's steering wheel.

"Morning," he called, not appearing the least bit concerned about having them both as passengers for the day.

Mariella thought about when she'd first met Cam. He'd still, for the most part, been a hermit, only drawn out of his solitary existence to help the sister of his late wife, who was the first bride to be married at the Wildflower.

By doing that one good act, everything had changed for both Cam and Emma. Opposites on the surface, they'd fallen deeply in love and he'd rediscovered his passion for building custom furniture in addition to helping Emma as the inn's unofficial resident handyman.

There was a lesson in the two of them coming together, something about finding your own inner strength and never giving up. Mariella had never been a fan of school and wasn't much in the mood today for learning.

Especially when her body was so distracted. Alex's steady presence at her side and the clean scent of his soap were a combination that seemed to make her lose all her good sense.

She'd chalked up their kiss to a silly loss of control for both of them. After all, he hadn't called her or asked to see her after said interlude. And thanks to the interview that appeared in the paper, his name was once again linked to hers. She couldn't imagine him liking that.

What she could imagine was him wanting to keep their interactions to a minimum. That was fine. She wanted the same thing.

*Liar*, her body screamed. Strangely, the voice sounded like her mother's. Her mom had never let something trivial like a conscience or good sense keep her from acting on whatever her body wanted.

She would have been very disappointed in the maturity and wisdom Mariella had gained since coming to Magnolia. Maturity didn't run in her family. Even so, she would be the bigger person and not worry about the way Alex made her feel.

Simple enough to manage. She could do that easily. No problem. They were there to fish and enjoy a day on the water. Since she'd been spending more time at the ocean, she'd asked Emma about going out on one of their excursions. The water and waves appealed to her despite her fear, and she wanted a chance to see them from a different perspective. She wanted to stop being afraid, and a boat trip felt like a big step to accomplishing that goal.

Despite her wariness about Alex, he seemed to be just as interested in making it a good day. Once they got on the boat and motored into open water, there was very little awkwardness. Even her nerves disappeared.

Cam showed her how to rig a line after she'd made it clear that she wanted to learn instead of asking him to do the hard stuff for her.

It was a gorgeous day with the sun shining and wind blowing in her hair. The open water was choppy in some parts and gentle in others. In the distance, the horizon beckoned, and Mariella felt much of the tension held tight inside her recede like a wave pooling away from the shore.

All four of them wore hats to protect their faces from the harsh glare. Another thing her mom would have chided her for. Janice had always been a fan of sunbathing even after her first battle with melanoma, the deadly cancer that would eventually claim her life.

As the temperatures warmed, both Cam and Alex took

off their shirts in order to jump off the side of the boat for a relaxing swim.

"You doing okay?" Emma asked when it was just the two of them.

"It's fine. I'm not even scared of the water. Maybe I'll swim. Cam has life vests, right?"

"I was talking about you and Alex."

"We're both going to live in this town so we need to grow accustomed to seeing each other."

Emma studied her for a moment.

"What?" Mariella demanded as she forced herself not to squirm under Emma's scrutiny.

"It seems to me that Alex is doing more than growing accustomed to you. I keep catching him looking at you."

"It's not a huge boat."

"That's not what I mean. He's looking at you like you're a piece of key lime pie and he just sat down at the dessert buffet."

Mariella snorted even though the idea of that had butterflies dancing across her stomach. "I think you're imagining it."

"No. He likes you. I think you like him, too."

"Don't confuse like with trying to keep the peace. I think Alex and I have come to an understanding. We live in a small town and we have a lot of the same friends. There's no point in us being at war."

She didn't mention that part of their new truce had involved his steamy kiss.

"I'm glad to hear you say that." Emma handed her a can of sparkling water from the cooler. "This means you're not thinking of leaving Magnolia, right? Not because of Alex or a disgruntled inn guest or for any reason. This is your home, Mar."

"Let's just enjoy the day." Mariella popped open the can and then rolled her eyes when Emma's glare turned severe. "I'm not thinking of leaving," she conceded. At least not at the moment.

"Good, because Angi and I would drag you back, tie you up and stuff you in the basement of the inn if that's what it took."

"Such caring friends I have," Mariella said with a laugh. But her heart warmed at the thought that they cared enough to consider kidnapping her. She really did have a warped sense of relationships.

Despite the upheaval of the past week, Magnolia felt more like home every day.

BY THE TIME Cam maneuvered the boat back into its slip in the marina, Mariella realized she'd laughed more today than she had in ages and felt as relaxed as she had in—well, possibly forever.

Sometimes she believed she wasn't built for relaxation. Whether it was her laundry list of insecurities about getting her needs met as a child or some inherent drive not to fail, she'd become a striver. She was always working toward the next goal or achievement.

Even after leaving behind her business, it had only taken a few months before she'd set her mind to opening the store in Magnolia. Although she had plenty of money to live on left over from the money she'd made at Belle Vie, she never wanted anyone to think she wasn't a hard worker.

Emma and Angi were much the same way, even though they were motivated by different things. The three of them had bonded over getting the inn up and running and solidifying its reputation by attracting a steady stream of guests and wedding clients.

Today had been about fun and it made clear the ways she'd suppressed the part of herself that looked at fun as a legitimate pursuit. She reveled in the excitement of reeling in a big fish and the pleasure of lying back on the bench seat on the front of the boat to enjoy the warmth of the midday sun.

Mike, her down-home Hemingway, was standing at the edge of the dock and grabbed the rope from Cam to tie off the boat.

"How did you do?" he asked Mariella.

She gave him two thumbs up. "I might usurp your position as the local fish whisperer," she warned with a wink.

"Is that so?" He gave her a thorough once-over. "Well, I can tell the open water agreed with you. You don't look so much like you're smuggling a stick up your back end as you did this morning."

Mariella heard Alex let out a startled bark of laughter behind her.

"You have a way with the women," she told Mike.

"That's what two out of three of my wives said," he answered, scratching his belly. "The first one married me when I was in med school so she thought she was hitching her wagon to a future doctor. Didn't really take to the coastal life when I dropped out to run charters."

"Her loss," Mariella assured him.

"Appreciate that, especially coming from a beautiful woman like yourself. My offer still stands to take you out on the water. If you think Cam is a great instructor, wait until you check out my fishing moves."

He turned his attention toward Cam, which was helpful because Mariella felt a blush creep up her cheeks. She didn't want to think about Cam's moves or Mike's moves. And she couldn't stop thinking about Alex's potential moves, so overall, she was a discombobulated mess. A relaxed and happy mess, but a mess just the same.

While Cam and Mike worked out the details of a fishing charter Mike wanted Cam to take out the following week, Mariella joined Emma and Alex in carrying the coolers and towels and leftover food up to the parking lot.

"You do look lovely right now," Emma told Mariella.

Mariella grimaced. "All this effusive complimenting makes me wonder how bad I looked before."

"You are always beautiful but you're also wound a bit tight normally. Now you seem happy. It's good to be happy. I'm glad you asked about coming out on the boat. That was a nice surprise."

Emma headed for Cam's truck while Mariella walked to her car. She wasn't sure how she had missed the fact that Alex's hulking Land Rover was parked only two spots from hers.

"Some people like surprises," he said casually when they got to the back of her car.

"Do you also want to tell me how I looked like I had a stick up my butt before today?"

He shook his head slowly. "That was never what I thought when I noticed your butt."

She couldn't help the laugh that escaped at his words. "Are you objectifying me?"

"I wouldn't dare."

"Good." She placed her bag in the trunk then turned. "Thank you for not making this day awkward."

"Despite what you might believe, I'm not out to get you."

"It's easier for me to believe you are."

"Why is that?"

"I don't want to like you, Alex. I sure as hell don't want to want you. That would be stupid for both of us."

"But you do?"

She rolled her eyes. "Maybe you don't remember our kiss. I think I made it pretty obvious how I feel about you."

"Trust me, I remember. I also know we were both there for it. But you were the one who called it a mistake."

"You were the one who said it would never happen again." She held up a hand before he could speak. "And I agree with you."

"That's a first."

Cam and Emma approached the two of them. "We're taking off," Cam said. "Good job not clawing each other's eyes out on the boat today."

Emma smacked his shoulder.

"What?" he demanded. "You know it's true. They're sworn enemies."

"That might be taking it a bit far," Alex said, rubbing a hand over the back of his neck.

Cam chuckled. "We'll leave it at a good day all the way around."

Emma came forward and gave Mariella another hug before walking away hand in hand with Cam.

"They are annoyingly cute together," Mariella said when she and Alex were alone again.

"Another thing we agree on," he told her with a smile. "This is becoming a habit."

"We are not enemies." She wasn't sure why she felt the need to confirm that, but it seemed to make Alex happy.

"Would you like to get dinner?" he asked suddenly. "It doesn't have to mean anything other than we're not enemies. I know this great little seafood joint down here that has the best oysters you've ever tried."

She wrinkled her nose. "Yes on dinner, no for oysters. They remind me too much of eating snot."

His grin widened. "Snot, huh? I can see why that isn't appetizing. Why don't you leave your car here and we can drive down together? I'll drop you off later."

If someone had asked her a few weeks ago about the possibility of having a friendly meal with Alex Ralsten, she would have laughed. Now she nodded.

She could tell herself all she wanted that she was just doing this because she had no other plans but it wasn't the whole truth.

It didn't take into account the part of her that simply wanted to spend more time with Alex. That part held sway more than any other, and she was tired of trying to find a way to ignore it.

# CHAPTER ELEVEN

MARIELLA BECAME MORE appealing every minute Alex spent with her.

He'd suggested dinner on a whim because he didn't want the day to end. He liked Cam and Emma, and although it had been a shock to realize Mariella was joining them on the boat, it had made their time on the water even better. He appreciated her enthusiasm and the way she'd wanted to learn every aspect of being on a boat and fishing.

Enthusiasm attracted Alex more than anything. People who were excited about something—their work or a hobby—he wanted to be around those kinds of people. It didn't matter if it was scaling a mountain or an obsession with training bonsai trees. He admired passion, and this Magnolia version of Mariella had it in spades.

The only thing Amber had been excited about during their time together was being seen at a trendy hot spot either in NYC or LA. She complained about the press, but instructed her team to make sure there were paparazzi at the ready to snap a few pictures. It was as if the things they did as a couple didn't count unless they were later documented and dissected on one of the popular gossip sites or could be used for a social media campaign.

At the time, Alex figured it came with the territory of dating a celebrity but he didn't realize how weary he'd grow of having his life out there for public consumption until his move to this small town.

Mariella seemed as interested in him she was in keeping a low profile, although she garnered notice the way a colorful butterfly might in a room filled with plain moths. She and Amber had that in common—an inherent brightness that drew people to them. And it wasn't just men. Despite all of her sharp edges, when she let her light shine, Mariella connected with everyone she met.

In the same respect, Alex understood she could never be for him. Not only because of the past they shared. He didn't possess the radiance that Mariella deserved in a partner.

He had success and money, but those were easy enough to come by for someone with his background. Deep in his soul, Alex was ordinary. His past and his family had made that clear. Part of him wondered if that had been what attracted him to Amber in the first place. If he could gain the notice of a movie star of her caliber that would prove to his family he was interesting and worthy of love and respect.

Some piece of him believed that soaking up the glow of her bright light would make people believe some of that sparkle actually came from him. He'd never understood how to achieve it on his own. Then Amber had cheated and turned the ensuing fallout into an indictment of him. She hadn't been subtle about it either.

He didn't know how much was her true belief and what part was about repairing her tarnished reputation, but she'd made it clear in interviews and snippets dropped into the tabloid stories from unnamed sources that he'd held her back. It had been a blow to Alex. During their time together, he'd shared the insecurities he'd had growing up and she'd exposed his weakness on a national stage.

He'd trusted her implicitly, which had been a huge mistake.

If he allowed himself to fall in love again, which was not on his current radar, it would not be with a shining star. He would find a woman with her feet firmly planted on the ground who wanted the same kind of normal, boring life that he knew embodied his real comfort level.

The funny part about Mariella was although he could see her brightness, he didn't think she recognized that quality in herself. She seemed to enjoy their low-key night at a local hangout as much as he did.

They drove back to the empty parking lot at the marina in companionable silence.

As the evening progressed, his physical awareness of her had grown until he felt it with the power of a tidal wave. It was all he could do not to reach for her and pull her into his arms.

He barely resisted the urge because even more than desiring her, he was starting to realize he wanted her as a friend. He wouldn't take the chance of pushing her away by asking for something she couldn't give him. Something that could only end in pain.

His phone rang as they entered the lot, and a local number he didn't recognize appeared on the screen.

He ignored the ring the first time. As soon as the call went to voice mail, the phone started chirping again.

"You can answer it," Mariella told him with an incredulous glance. "Maybe it's a woman offering a Saturday night booty call."

"No one is phoning me about a booty call," he said.

"Are you sure?" she asked when the phone continued to ring. He pulled to a stop at the back of her car.

"Just answer it, Alex. You're fine. It's not like you need to walk me to my door."

He accepted the call, at the same time holding up a finger to Mariella. He didn't want to end the night with the impression he was going to drop her off and then head to some late-night date. He suspected she was acting this way so she'd have an excuse to take off in a snit. He should probably let her. It would allow him to get his swelling need under control.

He was surprised to hear Jack Grage, one of the first employees he'd hired to the Fit Collective, on the line. Alex couldn't figure out why the project manager would need to get ahold of him so urgently. "What's going on?" he asked, trying not to sound as irritated as he felt. Ice ran through his veins as the man explained the current situation. "Slow down, Jack. Is Heather okay?"

Mariella stilled in the process of exiting his car. "What's going on with Heather?"

He held up a finger again and listened as Jack went into more detail. "It's good you called me. I'll be there in twenty minutes. Make sure she knows she's not alone right now."

Alex disconnected the call then turned to Mariella, who had returned to the passenger seat and shut the door to the car.

"I've got this," he said. "She's fine. A little rock-climbing accident. Nothing serious."

Mariella gave him a tight nod. "You can tell me about it on the way. Start driving."

"You don't have to get involved."

"She's my daughter whether she wants to be or not. I'm already involved."

Alex could hear the tension in her voice, but she didn't seem inclined to make eye contact with him. It wouldn't take an emotional-IQ genius to deduce that Mariella was upset, and he questioned whether letting her come with him was the best idea.

He also didn't want to waste time arguing so he put the car into gear and started toward the direction of the local hospital.

"A group of employees from the company went rock climbing today. Heather was involved in a fall."

"How far?" Mariella asked, her tone even again.

"About five feet," he said with a wince. "She broke her left arm and two ribs."

He heard Mariella's sharp intake of breath even though she was staring out the window, her face hidden from view. "Is that all?" she asked in the same steady tone.

"Jack thinks she might have punctured a lung. The doctor is with her now."

"What kind of irresponsible group was she with on this climbing excursion? Somebody should have been looking out for her."

"It was an accident, Mariella. Jack is a senior project manager and responsible beyond his years. From the little he told me, she keeps saying he can go home. She's fine on her own. He's not leaving her."

"That's ridiculous," Mariella muttered. "She can't be fine when her injuries are that serious."

"Sounds to me like she takes after her mother with that fiercely independent streak."

"I didn't realize you knew her mother."

He gave her a sidelong glance. After a few seconds, she nodded. "Right. You were talking about me."

"She's going to be okay," he said again. "We'll make sure she's okay. The company has great health insurance, and she can have whatever time off she needs. I'll take care of her."

He said the words as much to himself as to Mariella, needing to believe they were true. This was the first time he felt like the responsibility he'd taken on with the Fit Collective might be too much. Financial responsibility he could handle. He didn't discount the fact that his employees were counting on him for their salaries.

Acting as someone's emergency contact ramped up the responsibility to a different level, one so serious it terrified him. As if reading his mind, Mariella reached over and took his hand.

"No one who worked at Belle Vie would have called me in an emergency. That says something about you, Alex. Something important. They trust you. It's in keeping with the type of company you want to build that your staff relies on you at this level."

"Thank you," he said quietly. "But that isn't much of a comfort when one of them is hurt."

"Do you think she called her parents?"

He shrugged. "I don't know but if she hasn't, I will. They sound like the kind of people who would want to be called after their daughter was in an accident."

"Yes," Mariella agreed. "I'm glad for that. I'm glad she has those kind of people in her life."

"Me, too."

"I met your mother once." Mariella offered the barest hint of a smile as she revealed that.

It shouldn't have shocked him, but somehow he hadn't expected it. His mom had been overly involved with the plans for his wedding. "My mom is a snob, but people thought it was a big deal that I was dating America's sweetheart. That made her like Amber. She liked that I had found somebody who would make me more interesting."

"She didn't make you interesting."

He tried not to cringe as he wondered whether Mariella had just handed him a compliment or an insult. "She's a star. My mother's friends were impressed by her fame. Not to quote country songs, but I didn't impress them much."

That drew more of a smile. "The fact that you can quote Shania Twain is legit impressive. Besides, you went to an ivy-league school and you're a success in your own right."

"I graduated from an ivy but didn't distinguish myself the way my half brother did. I wasn't part of some secret society or an exclusive club. Those things didn't matter to me, although they are important in my family and the social circles my mom inhabits. I worked hard enough and got decent grades. But they expected exceptional things. All I managed was decent which wasn't enough. Amber was a great catch according to my mom."

He felt his jaw twitch with remnants of the bitterness he'd felt at the time and watched out of the corner of his eye as Mariella processed his words. He didn't want sympathy for his rich-kid problems.

Instead of responding directly to what he'd told her, Mariella shook her head. "Your mom didn't like Amber."

He blinked. "Of course she did."

"Nope. She called her a twiddlehead. I remember it because I'd never heard anyone use that term."

Alex let out a surprised laugh. "To the best of my knowledge, it's a term my mom made up. I thought she reserved it for my cousin, Henry. He's the kind of person who makes a brick seem like an extraordinary genius of monumental proportions. He gave my aunt no end of heartbreak. After a while, my mother refused to speak his name. She would only call him the twiddlehead."

"She put your ex-fiancée in the same category."

"I just can't believe that. She was always nice to Amber. And Amber loved to tell me how much my mom adored her. She loved to tell me how much most people adored her."

"I'd be curious," Mariella said after a moment, "to know how many of the people who adore her are also on her payroll in one way or another. I worked with a lot of famous people. There was a certain type who liked to surround themselves with—not exactly sycophants—but yes-friends to be sure."

He chewed on this piece of information for a few seconds and found that it sat in his belly with the weight of a lead balloon. "You think Amber is one of those?"

"I don't think it, Alex. It was a well-known fact."

"I wish somebody would have let me in on that little secret."

"It sounds to me like you saw her in the light you wanted to. I did the same with Jacques and it worked out for me as well as it worked out for you. To your credit, you handled it better."

"You're doing okay now."

"Some days," she agreed then chewed on her lower lip as he pulled into the hospital parking lot. "I think you should go into her room without me. She's already had a rough night, and I don't want to upset her more."

He nodded, hating the pain he heard in Mariella's voice but respecting her for that choice. It was the way mothers were supposed to be. Unselfish and putting the welfare of their kids before their own needs.

Mariella was hard enough on herself, and he wasn't going to dispute whether she had made the right decision putting Heather up for adoption. But he had no doubt that if she'd kept the baby, she would have found a way to make it work. That's what moms did and she would have made a good one.

No matter what she believed.

MARIELLA SAT IN the waiting area of the hospital's small emergency ward. Her foot tapped against the floor as she tried to calm the tumultuous emotions rolling through her. Wave after wave they came, sending her into a spiral of swirling uncertainty.

She hated waiting. Patience had never been one of her strongest characteristics. She hadn't seen the value of it. As far as she'd been concerned for most of her life, patience was for wimps and people who weren't willing to charge forward and get the job done.

Mariella had painstakingly shaped herself into a charge-forward sort of person.

Maybe it was something she would have learned earlier if she'd really been a mom. Because in the past few weeks, she'd had more lessons in the value of patience than she'd been granted for her previous thirty-plus years on the planet.

Only one other person sat in the waiting area, a woman who looked to be in her midseventies. The woman had arrived fifteen minutes earlier, following in a gurney with her husband on it. He'd been surrounded by EMTs and hospital staff, then quickly wheeled into the back.

"We told him to lay off the cheese," the woman said when Mariella accidentally made eye contact with her. "That stuff is crap on your heart, but he wouldn't listen." Her voice broke on the final word.

Mariella didn't want to bear witness to this woman's

emotions when hers were teetering on the brink of control. She gave a tight nod. "I hope he's okay."

The woman compulsively shredded the tissue she held between her fingers. "He fell over right in the middle of *Jeopardy.* My Thomas is great at supplying those questions. He's so smart. I told him he should try to get on there. I would have loved to meet Alex Trebeck back in the day. It's too late for that now and maybe Thomas won't even have a chance to answer another Final Jeopardy! question."

Oh, God. This was a nightmare. Having to comfort somebody in such emotional distress. "I'm sure he'll have many more moments with Final Jeopardy. I'll…um…pray for him." She didn't have much experience with prayer, but she'd be willing to try if it meant this nice old woman would get her husband back.

"Thank you," the woman whispered. "Who are you waiting on?"

The words *my daughter* almost slipped out of Mariella's mouth, but she didn't allow herself to say them out loud. She hadn't earned those words. "A friend had an accident while rock climbing. She'll be okay though."

"It's nice of you to be here," the woman said. *Nice* had never been a word Mariella associated with herself.

Alex came through the big double doors at that moment.

He'd sent home Jack, the employee who had stayed with Heather, when they first arrived. Mariella had been tempted to rail at the guy for putting her daughter in danger, but he looked so young and miserable that she hadn't bothered.

As Alex approached, she wondered if he'd already called Heather's parents. They would know Mariella, and Magnolia was a small enough town that it would take some effort to keep her presence a secret if they came down to be with their daughter during her recovery.

*One moment at a time*, she reminded herself as she stood up to greet Alex.

"How is she?"

He nodded as if to reassure her, but his mouth was tight. "She's okay. Banged up but doing okay. The drugs are helping take the edge off."

"Can I…?"

"She'd like to see you."

Mariella let out a shaky breath. This was what she wanted, so why did she have the almost insurmountable urge to run away? It was terrifying to think that she might do or say something wrong. This moment wasn't about her, she reminded herself. She was here to support Heather.

She took a step forward then stopped and turned back to the older woman. "I really will pray for your husband."

The words coming out of her mouth should have been a shock, but the old woman didn't realize that. "Thank you. I'll do the same thing for your friend."

"I didn't realize you were one for prayer," Alex said as he led her down the hall.

"Me neither. But lightning hasn't struck me down so that seems like a good sign."

He placed a hand on her arm, whether in comfort or warning she couldn't quite tell. She appreciated his steady touch nonetheless.

"I'm going to call her mom while you're in there. I wanted you to know."

"Of course," she agreed. He stopped in front of a door halfway down the hall.

"I probably won't be long."

"Okay." She appreciated that he wasn't pushing her. Once again, she thought about Amber and how that woman must be the biggest idiot on the planet to have squandered what she'd had with Alex. The guy was handsome, smart and had a caring streak a mile long.

Any woman would be lucky to have him. The dawning realization that she truly wanted him hit Mariella like a mallet to the temple. It simply wasn't going to happen.

"You okay?" he asked when she didn't move for a few moments.

"I've got this," she answered, unsure which one of them she was trying to convince.

The room was quiet when she entered. Heather was propped up in the hospital bed with her eyes closed. Her left arm was in a cast and there was a bandage on her cheek. Mariella figured the girl was lucky she hadn't scraped her face worse in the fall.

She looked at once younger and somehow more world-weary than the last time Mariella had seen her. She seemed fragile, which was terrifying. Mariella tended to be a bull in an emotional china shop and didn't want to do anything that would hurt or upset Heather more than she was.

"I'm fine," the girl said as her eyes fluttered open.

Mariella nodded. "Clearly you showed that rock face who was boss."

Heather laughed softly and then winced. Mariella immediately regretted her lame joke.

"What hurts the most?" she asked.

"Probably my pride."

"Really? Because I've heard broken ribs can make breathing not the greatest."

Heather ignored the comment and continued, "I don't even think they wanted to invite me. That's the problem with being younger than everybody. I don't fit in."

"You don't have to be younger to have that problem." Mariella felt a pinch in her chest that she almost wanted to describe as maternal. "I'm sure they wouldn't have invited you if they didn't want you to be there."

"I kind of invited myself," Heather admitted. "Then I ruined the whole day."

"Did somebody say that? Because what happened to you was an accident. You didn't ruin anything. Tell me who said that and I will have a conversation with them."

Heather shook her head, a strand of limp blond hair falling into her face. She didn't bother to push it away. "You're talking like a mom."

Mariella drew closer to the bed and tucked the hair behind Heather's ear. "I take that as a compliment. Your real mom will get here as soon as she can. I know I'm not a substitute and I'm not trying to be, but if there's anything you need—"

"I don't want her to know about you being in town."

Mariella took a small step back. She'd expected that but hearing Heather say it out loud still stung. It wasn't as if she thought she was going to get invited to dinner with her daughter's adoptive parents or that she deserved anything different.

She pressed two fingers against the ache in her chest. "I can't exactly disappear," she said, "but I'll do my best to lay low while they're in town. I don't want to cause you pain, Heather. Any more pain," she clarified.

The girl nodded. "I doubt they'll be able to get here until tomorrow morning, and the doctor is releasing me today. I don't want to spend the night alone. Not that I think anything bad is going to happen. Maybe I'm being a big baby but—"

"You can stay with me." Mariella tried to keep her voice even as she made the offer even though her heart was beating like the frantic wings of a trapped bird. "I have plenty of room."

"Thanks," Heather said and closed her eyes again.

Mariella drew in a deep breath. One step at a time, she reminded herself as a fragile sort of hope filled her heart.

# CHAPTER TWELVE

MARIELLA PULLED INTO her garage and turned off the car, glancing over at Heather, who was resting her head, eyes closed, on the back of the seat. They hadn't spoken much on the drive from the hospital, which left Mariella time to ruminate over the implications of having her daughter stay overnight.

"Here we are," she said as if it wasn't obvious. "Are you doing okay? Is there anything I can get you?"

The girl unbuckled her seat belt without making eye contact. "I'd like to start by getting out of the car. You sound nervous. If you're worried I'm going to stab you in your sleep or something, I don't have the energy for that right now."

Mariella winced. "That's comforting."

"I'm also all out of warm and fuzzy."

"Duly noted." The girl's attitude was almost a relief. Mariella had never found a groove with warm and fuzzy. She was also anxious about being in any sort of a caregiving role. Probably the first thing she should do when she walked into the house was reapply deodorant.

They'd stopped at Heather's small guest house on the way over, and Mariella grabbed the duffel bag from the back seat then hurried around the car to help Heather out.

"I broke my arm," the girl said through gritted teeth.

"The doctor said the lung is bruised, not punctured. I'm not an invalid and can get out of the car on my own."

Mariella didn't argue although it was obvious Heather was in a significant amount of pain. They'd already picked up a prescription the ER doc had called in for some fairly heavy-duty pain meds. The kind Mariella had favored back in her wild days.

They walked into the house in silence. Mariella flipped on the light and automatically walked over to the kitchen counter to greet Millie. "How's my best girl?" she asked and dropped a few flakes into the bowl. Millie darted to the top of the water to grab her dinner then floated back down toward the castle Mariella had arranged in the center of the small tank.

She turned, shocked to find Heather directly behind her staring between the goldfish and Mariella. "Did you talk to that fish like it's a dog?"

"No. I talked to her like she is the most perfect fish that has ever lived, which is the truth. Heather…" She gestured to the bowl. "Meet Millie."

"It's a goldfish."

"Do you have a problem with fish?"

"No. I wouldn't have guessed you to be the pet type. Not much of a caregiver."

Mariella wondered if the girl had any idea how her observations bit like the sharp crack of a whip and gave voice to Mariella's own fears about her shortcomings. She doubted it.

Heather didn't seem to have the same animosity toward her as when they'd first officially met. Mariella appreciated the change, even it was subtle.

"As you said, she's a fish. Fish don't take a lot of work." She didn't mention that Millie was the most loyal companion she had in her life. And how much comfort she took from her pet.

"How do you know it's a girl?"

"I'm sure there's an anatomical way, but I know because she has girl energy."

"That's not a thing."

"Can I show you to your bedroom?" Mariella wasn't in the mood to be judged on her relationship with her fish. "You said your parents will be here by ten tomorrow morning. You probably want to get to bed early so we can have you back in your place before they arrive."

Heather nodded and looked away. Mariella wasn't sure if the girl was embarrassed to be hiding Mariella from her adoptive parents, but she needn't have worried.

Mariella did not want to come face-to-face with the people who had done so much better of a job with her daughter than she could have. Insult to injury and all that.

"You have a nice house," Heather said, almost reluctantly. "Thanks for letting me stay here tonight. I probably could have called Mary Ellen and—"

"I'm glad you're here, and it's fine that you want me hidden from your parents. I don't blame you." Both sentiments were true, which didn't stop the pain they caused. Mariella could deal with pain. "I'm not going to make things difficult or cause a scene."

Heather nodded and followed Mariella toward the back of the house where the bedrooms were situated. "I didn't think you would. I'm sure you don't want anybody to know that we have a history. It's easier that way."

Mariella turned to stare at the girl, whose delicate features appeared even more fragile in the glow from the hallway light. Her pale skin was pink around the edges of the bandage covering the scrape on her forehead.

"A history? You are my child. You may not feel that way and I didn't expect you to come back into my life, but it doesn't change the fact that you are my daughter."

Mariella might not have earned a place in Heather's life, but that didn't stop her heart from craving a connection. "I'm not going to tell you this is easy or ask for understanding of why I made the choice I did. My feelings aren't important right now. You are running this show, Heather. Whatever you need, I will agree. Hiding me from your parents is small potatoes compared to what I'm willing to give you."

"And if I decide that I like it in Magnolia and don't want to move to Chapel Hill in the fall but it's hard having you here? What if I want you to leave?"

Mariella shrugged. "Then I'll go."

"But I followed you. This is your home."

"Not if you don't want me here." Mariella still wasn't sure how to be a mom or what sort of relationship she wanted with Heather, but she wasn't lying when she said her needs didn't matter. It might hurt, but she'd do what Heather needed. The idea of acting unselfishly actually calmed her nerves in ways she couldn't quite explain.

The girl's sky-blue gaze flicked away "It's okay that you're here," she said into the silence. "I don't mind."

"Okay," Mariella answered. As responses went, it was lame at best. But there were too many emotions coursing through her to come up with something better.

She continued down the hall, trying her best to ignore the hope welling inside her. She didn't know what tomorrow would bring or if Heather's unexpected vulnerability was due more to the trauma of the accident and the drugs they'd given her at the hospital than any lasting sentiment.

It didn't matter. This moment of connection with the daughter she'd never expected to know was more than she could have asked for.

She pulled down the sheets and comforter on the full-size guest bed.

No one had stayed in this room before now. Mariella hadn't kept friends from her previous life. She wasn't even sure why she'd furnished it up until this moment. Now she was glad she had.

"Do you need help?" she asked as she straightened the base of the lamp that sat on the nightstand. It was already straight.

"I'm fine."

"I'll leave you to it then." She thought about hugging Heather but that seemed like it might be pushing her luck. Plus, she wasn't much of a hugger to begin with.

"I thought I was going to die," Heather said just as Mariella got to the doorway. "I didn't mention that to the people from the office because I didn't want to seem like more of a spectacle than I already was with the injury. But the first few seconds after the cord released, I thought it was the end."

"That must have been terrifying." Mariella tried for a supportive smile and hoped she succeeded. "I don't think you have to worry about your coworkers thinking you made too much of it. Any normal person would have just about pooped their pants given the situation."

One corner of Heather's mouth lifted. "Have you ever thought about dying?"

"I have." Far too often at one point in her life. "It wasn't my time. Or yours. You have a long life ahead of you, Heather. With the little I know about you, I bet it's going to be amazing."

The girl nodded. "Thank you for your help tonight."

"Anytime." Mariella cleared her throat when her voice cracked on that one word. It was a simple answer but a vow she took seriously. Even if tonight was the closest she ever came to having a relationship with her daughter, Mariella knew that she would do anything for Heather. Even if it meant dismantling her own life in the process.

ALEX ROCKED BACK on his feet as he waited on the doorstep of Mariella's front porch two nights later. Although he hadn't spoken with her directly, he knew from talking to her friends that she needed an intervention at the moment.

He heard shuffling from inside and somehow sensed her standing on the other side of the doorway. It was a tingle along the back of his neck, the way his heart always beat a little faster when she was close. "I know you're in there. I can feel your nervous energy."

The door opened, and she glared at him. "My energy isn't nervous. It's annoying because you're here and bothering me so now you can leave."

"You look like hell," he said and her eyes widened slightly. It wasn't true. He wanted to get a rise out of her. Mariella could spend two weeks camping in the wild with no shower, and she'd still walk out of the woods beautiful.

But the past forty-eight hours had taken a toll on her. Her eyes were red-rimmed and her hair fell in tangled waves over her shoulders. There was a crumb stuck to the edge of her mouth that his fingers itched to flick away.

"Have you been crying?" he asked gently.

"Of course not. Crying is for wimps."

"Have you left the house since dropping off Heather?"

"I'm taking a mental health day or two."

"How's that working for your mental health?"

"Did you come here for the sole purpose of giving me grief because if so you can—"

He held up the brown paper bag he was carrying. "I brought dinner."

"I have food," she said with a sniff.

"Not Angi's chicken pesto ravioli. She included an order of cheesy garlic knots and an extra-large slice of tiramisu."

Mariella perked up. "I guess since you're here, you might as well come in."

Alex resisted the urge to smile. That would just put her on edge again. But he wanted to grin like a fool. Mariella was funny when she turned prickly. He almost liked her better this way. Now he'd seen her soft side, the vulnerability she didn't let show very often. It made him feel too tender and exposed. Snarky banter he could handle.

As if to confirm his opinion, she closed the door behind him and asked, "How's Heather?"

"She's doing better. She seems to be adjusting to the cast and the pain isn't as bad as it was. She's all the talk around the office. That accident has made her famous at the Fit Collective."

"What are you talking about?" Mariella demanded as she followed him into the kitchen. "Is somebody being mean to her or hazing her for what happened? Because people fall and get hurt rock climbing all the time. That could have happened to anyone and if they—"

He placed a finger against her mouth to silence her. He enjoyed the touch far too much and quickly pulled away his hand. "No need to bring out the mama bear," he told her. "She's dealing with the accident like a trooper, which is making her a bit of a water-cooler legend. She's gone from falling a few feet to nearly toppling down the side of the mountain and getting up without complaint despite the severity of her injuries. Our summer intern is half in love with her at this point."

Mariella frowned. "She's too young to date. You should have a policy against fraternizing among your staff. Dating can wait until she gets to campus."

"I'll keep that in mind, although the dating part isn't any of my business."

He placed the bag of food on the counter and Mariella stepped closer to him. The kitchen, decorated in a charming farmhouse style with stone countertops, painted cabinets and stainless-steel appliances, was littered with dirty dishes and half-eaten bags of chips and cookies.

"You're really taking this laying low seriously," he told her.

"I promised Heather. Have you met her parents?"

He nodded. "They're nice people who clearly adore her. She has a great family, Mariella. Her dad went back this morning, but her mom is staying through the weekend. I think she's happy for an excuse to fuss over her daughter. The way they make it sound, she's always been fiercely independent and self-sufficient."

"Which probably comes from being abandoned as a baby. My fault."

Mariella's voice sounded hollow, and he wanted to pull her close. Instead, he took the containers out of the carryout bag to keep busy. "Self-sufficient isn't a bad thing. And you didn't abandon her. You put her up for adoption and she was chosen by a great family."

"It's what I wanted for her."

"Are you going to hide out in your house until the weekend?"

"The plan was to lay low for a couple of days. If her

mom is now staying until the weekend, then I'm keeping the curtains drawn."

"Do you think that's a little excessive? You could go for a walk around the neighborhood to get some fresh air." He reached out and patted the top of her head. "Potentially shower?"

"Yeah, yeah, point taken. I've been… Well…it's been a rough couple of days to be honest."

"Tell me about it," he said, truly wanting to know. To understand what made this fascinating woman—with her dichotomy of edges and vulnerability—tick.

"You know she spent the night here."

"I do."

"I barely slept a minute. I laid in bed all night listening in case she called out to me. As if she were still a toddler." She started to run a hand through her hair then cringed when her finger immediately got tangled in it. "It was ridiculous but not as absurd as the fact that last night I slept in the guest bedroom."

"Why did you sleep there?"

"When I gave her up, I did my best to set aside any attachment I had to the person she would become. Sometimes my mind would try to imagine her as a child. Birthdays— April thirteenth by the way—were particularly difficult. I would pay attention to other girls who seemed to be around her age. I wanted to imagine my daughter growing up."

She rolled her shoulders like that would displace some of the tension she clearly carried there. "Drinking helped me not to think about her. The drugs and the booze enabled me to tamp down my curiosity. Then the business got bigger and my life got busier. I managed to tamp down thoughts of her, which made me feel even worse. What kind of a mother could let her child slip from her heart?"

"I don't believe you did that." Unable to resist any longer, Alex reached out and drew her to him. He expected her to fight him, but she came willingly. A testament to how much she was struggling right now that she wouldn't rebuff the comfort he offered.

She didn't exactly sink into him but rested her head on his chest. He drew circles on her back with the palm of his hand, hoping to help her feel better.

"You're right," she said against his shirt. "It took more work and more drinking and more…of everything to keep myself shut off from thoughts of her. When I came to Magnolia and I didn't have any of those crutches, regret and what-ifs ran me over like a freight train. But you know what happened?"

"What's that?"

"I made peace with them. Not with what I had done or my guilt over giving her up. Instead, I allowed myself to imagine who she would have become."

She pulled away and looked up at him. "Then she was here and more amazing than I could have imagined. I have no right to want a relationship with her, but I want it with every fiber of my being. So I'm going to hide out here with the curtains drawn unless the store catches fire or zombie apocalypse rains down on us."

"At this point, nothing would surprise me."

Mariella laughed before turning serious again. "As much as Heather wants to keep me a secret from her mom, I don't think I can handle seeing the woman who raised my daughter. I owe her and part of me hates her because she succeeded where I failed. She's a living reminder that I'm a failure. I hate myself for it."

"No." He cupped her face between his hands. "Don't say that. You chose what you believed to be the best option for your baby. You can't hate yourself for a decision you made from a place of pure love."

She seemed to consider that for a moment. "You make more sense than I'd like to admit."

"I'm brilliant," he told her. "One hundred percent genius."

"Also humble," she agreed with another laugh. "Have I mentioned yet today that Amber was an idiot? Because I knew what she was trading for when she gave you up. Jacques is not only a subpar boyfriend, but he has a tiny you-know-what."

Alex choked out a laugh. "That's more information than I want. My corneas are burning."

"You're welcome," she told him then lifted her arm and sniffed under it. "Lord, I need a shower. Do you care if I take one before the ravioli? I don't think I'll be able to truly enjoy our scrumptious meal if I'm distracted by my own smell."

She really was something. "Have you ever had a filter?" he asked.

"Sure, I have one." She started toward the hallway that he assumed led to the bedrooms. "I choose not to utilize it."

"Good to know," he said as he watched her walk away.

MARIELLA RETURNED FROM the shower fifteen minutes later and let out an appreciative gasp at her newly cleaned kitchen. "You do housework, too? The next time I decide to get married I'm choosing you as my groom."

She regretted the words as soon as they were out of her mouth. She and Alex weren't exactly at the place where they could joke about marriage.

He laughed awkwardly. "I'm not getting married so no need to worry."

"What makes you say that?" she asked as she moved toward the rough-hewn oak table, which had been set for two.

"Not much interest in it," he told her. "You think you'll get engaged again? Could you even consider another trip down the aisle?"

"Honestly, I can't imagine it, but stranger things have happened, I suppose."

"You wouldn't want to pick me anyway," he said, avoiding her gaze as he brought aluminum serving trays to the table. "I'm boring. And apparently too needy in relationships, which is crap but whatever."

"Amber's parting shots," she murmured. "She blamed you because it made her feel like less of a jerk. The truth is she was a jerk."

Alex didn't look convinced, but it also didn't seem like he wanted to linger on the subject.

Mariella had plenty of things she would prefer not to discuss so chose not to push it.

"You smell nice," he said as they dished out the portions. "Not sure how that's going to help you focus on eating, but if it works then more power to you."

"It makes me feel better. I should have showered before now. Thank you for coming over. You didn't have to do this."

She dipped her finger in the sauce that oozed across her plate and sucked it into her mouth. A glance at Alex, whose eyes had gone dark as he watched her, made her quickly wipe her finger on a napkin. She hadn't meant for the gesture to be suggestive, but an answering heat pooled low in her belly.

He cleared his throat. "I wanted to," he said like it was the most normal thing in the world. "Angi told me you were refusing visitors, but I had a feeling her ravioli would be too hard to resist."

Mariella didn't mention that the company was as irresistible as the food. As they ate, their conversation was easy and natural, which should have surprised her. At this point, virtually nothing about Alex surprised her because everything was unexpected.

She told him he didn't have to stay to help clean up but he did. He was, quite possibly, the most even-keeled person she'd ever met. Given her past, Mariella found that incredibly appealing as she walked him to the door after the remnants of dinner had been put away.

Mariella realized she didn't want him to leave. Not only did she want him to stay, but she wanted him in her bed.

She knew it couldn't mean anything. Despite what Alex told her about not wanting to marry, he was a white-picket-fence kind of guy. She had no doubt he would meet some sweet small-town woman who'd help him get over Amber and the issues he harbored from the way his family didn't seem to value him.

She tried not to think about how it would feel to watch him fall in love with someone else now that they had this strange and wonderful friendship thing going on.

Her life was better if she didn't focus too much on the future or think about the past. Present moment. That was the safest, and in this moment, she wanted very much to be with this man.

She took his hand and tugged on it. When he turned back, she leaned in and kissed him. She tried not to put all the need she felt into the kiss. To have it be more of an open-ended question. He could choose to move forward, but if he backed away she would respect his decision. She wasn't going to throw herself at somebody who didn't want her.

To her great delight, he threaded his big hands through her hair and angled her head so that he had better access to her mouth. His tongue melded with hers, and he pulled her close as he continued to deepen the connection until their bodies were pressed together.

She pulled his shirt up and over his head, feeling that she might explode if she couldn't get her hands on his skin.

He let out a ragged moan when she drew her fingernails over the hard planes of his shoulders.

As if he craved the feel of her skin with the same driving desire, he reached under her shirt and spread his hands over her back. When his teeth nipped at her earlobe, need spiraled through her with the force of a tornado. It threatened to undo the protective layers she'd fashioned into the foundation of her life, ripping through the segments like they were nothing more than a stack of children's blocks.

"Bedroom," she whispered, shocked when the word came out on a needy pant.

He let out a knowing chuckle when she all but sprinted down the hall, towing him along in her wake. "Where's the fire?" he asked.

She glared at him over her shoulder but didn't stop moving. "I'm not giving you the satisfaction of the 'in my pants' answer."

As they entered the bedroom, he stopped and spun her to face him. "I want you, Mariella."

His hair was messed, his muscled chest rising and falling in unsteady breaths and his gaze a little wild as he studied her.

"Ditto," she said then cringed. She sounded like a fool. She reached between them and cupped his erection through his jeans. "I get that in a big way. Emphasis on big."

"Mariella." He gently pulled her hand away from him and linked their fingers together. "I want to be with you."

The words were simple, but the intensity in his voice lent more meaning to them, a gravity she hadn't expected.

He liked her. She liked him. The heat between them was enough to warm the whole of the arctic during a long winter.

"Ditto," she repeated then licked her dry lips. "I want to be with you, Alex." The sentence left her feeling both exposed and exhilarated.

Alex's dark gaze intensified, both sexy and somehow reassuring. Mariella realized she felt safe with him. She wouldn't have guessed that mattered, but her chest tightened and goose bumps erupted along her skin. Safe was a turn-on. Who knew?

She took a step back and shed her sweatshirt. "Tell me more about wanting me. I'm detail-oriented, you know."

He looked like he wanted to smile but then his gaze raked over her body and his expression went serious, almost reverent.

"That makes two of us," he said as he closed the distance between them and cupped her breasts. He peeled down the lacy edge and swirled his tongue over one pebbled peak.

Detail-oriented didn't do him justice, she realized as he lavished attention on her body. She hadn't ever considered the possibility of finding release just from second base, but her knees went weak as he continued his ardent ministrations. His tongue did the most amazing things, quickly followed by nips and kisses.

He wrapped a supportive arm around her as if he knew she was about to melt into a puddle of lust at his feet.

At this point, she didn't even care about holding back. She wanted him. Every part of him.

They made it to the bed, and he curled his fingers in the waistband of her cotton pants. The air felt cool on her fiery skin as he pulled them down her legs.

He toed off his shoes then stripped out of his jeans with practiced efficiency to join her. The first man she'd allowed into her bed since her broken engagement.

The only man she could imagine wanting there.

He'd pulled a condom packet from his wallet, so she expected things to move fast from there, but once again, Alex did the unexpected.

He gave her a long, deep kiss then trailed his mouth down her body as if he wanted to memorize every inch of her by taste and feel. When he stopped at the apex of her thighs, she thought about protesting.

That was too much, too intimate, too vulnerable for her. But she couldn't find her voice or the real desire to make him stop. In fact, she heard the word *yes* escape her lips, the answer to a question she wasn't even sure he'd asked out loud.

The encouragement seemed to be exactly what he wanted, and he licked along her center, sparks shooting through her as he teased and coaxed her with his tongue and teeth.

Oh, he knew his way around a woman's body. Or maybe it was just her reaction to him. He hummed her name, and she fisted her hands in his hair. Her back arched as he drove her out of her mind with pleasure. She lost herself to it, shocked when the explosion pulsed through her, far more quickly and with more intensity than she could have imagined.

She hadn't ever imagined feeling the shuddering bliss Alex gave her.

When he moved back up her body, she reached out and grabbed the condom he'd tossed onto the bed next to them.

Because as amazing as her release had been, she still wanted more.

Rolling the condom over his hot length, she nudged him between her legs, reveling in the heat she felt rolling off him in waves.

"Tell me again you want this," he said, his voice hoarse with need.

"More than I want my next breath," she answered. She cradled his face between her hands. "I want you, Alex."

"Ditto," he told her then gripped her hips and plunged into her, filling her in a way that felt so right.

They set the rhythm together, steady as they moved as one. Emotions shimmered through her like hummingbird wings, delicate in a way that could terrify her if she let them. So she concentrated on the sensation of their joining, the way he whispered her name like a prayer, and the passion that flamed between them.

She wasn't inexperienced, but this felt new and precious. Her eyes drifted closed as the release washed through her, not as sharp or surprising as the first time. It was like being bathed in golden light and she cried out Alex's name then heard his answering groan as he found his own climax.

After, he relaxed next to her, pulling her close until she was wrapped around him.

"You okay?" he asked. She knew he wasn't talking about physically.

"Yeah," she answered, surprised to find it true. "I'm good."

"Me, too." His fingers gently stroked along her back as their breathing returned to normal.

Questions pinged through her mind, but none of them needed answering at the moment. Right now, she wanted to simply enjoy this...whatever it turned out to be.

# CHAPTER THIRTEEN

MARIELLA WAS IN the shop's office Saturday morning when she heard voices coming down the stairs, two of which she recognized despite her shock. She'd guessed who the third voice belonged to even before Heather laughed and called out the word *mom* in a teasing voice.

Her heart felt like it was going to beat out of her chest. She'd given Jasmin the day off because she couldn't stand to spend any more time alone in her house but didn't want to take the chance of running into Heather or her mother if the girl felt up to babysitting little Isabella.

She would have liked to spend the remaining days of her confinement wrapped up in Alex, but he'd received a call from his half brother the morning following their night together that his mother had suffered a mild heart attack. He'd immediately left for the airport to fly back to New York City.

She'd texted him late that night to check in, and he'd shared that they were putting a stent in her mother's chest then sending her home. She was expected to make a full recovery.

Mariella's mother had died at the hands of an aggressive melanoma a year before Mariella lost the company.

According to the doctors, her mother probably had symptoms that she ignored for months or longer leading up to the diagnosis. By the time they found the cancer, it had metastasized throughout her body.

Mariella had wanted to believe the understanding of what her mother was facing would help them bridge some of the difficulties in their relationship. That hadn't been the case. Her mom had been just as bitter and cantankerous as ever, lamenting that it was no use having a successful child if that child couldn't use her wealth to make her mother's treatment options more favorable. As if Mariella was to blame for the cancer.

She hoped Alex found a way to make peace with his family while he was in New York City. There'd been several moments in the past couple of days when she'd wanted to call him. To hear his voice and offer whatever comfort she could. But she hadn't, chiding herself for being a fool for even thinking she had a right to.

Mariella knew better than most people that having sex didn't mean she was suddenly close to a man or had any claim on his life or affections.

The connection between her and Alex was physical. She wouldn't jeopardize their burgeoning friendship by demanding something he'd already told her he had no intention of giving.

She hadn't called. Instead, she'd become antsy in her house. Emma had offered to give her a room at the inn until Heather's mom left so at least she wouldn't be alone, but Mariella didn't want to talk to her friends about how she was feeling. Part of her wanted to run away—that cowardly sliver of her soul that couldn't give up the idea of taking off as an option to avoid the difficult parts of her life.

She didn't want to be the type of person who ran away from her troubles any longer.

She also didn't want to come face-to-face with Heather

and her adoptive mother. Coming into the store seemed like a safe option, especially when Heather's mother was leaving town that day.

It wouldn't surprise Mariella if Heather had wanted her mom to meet Isabella. The girl loved that baby. She didn't think her daughter would bring her mom into A Second Chance if she thought Mariella might be there.

It was barely eight in the morning. Hours earlier than Mariella would normally show up to open the shop.

So she did what any person determined to be braver would do and dropped from her chair to wedge herself under the desk.

If Jasmin was giving Heather and her mom a tour of the store for lord knew what reason, they wouldn't need to come to the back. Maybe she wouldn't venture to the office.

"I think we have one of the vanilla-lavender candles in back," she heard Jasmin tell Heather and her mom.

Mariella glanced to her right at the row of metal shelves that held overflow inventory. She'd left the door to her office open and prayed Jasmin wouldn't notice her as the young woman searched the shelves for the candle she wanted. She cradled Isabella in one arm, and Mariella offered up another quick prayer that the baby would burst into tears and distract the trio of unwelcome visitors to her office.

She'd been doing a lot of praying recently and wondered if the big guy was having a good laugh at her expense.

"I appreciate looking behind the scenes," a soft voice said from the doorway.

Heat flooded her face. Her daughter's mother was standing a few feet away.

"Mariella has…" Jasmin's voice trailed off as she turned

and noticed Mariella crouched behind the desk. Mariella shook her head sharply.

Jasmin stood stock-still for several long seconds then turned with a brittle smile. "We should head out into the store. If you like the scent of this candle, the same company makes a line of soap I'd love to show you before you get on the road."

"Did you say Mariella?" the woman demanded.

"Mom, we should get going. I want to take you to the bakery one more time to pick up pastries for the girls before you head out."

"Are you talking about Mariella Jacob?"

Jasmin glanced at Mariella out of the corner of her eye and then back toward Heather and her mom. "I think you're really going to like those soaps. Plus a lotion bar to die for."

"Mom, let's go."

"Heather, who is the owner of this shop? Tell me again why you decided to spend this summer in Magnolia instead of going straight to Chapel Hill."

"Mom, it's okay."

Mariella heard the thread of panic in her daughter's voice. She didn't want Heather to get into trouble for seeking her out. She wasn't exactly sure how Kay would react, but she had no doubt that things would go better if the woman had an outlet for her emotions other than Heather.

Mariella slowly rose from under the desk. If she could give Heather nothing else, she could be a fall guy at this moment.

"They don't make earring backs like they used to," she said, looking at Jasmin as she fiddled with her lobe. Based on the incredulous look her employee gave her, the excuse for why she'd been hiding behind the desk sounded as lame as it did to her own ears.

*Push through. Don't show weakness.*

She shifted her gaze to Kay Garrison, who had gone white as a sheet and was staring at Mariella like she'd just done that exorcist head-spinning trick.

Mariella didn't bother to pretend they hadn't met before. She was certain those few minutes were etched in Kay's mind as much as they were hers. Kay looked much the same as she had back then, albeit with a few more wrinkles and streaks of gray in her dark hair, which was pulled back into a low bun.

She looked like the version of a mother Mariella could never be, with a kind smile and gentle brown eyes. She wore a striped blouse and jeans that seemed to have a bit of stretch to them. Stylish but appropriate.

"You've raised a lovely daughter," Mariella said.

She hadn't seen the woman since that day eighteen years ago. Even with the recent popularity of social media that made cyber-stalking feel like a normal activity, she'd never googled Kay or her husband. She'd been resigned to honor the choice she made, as difficult as it was.

Now something shifted inside her, and she wasn't sure she could give up the possibility of a relationship with her daughter. What if Kay demanded that? What if that was the only choice Heather had?

"Did you do this?" The woman's voice was eerily quiet. "Did you track her down?" She lobbed the questions at Mariella as if her mind refused to consider any other possibility.

"No, I didn't. I honored the terms of the adoption. I never reached out to her. I never would have tried to find her."

Heather had come to stand next to her mother. Mariella saw her flinch slightly at those words and realized how they sounded.

How could she explain to the girl that it wasn't as if she hadn't wanted to know her or been curious? She'd needed to cut things off. Imagining her daughter's future had been soul-wrenching enough without being privy to the details of Heather's life. She'd understood the need to not open her heart to the kind of pain it was feeling now. The kind that could crush her if she let it.

"It was me, Mom." Heather put a hand on Kay's arm. "I found an old letter from her in Dad's office. I figured it out from there, and I came to Magnolia to find her."

Mariella thought she understood pain. She'd experienced enough of it in her life. But the look of anguish on Kay Garrison's round face when her daughter admitted to seeking out Mariella went beyond anything she could have imagined. Mariella glanced away. Jasmin had taken a step closer to her.

"Heather is…" Her employee and friend started to ask. She didn't need to finish the question.

Mariella nodded, not trusting herself to speak at this moment.

"Why?" Kay whispered to Heather. "Am I not enough? Did I do something to push you away? I know you had to look after your sisters a lot but I thought…"

"It's not that," Heather said softly. "It has nothing to do with you."

Heather was openly crying now and the sight of it broke Mariella's heart.

"She has said wonderful things about your family," Mariella offered. "It's clear that you—"

Kay held up a hand. "You have no business offering an opinion on my family or what we have or haven't done. You made your choice in that hospital, and I will always be grateful because your choice made me a mother. You gave up your right to anything else."

"She came to me," Mariella couldn't help but point out. She wasn't trying to be cruel, but it was the truth. "I'm happy to know her and I'm grateful to you as well. You are her mother."

"Damn right," Kay said through clenched teeth, showing more spine than Mariella would have expected from her with her quiet voice and unassuming demeanor.

"This wasn't supposed to happen." Heather sounded miserable. "It's early and I just wanted you to meet the baby. I didn't tell you about Mariella being in Magnolia because I knew it would upset you."

"There are consequences to actions," Kay said. "You're young and smart, but you convinced us that you wanted this chance to live on your own under false pretenses. You also made a choice, Heather. Now we're all going to have to live with it. I love you, but I need some time right now."

Kay turned and walked away. Heather stood in the doorway quietly sobbing.

"Go after her," Mariella urged. "You need to talk this through before she leaves."

"She's too mad. I hurt her so badly. This is all my stupid, selfish fault."

Mariella wanted to step forward and comfort the girl, but it wasn't her place to inject herself into Heather's relationship with her adoptive mother.

She had too much respect for Kay to take advantage of this moment. "Go after her. Talk to her," she said again. "You'll work it out."

Heather didn't look convinced, but with a shaky nod, she followed her mom.

"Are you okay?" Jasmin asked softly when they were alone again.

Mariella shook her head. "I don't think I've been okay since I let strangers walk out of a hospital with my baby." She reached out to trail a finger over Isabella's soft head. "But not being okay is my normal, so I'll manage."

"Is that why you were so nice to me when I showed up pregnant looking for work?"

"You're a great employee and a wonderful mother," Mariella answered. "You deserve the chance I gave you."

"I wish you would have had somebody like that in your life when you needed it."

"No. You've met Heather. She's wonderful. Her adoptive parents loved her and raised her into the person she is today. Who knows what would have happened otherwise? She's had a great life with people who gave her every advantage. Even with help, I was sixteen and had no business raising a child."

She wrapped her arms tightly around her middle like that would stop the pain she felt. "Kay is right. I have no business inserting myself into her life now."

"She came here. She came to find you."

"I should have turned her away. I should have pushed her back toward the family she knows and loves. The family that's better for her than I could ever be."

"Don't you think she gets to decide that for herself?"

Mariella shrugged. "Only if she's going to make the right decision."

"I'm sorry, Mariella. Heather's mom complimented the scent in the apartment, so we stopped in to look for a candle. I never would have brought her if..."

"I know."

"Do you want me to stay? I'll find somebody to help with

Isabella and I can take over the front of the shop today. I don't think you—"

"I'm fine," Mariella promised. "In a lifetime full of low moments, this one barely even registers. Enjoy your day off and that sweet baby girl. I'll see you here on Monday."

Jasmin looked like she wanted to argue but nodded. "If you change your mind, text me. I'll be right upstairs."

Mariella smiled, but she knew she wouldn't reach out. There were some things she simply had to get through on her own. The possibility of losing her daughter only weeks after finding her again fell into that category.

Luckily the store was busy for most of the day, so it was hard to wallow in self-pity for any long stretch. She did have time to check her phone over and over but there was no message from Heather. Not that she expected one. But hope was a wily mistress, and Mariella was all out of tricks for keeping her heart protected.

She shut the door late that afternoon as the final customer left the shop. Flipping the sign in the window to closed, she was about to lock up when a soft knock sounded. Her heart swooped and dived like a gull sailing over the ocean waves when she glanced out to see Alex standing on the other side.

She opened the door and could tell by the look on his face that he'd heard about Kay. "How did you find out?"

"Heather texted me. She's taking a couple of days off to go back home with her family."

"Everyone is leaving to be with their family." Mariella laughed without humor. "Some of us don't have those options. We don't have a family."

Alex didn't argue. He simply wrapped his arms around her and drew her into his warm embrace. She didn't try to fight it but went willingly.

She might not have family. She might be alone in the world, but she would take whatever comfort he could give her.

"How is your mom?"

"Fine. She's fine. I don't want to talk about her right now, Mariella." He reached back and flipped the lock on the door. "I don't want to talk at all."

"That works for me." Her body immediately revved into overdrive. With one sexy look, Alex could dazzle her.

She linked their fingers and led him through the store and into the back office, kicking the door shut when they were both through. They kissed until she felt drunk with desire, then she pushed him toward the old leather sofa that sat against one wall. He shucked off his shirt and boots and pulled his jeans down as he stood in front of her.

Mariella stripped down just as quickly and watched as he lowered himself onto the sofa and then sheathed himself. Need making every inch of her pliant with need, she straddled his strong tights. He kissed her as she sank onto him, filling herself until she was momentarily sated.

She'd be a fool to think this meant more than it did, but there was no denying that when she was joined with Alex, it felt as though the lonely places inside her weren't so hollow.

He let her set the pace and held her as she did—like she was precious to him. He made her feel cared for. She could get used to that. She could become as addicted to this man as she'd been to the wine and the pills.

And she knew going cold turkey from him would be the hardest detox she would ever experience. She put aside those fears and the reality of what could be as they moved together. This moment was enough. It had to be.

And she would enjoy every moment of it. Every moment

of him. He covered her breast with his mouth, both gentle and demanding as he licked and sucked.

She sighed and moaned as the pressure built and when she couldn't control it any longer, she let the release wash over her as he quickly followed. She reveled in the mindless pleasure and the soul-deep knowing that at least for a few minutes she had found a connection.

It didn't matter how long it lasted or what would happen on the other end. All she cared about was the moment. Even as she told herself the lie, her heart silently protested. It wanted more. Despite years of trying to convince herself she could ignore her feelings, the damned organ would not be silenced.

She separated from him and quickly got dressed while he took his clothes to the bathroom connected to the office.

She was ready to make a joke about a quickie or a booty call when he returned, but his gaze was so open and vulnerable that she didn't have the heart to ruin this.

Not when it seemed to mean so much to both of them.

He took her in his arms again and just held her until she finally let go and relaxed against him. It felt good to give herself over to the comfort he offered. She felt safe enough to ask, "Do you think Heather will come back? What if her parents demand she not return to Magnolia because of me?"

"She's an adult and can make that decision for herself."

Mariella sniffed. "Come on. You know how family pressure can be."

His whole body went rigid and he pulled away. "I do."

"What happened in New York, Alex?"

"I visited my mom."

"Things were okay with her?"

He nodded, but his gaze became guarded when moments earlier it had been completely open.

"They want you to come back?" She wasn't sure why she felt so certain with that guess, but she did.

"My stepfather offered me a position on the hotel group's executive management team. Basically, the role I thought was my dream job."

"You aren't considering it, are you?"

He grabbed his shoe from the doorway and bent over to put it on without answering her.

"Tell me you aren't considering this," she said, giving him a not-so-gentle shove. He stumbled a step.

"Hey, that was unnecessary."

"Was it? Not nearly as unnecessary as you thinking about leaving your company and this town behind. How's that going to work, Alex? You get everything going here and then just desert them?"

"You left your company," he pointed out.

"I had to," she reminded him. "For a justifiable reason. They've done fine without me."

"I'm not saying I'm going to leave the Fit Collective behind. I didn't say yes to my stepfather, but it's the first time he seemed willing to consider giving me a real role in the family business. For years, that was all I wanted."

"Doesn't that feel like kind of a coincidence? When you finally move on with your life, he throws you a bone."

"Is that what you think?"

"I don't know what it is, but I do know that you made commitments to the people here." In truth, she wasn't sure why she cared. Two weeks ago she would have been happy to hear Alex was considering leaving town. It meant she wouldn't have to deal with him plus she'd have the bonus of him turning into the bad guy in Magnolia so everyone could forget about her villainous past.

"Like I said, I wouldn't leave the company. I've invested

too much in it. I care too much about making it a success. But I could oversee things while still helping out in New York City and find somebody to run operations on the ground down here. Somebody who had experience with a successful retail operation."

"Get out," she whispered.

"Just consider it." He held up his hands. "It's not like I've made a complete decision. I'm weighing my options."

"Is that what this was?" She gestured toward the couch. "You placating me with sex so that I'd agree to take over managing your company? Are you and Luann working together to tag-team me? Just so you know, she's not my type in case that was also part of the deal."

He ran a hand through his hair. "Stop it. This doesn't have anything to do with what's between us. You know that."

"Do I? I thought you'd come here for me. I guess I should have known better. Honestly, it's probably my due where you're concerned."

He growled in frustration and took a step toward her, but she backed away, shaking her head.

"This isn't revenge," he insisted. "It isn't like that. I'm working through things."

"Sure. Besides, most men think better after a nice release." She gave him a thumbs-up. "I know Jacques always did. Although I think he preferred me on my knees. At least I should be grateful you didn't immediately go that route."

"Mariella, stop."

"Alex, get out." She couldn't do this. It was impossible to have this conversation after feeling so vulnerable. It would split her in two.

"I'm sorry I said anything." He sighed. "You're right. I've made a commitment here and I don't want to leave.

It's just that I never dreamed my stepfather might give me a chance like this. Do you know what it's like to have an opportunity for something you wanted with every fiber of your being and never thought would truly happen?"

"Yeah," she said on a shaky breath. "It's called a relationship with the daughter I gave up for adoption."

He cursed. "I'm sorry."

"It's fine. Go. Please, Alex. Just go."

She turned away and stared at the bookcase next to her desk, concentrating on a framed photo of her, Emma and Angi. Emma had given it to her for Christmas. The three of them sat in the kitchen of the Wildflower Inn after Holly's wedding, the first of their successful events they'd managed together.

She reminded herself that she had friends. The people in her life cared about her despite her flaws. She didn't need a man to make her feel special. That could be accomplished on her own, and her friends could help if she needed it.

Alex opened the door to the office and let himself out. A moment later, the chimes connected to the front door dinged.

She could tell herself all she wanted that she didn't need any man, particularly not Alex Ralsten. But based on the way her chest ached in the hollow silence of the empty store, her heart would take a bit more convincing.

# CHAPTER FOURTEEN

Alex was shocked when he arrived at work on Tuesday morning to find Heather already seated at her desk.

"I thought you were taking a few days with your family?"

"I got back last night. There's a lunch meeting today at the town hall about the Magnolia Blossom Festival. I didn't want to miss it."

"I could have handled that," he told her. "Heather, you don't have to—"

"It's okay." She glanced up at him, giving a little wave with a casted arm. The scrape on her forehead no longer required a bandage and had turned into a pale bruise.

Even with the tension he could read around the corners of her eyes, she had more color in her cheeks than she'd had the night of the accident. "Is everything okay with your family?"

"I think so. I should have told them before coming down here. My mom is still freaked out about the whole thing, but she's trying to understand. Heck, I'm still trying to understand why it's important to me that I know the person who didn't want me when I was a baby."

Alex shouldn't feel any need to defend Mariella at this point. Based on how they'd left things Saturday, he wasn't sure she'd ever speak to him again. "I don't think it was a matter of not wanting you," he told the girl.

"That's how it felt," Heather said, "when I was growing up. Like I'd been disposable to her."

Alex wasn't going to pretend he understood the emotional turmoil of someone who'd been adopted, but he could relate when his mother had been happier with her second husband and second baby. Alex sometimes felt like her life would have been easier if he hadn't been born.

He reminded himself that he was there to support Heather not to wallow in his own past. "What about now that you know Mariella?"

Heather ran a hand over the purple cast that covered her left arm up to her bicep. "I guess it's more complicated now that she's involved."

Alex smiled. "I'm not sure anything with Mariella is simple."

Heather snorted her agreement and gave him a curious glance. Before she could raise the question about the nature of his relationship with Mariella, Alex turned the conversation back to business. "Can you get me projected sales numbers for the fall season? And when you see Luann, tell her she needs to finalize which pieces she wants to focus on when we see the New York buyers."

"New York? I thought you were doing the launch at the Magnolia Blossom Festival."

Alex nodded. "Yes, but we still need to go with some of the big retailers. I've set up the business model so that we'll rely mostly on sales from the website and our social media links. We're also going to do some work with major retail outlets."

He studied her as she fidgeted. "You don't think it's a good idea?"

"It's not really my business. I'm just an administrative assistant."

"You aren't going to play the not-involved card now. You pretty much run my life at this point. I know you have thoughts on the business."

She flashed him a small smile. This time it reached her eyes, which gave him no small sense of accomplishment. Then she told him her ideas for the collection and how to launch it most effectively. He was amazed, once again, by her maturity and insight.

"You're going to set the world on fire." He didn't know anything about Heather's adoptive parents but could see so much of Mariella in her. He imagined this was how determined and focused she'd been coming to New York City on her own to make her mark on the fashion world.

He still wasn't quite sure what to do with his feelings for Mariella.

Alex liked emotions simple and straightforward, and she was neither of those. But he could appreciate the adventure of discovering where it might take the two of them if their argument hadn't ended things before they truly got started. As strange as it was that their lives intersected on so many levels, he wouldn't change a thing about their connection.

Well, he would change how angry he'd made her on Saturday, but all he could do was find a way to fix that.

He kept an eye on Heather to make sure she didn't seem strained or stressed as she went about her day.

Even after she returned from the meeting, which he assumed Mariella would have also attended, the girl seemed to be in good spirits.

It probably wasn't his place, but he sent a quick text to her mother to express that Heather seemed to be doing well, feeling great and keeping her energy level high. He would have wanted to know that about his child.

Kay texted back a thank-you almost immediately and

another text came in at the same time. The second one was from Mariella, asking him to meet her at the beach later that afternoon.

His heart gave a little leap of pleasure that she'd reached out, although for all he knew she would try to lure him to the ocean so she could drown him.

It was worth the risk without a doubt. Alex counted down the hours until he could leave the office and head home to change into shorts and a T-shirt before meeting her.

The temperature had climbed into the low eighties on this balmy late-spring afternoon. Alex loved the way the town was alive with blooming trees and great swaths of wildflowers along the open fields lining the road on the way to the shore.

There were a few areas of beach on the south end of town that were more popular with tourists, but Mariella had told him to meet at a somewhat remote area, just behind the Furever Friends animal rescue property.

He'd thought about adopting a dog but had never gotten around to it. Even that had felt like more of a relationship responsibility than he was willing to take on in the early months of launching the company.

He'd met Meredith, who ran the rescue, several times and she'd told him that whenever he was ready she would help him find the perfect pet. The woman reminded him of a matchmaker for animals. And that might be part of the problem.

Sad as it was, Alex no longer had much confidence in his ability for lasting commitment. Even to a dog.

He parked his Land Rover behind Mariella's car. It looked like she'd arrived and already headed down to the ocean. He drew in a deep breath of the salt air as he walked along the weathered pier. Nerves and anticipation coursed through him. But at the same time, he found it difficult to hold on to any anxiety as the wide expanse of sea greeted him.

There was something humbling about the ocean. The waves had lapped upon this shore for longer than he could even imagine, and they would continue long after he was there to witness it.

In the day-to-day business of life, it was easy to get wrapped up in his own struggles like he was the center of the universe. The ocean reminded him of his insignificance in the grand scheme of things.

As he'd suspected, this part of the beach wasn't crowded. One family, a mother and father and their two small kids, were building sandcastles in the area of hard sand on the top section of the beach.

He looked past them and saw the woman standing at the edge of the water, her back to him. Her long blond hair whipped in the wind but she didn't seem to notice or care. She stood as still as a statue staring out at the horizon.

Alex's heart fluttered and then settled, somehow soothed by the sight of her.

The same word that had whispered through him the first night he'd taken her in his arms filled his brain once more.

*Mine.*

He shook his head to dislodge that idea. She was no more his than the sand belonged to those kids forming it into stiff peaks while their parents looked on and smiled.

He could do his best to claim her while understanding that, at any moment, she could slip from his grasp and be carried out into the larger world leaving him behind.

He was always being left behind.

The crash of the waves and the whistle of the wind muffled his approach, but Mariella didn't seem surprised when he arrived at her side. Of course she'd known he was coming. He'd texted her when he left the house.

But it felt like something more. It felt as though she'd sensed his arrival, and he liked the idea of that. He wanted to believe he wasn't the only one who couldn't deny their connection.

"Come here often?" he asked then silently chided himself on the inane line. What was it about Mariella that made him feel like an inexperienced schoolboy trying to impress his first crush?

She glanced up and gave him a look that—while not quite withering—clearly communicated that he was going to need to up his game.

If only he had any game where she was concerned.

"I didn't used to," she said, surprising him by answering his dumb question like he'd meant it seriously. "The ocean and I are working out some past issues. Recently I've started walking the beach several times a week. I like how the waves put everything in their place. I like the idea that in the greater scheme of things, I'm just a speck of sand and don't really matter."

"You matter," he told her. "Every tiny piece of sand matters. Try getting one stuck in your shoe. It might be tiny, but one speck can make a big impact."

She tucked a strand of hair that had blown across her face behind one ear. He could see a smattering of freckles across the bridge of her nose that he hadn't noticed before. Maybe they'd been there or perhaps her time walking in the sun had brought them out. Either way, he found them adorable.

"Did you just compare me to an irritant in your shoe?"

He chuckled. "Yes, but I meant it as a compliment."

She returned his smile. "Then it's a good thing you're so

darn physically perfect," she told him. "It will help women have an easier time ignoring your gaping personality deficits."

The words were harsh, but she said them with such affection he couldn't even take offense. She might be tough and sometimes cantankerous, but those rough edges had found their way into his heart.

"I should probably start all my dates shirtless, huh? Get to the objectifying part of the evening right from the start."

"Definitely." She gestured down the beach. "Want to go for a walk?"

"Sure." He couldn't quite read her mood. She wasn't spitting mad the way she'd been on Saturday. He still didn't like how that conversation had ended.

"I wasn't using you," he felt compelled to tell her.

She kept looking straight ahead. "I know. That was just me lashing out because I was hurt and angry. Honestly, it would have been easier if you had been using me. I know what to do with that."

"But you don't know what to do with me?"

"Not at all."

"That makes two of us. How are things with Heather? She hasn't said much since returning to work, but she was in a good mood after the meeting today. You were there, right?"

"Yep. Did you think I was going to make her cry like I'm the big bad wolf or something?"

"I didn't say that, and it's not what I thought."

She continued to walk but her pace slowed slightly. "Heather was fine. Distant. Obviously, Luann and Mary Ellen don't know about the two of us, so we could act like surface acquaintances and no one is the wiser."

"Is that what you want?"

"People need to stop asking what I want." She scrunched up her nose. "At the end of the day, what I want is what's best for Heather. She hasn't asked me to leave town and she doesn't seem to have any inclination to pick up and take off herself."

"She's strong. You both are."

She stopped suddenly and turned to face him. "Do you believe that? Not about her but me? Because I'm not sure I've displayed any strength when it comes to my dealings with you. Certainly not at the start, and I've mostly been rude to you since you came to Magnolia."

"Not always rude."

"Right. Not when we were in bed together or on the couch of my office."

"Don't do that." He shook his head. "Don't make the two of us being together into something less than it is. I like you, Mariella. I like spending time with you and not just naked time."

He let out a breath as he looked toward the waves, taking comfort in the rhythmic sound of the surf. "Did you ask me here so you could make sure that I knew my place in your life? We're all square on that, which doesn't mean I have to agree with it."

She rolled her lips together as a myriad of emotions swam in those big blue eyes. Anger, confusion and just the tiniest bit of hope. "How can you know where you fit when I can't for the life of me figure it out? It's making me crazy, Alex. You don't even have a reason to like me."

"Yet I like you anyway."

"How is that possible when I've infringed on your life at every turn? You hire a business partner and she wants me to take over her part of the deal. You get pushed back into the wedding season limelight because somehow you're the poster child for jilted grooms and that's my fault."

"I don't blame you." The wind picked up his words and carried them away as soon as they were out of his mouth. She looked away from him as if she were trying to chase them down the beach like a child with a kite bobbing along in the breeze.

"I blame me. I blame me for Heather coming here, and you have to deal with the mess I've made of her life as well."

"Heather is a great kid. And I don't mind messes nearly as much as you seem to think I should."

"Stop being such a stand-up guy," she demanded, wagging a finger in his face. He wrapped his hand around that finger, and she clenched her hand into a fist.

They stood like that for several long moments.

He knew what she was doing. She was trying to take the easy way out. He'd thought about that a thousand times himself.

It had been easier when they'd been enemies, but he believed the words he told Heather. Nothing worth having was easy.

"I don't want to like you," she said finally. He felt her hand goes slack under his as she said the words.

He turned her palm to face upward. "I know." He linked their fingers together. "But you also like me anyway."

"Yeah, and not just because you're easy on the eyes."

"Good to know."

"But this can't be…anything."

Warning bells went off in his head. "Define anything."

"I mean we're not going to go steady or double date with Emma and Cam or hold hands walking down the sidewalk in the middle of town."

"What about hanging out with friends? It worked pretty well on Cam's boat."

"I guess that's okay."

He looked at their joined fingers. "Is holding hands on a deserted beach acceptable?"

"If it's truly deserted," Mariella whispered, "but only then."

He nodded. "I can live with that. But I have some parameters of my own."

Her brow wrinkled. "Is that so?"

"No more making this small. I'm not saying it has to be on a billboard in town, but I spent too long being publicly bashed by Amber and her legions of adoring fans. I'm not looking to be belittled either publicly or privately any longer."

"I didn't mean to make you feel that way," she said softly. "It's the reason I normally hang out with jerks. I'm not great at knowing how to treat people."

"You'll learn," he promised, utterly committed to making whatever this was work, and then kissed her. For now, it would have to be enough.

COULD SHE LEARN? Mariella's past had been littered with bad decisions and toxic relationships, starting with her mother who'd sucked all the fun right out of dysfunctional.

One thing she knew about herself was that she wasn't afraid of hard work. She simply needed to look at this relationship—if she could call it that—with Alex as a project. He would help her learn how to be a normal person, just like her friendship with Emma and Angi had.

"I guess I can live with your parameters. Can we take lots of walks on deserted beaches?"

"Lots and lots." Alex grinned and wiggled his thick

brows. He looked younger in this moment with the sun golden as it started its long goodbye for the night. The breeze had rumpled his hair and she could see the edge of a tan line around the base of his neck in that casual T-shirt.

She wanted to put her mouth to his skin, to taste the salt on him and breathe in his rich scent. She wanted too much based on who she knew herself to be and her history of self-sabotage when emotions took over. "For the record, I'm not sure I deserve your faith in me."

"That's the thing about faith, sweetheart. You don't have to do anything to deserve it. I'm giving it to you freely."

Her heart wanted to believe him, but she had so many doubts. "In my experience nothing is free."

"Maybe it's time to think about broadening your horizons."

He moved to stand behind her and wrapped his strong arms around her shoulders. She felt safe in his embrace, which both delighted and terrified her. Could she allow herself to trust this man?

"The beach is a good place," he said as he nuzzled her ear and pointed to the open water, "for appreciating new horizons. We'll start here. Back to the basics of dating, hopefully complete with lots of making out."

She smiled and rolled her eyes. It didn't matter how many roadblocks she tried to erect. Alex refused to be swayed by her doubts. And Mariella wanted nothing more than to truly put her faith in him.

## CHAPTER FIFTEEN

THE NEXT WEEK passed quickly with Mariella dividing her time between the shop and the inn. She was working on two custom dresses for brides who had booked the Wildflower as a wedding and reception venue. Although she'd feared they might change their minds after her mention in the article, both brides had assured her they didn't think walking down the aisle in one of her creations would equate to bad luck in any way.

"I told you it would be fine," Emma said.

Mariella was meeting with her and Angi in the small cottage on the property that Emma and Cam had moved into a few months earlier. Mariella had set up a sewing machine in one corner of Emma's office so she could do on-site alterations as needed.

The dress this weekend's bride would be wearing hung from a hook on the wall with a layer of protective fabric over it. The bride, along with her mother and bridesmaids, would arrive at the inn on Thursday to finish preparations and enjoy a couple of days of pre-wedding pampering before the big event on Saturday.

"How many weddings have you booked since the article?" Mariella asked.

Emma tapped a pen against her chin. "It's a slow season for bookings," she said, and Mariella's heart sank.

"That translates to zero."

"We're going to be fine," Emma assured her.

"Right," Angi agreed. "So long as we don't have any more brides or grooms hit the dusty trail before their trip down the aisle."

"It was an unlucky coincidence that those two situations happened in a row," Emma insisted.

"Unlucky for us," Mariella agreed, "but maybe not for the groom who was spared hitching himself to a cheater."

"I don't think we can use that as part of the marketing campaign. Come to the Wildflower and suss out whether your intended mate is a two-timing jerk." Emma shook her head as she grinned. Her thick dark hair was held back in a messy bun with a few tendrils framing her face. Despite the recent challenges, she looked serene and in control. The opposite of how Mariella felt.

"There's a certain benefit to knowing early," Mariella observed. "In hindsight, I'm glad I found out about Jacques when I did. Maybe we could get one of those carnival psychic booths for the family room."

"Yes." Angi nodded. "Like out of the movie *Big*. Have Zoltar tell your fortune."

"That's a terrible idea," Avery Atwell said from the doorway of the office. "Although you get points for creativity."

"We're all about creativity," Emma told the town's marketing director, rubbing two fingers against her temples. Maybe she wasn't as serene as Mariella wanted to believe.

Joking aside, these issues with the inn's reputation were stressing out her friend.

They'd asked Avery to meet to come up with a plan for garnering favorable media coverage for a few of the upcoming events. According to Avery, the best way for them to combat the negative press was with positive press.

Mariella should have thought of that a few years ago.

Amber certainly had. She'd spun the hell out of her cheating, throwing both Mariella and Alex under the bus in the process. Mariella could have taken a lesson from that but she'd been too upset to consider it at the time.

"I have an idea for a bit of creative marketing that might work better." Avery stepped farther into the room. "It's kind of out of the box, but I'd like you all to consider it."

"No reality shows," Emma said, shaking her head. "I've already fielded calls from a couple of slimy producers. We are not going in that direction."

"Agreed." Avery nodded. "No reality shows. I talked to Holly Carmichael last night."

Emma's face relaxed at the mention of the bride that had started the Wildflower Inn down this path. "Yes. Holly reached out to me as well. She said both she and Brett would be willing to give a quote for the inn's press kit about how perfect their wedding was here at the Wildflower and how they'd unequivocally recommend us."

"That's good," Avery agreed. Today she wore a sleeveless shirtdress in a Vineyard Vines print, embracing her Southern style while still looking far more big-city polished than Mariella would have expected.

She wondered if Avery and her sisters had ever considered modeling. They'd be perfect for a campaign featuring local residents.

"I also talked to Holly about something a little more radical," Avery continued. Mariella forced her concentration back to the topic at hand. "She met Drake Simpson at an event a few weeks ago. He's producing and starring in a movie filming about an hour south of here. The crew is scouting locations in the area, and she mentioned the Wildflower. Turns out they're doing a scene that is supposed to take place in a historic B&B. He wants to use the Wildflower for a few hours the weekend of the festival. He'd make an appearance in town as well. Possibly judge the pie contest or something equally photogenic."

Mariella felt her mouth drop open as Angi and Emma gasped. Drake Simpson was one of Hollywood's most popular leading men at the moment. Hugh Grant circa *Four Weddings and a Funeral* mixed with an amalgamation of the two most famous Hemsworth brothers. He was ultra-swoony and women all over the world were in love with him.

"Holly said he's a big believer in making your own luck, and he might even do a pull quote for the inn along those lines."

"That would be huge," Emma said.

"What's the catch?" Angi asked with a frown. "It feels like there's a catch."

Avery turned toward Mariella.

"What? Drake Simpson has never been married. It's not like I designed his ex-wife's wedding dress. I don't even know the man." She held up her hands when Avery continued to stare. "I've never talked to him. There isn't enough wine in the world to make me forget meeting a guy like that."

"Amber is his co-star in the movie," Avery said without emotion. "She'd be staying here as well."

"Hell, no." Angi shot up from her chair.

Emma also voiced her refusal to host Amber as a guest, but Avery's gaze didn't waver from Mariella.

She had a new respect for the sophisticated blonde. "I see small-town living hasn't turned you soft," she said with a nod.

Avery's mouth tipped up on one end. "I want what's best for Magnolia."

"We are not doing this." Emma stood and came around the side of her desk. "No way are we doing this."

"Yes." Mariella managed to keep her voice steady. She nodded again. "Make it happen, Avery."

"You can't agree on your own." Angi paced from one end of the office to the other. "Remember this is a partnership. We all have to decide what's best for the inn."

Mariella sniffed and did her best to look nonchalant even though her stomach twisted and pulled like it was stuck in a taffy machine. "You know what's best for the inn and the town. Having Drake here, especially if he's willing to say something positive, would be a huge benefit. He might even push us on social media."

"Until Amber ruins it by trashing you or the Wildflower," Emma said. "It isn't worth it, Mariella."

"You need to talk to Alex," Mariella said to Avery. "He's got more to lose when it comes to Amber."

"Why are you acting like this is an option?" Emma crouched down in front of Mariella and took her hands. Mariella could feel the warmth of her friend's fingers, but she barely registered the touch. All she could feel was the cold seeping through her. Not just at the thought of what Amber could do to her but also her uncertainty over Alex's potential reaction to having his ex-fiancé return to his life.

She forced a smile. "Amber and Jacques aren't even together anymore. They lasted about five minutes."

"This isn't about them." Emma's features were so gentle, and Mariella wondered what she'd done to deserve this kind of friend in her life. She thought about Alex's words—that faith wasn't something you had to earn or deserve.

Apparently, friendship could work in a similar fashion with the right people.

"It's okay," she said. "I'm not the same person I was back then."

"This is your home. We are your people. There's no business worth you being put in a position that makes you uncomfortable."

She appreciated the sentiment. She really did. "I want to do it as much for myself as for the inn. I need to know I've moved past what happened. I'm stronger than anybody in my old life gave me credit for. You are helping me see that."

"I don't like it." Angi stepped forward. "I don't trust America's sweetheart as far as I can throw her and my upper-body strength has never been the best. What if she's doing this for another publicity stunt? What if she wants to find a new way to hurt you?"

Mariella shook her head. "She might not know I'm here."

"She knows," Avery said. "Her publicist reached out to me after I spoke with Drake's people. They don't want any questions or mention of your shared past while Amber is in town."

"That's easy enough to accommodate." Mariella squeezed Emma's fingers. She wasn't sure if the heat she suddenly felt came from her friend or if some of the icy cold that normally surrounded her heart was melting.

"I can do this," she told Emma then glanced toward Angi. "We can do this."

MARIELLA LET HERSELF out of the store's entrance the following evening after closing. She scanned the street until she spotted Alex's Land Rover parked about a half a block away.

She started walking toward the car then noticed him coming in her direction. He'd texted earlier and invited her to go fishing at a nearby lake. His version of the beach, he'd explained, and how he recharged.

She tried not to read too much into the fact that he'd included her in an activity that meant something to him. Especially when he'd added a follow-up text that they needed to talk about Amber.

She'd known Avery was going to tell him, but Mariella wanted to discuss Alex's former fiancée with him like she wanted to stick a fork in her eye. If he needed to be convinced to agree to let Amber and Drake do their little PR event as part of the Magnolia Blossom Festival, then she'd do it.

She knew how much the press would mean to the town and specifically to Emma and the Wildflower Inn.

Faith might not need to be earned, but she wanted to be worthy of it nonetheless.

"You know, Magnolia is a fairly safe town," she said when he was only a few feet away. "I can make it to your car on my own."

Tonight he wore a faded gray T-shirt and jeans that hugged his muscular thighs. A baseball cap turned backward sat low on his head, and she could see a strangely sexy five-o'clock shadow darkening his jaw. The man was as handsome in fishing attire as he was in a sophisticated suit. Her body tingled in approval as she watched him move closer.

He gave a tight nod. "I know. Heather is joining us," he said without preamble.

Mariella tried and she guessed failed at looking unfazed by the news. "You invited Heather?"

"Not exactly. She invited herself, and I didn't feel like I could say no."

"Does she know I'm going?" They'd gotten along at the meeting surrounded by other people, but Mariella could not imagine a world where the girl would want to purposely spend time with her.

They already had to see each other regularly for work on the festival, but normally Mary Ellen or Luann were with them, which took the sting out of some of the potential awkwardness.

He nodded. "I think that's what made her want to go in the first place." He sounded as stunned as Mariella felt. "Although she's kind of playing it off."

"It's a big deal." She schooled her features and started toward his car. "Let's not make it weirder by standing here."

"It is weird." He fell into step next to her.

"One hundred percent," she agreed, "but Heather makes the rules."

"You really have changed," he said and for just a moment, he placed his hand on her back. The touch was both comforting and made her heartbeat pick up speed.

She didn't remember ever caring about somebody's opinion the way she did about the way Alex saw her.

Could she live up to his positive opinion? Debatable, but she was learning to take things on faith no matter how foreign a concept that was.

"How's the arm?" she asked Heather as she climbed into the front seat.

"I know you were talking about me."

A weight settled in Mariella's heart as she heard the doubt in Heather's tone.

"If you don't want me here, you guys can just drop me off at my house. I'm just a little sick of sitting at home by myself. I can't do anything fun with this stupid cast on."

"You bet I want you here." Mariella turned around in her seat to look at the girl as Alex pulled away from the curb.

"I bet I can't out-fish Alex, but you're one-handed so I can for sure take you on."

Alex snorted out a laugh. "You know that everything doesn't have to be a competition."

"I can catch more than you one-handed," Heather said. "My dad used to take me fishing all the time."

Mariella smiled. She wondered if the girl thought the mention of her parents would bother her birth mom.

The opposite was true at the moment. Mariella appreciated the reminders that her daughter had been raised by loving people. She certainly understood that a girl's relationship with her father was a huge influence on her life.

Mariella hadn't known her dad. Maybe if she had she wouldn't have felt like she needed to earn the attention of random boys in the neighborhood when she hit puberty. Maybe she actually would have had some self-respect. Maybe Heather would have never been born.

Her stomach clenched even considering that possibility. There was the reason Mariella didn't put too much stock in regret.

It was like the butterfly effect. Small things that can change a complex system. She could go back and change the past but if she did, where would it leave her present and potentially her future?

Still, she felt fully alive with both Alex and Heather. "Want to wager on the fishing?"

"Seriously?" Alex asked.

"Whoever catches the least has to be in charge of the porta-potties the entire weekend of the festival." Mariella looked into the back seat via the passenger side mirror.

Heather didn't notice her watching, but a small smile played at the corners of the girl's mouth.

"That's brutal," Alex said, glancing in her direction. He

flipped a look at Heather in the rearview mirror. "Don't fall for it, kid. You've got a great excuse with that arm to get out of whatever nasty volunteer assignment you don't want to take on. I would think poo duty would top the list."

"He's right," Mariella agreed. "If you want to play the poor, injured flower card."

Alex shook his head. "She's baiting you," he warned Heather. "Which is not maternal or mature," he reminded Mariella.

"I don't need to play any card," Heather told him. "I can win on my own as long as we're talking about fish and not catching a hangover or potential disease picked up from a random guy in a bar."

"Whoa," Alex murmured, but Heather wasn't finished.

"I heard those were somebody's favorite pastimes back in New York City."

It said something about Mariella that she liked her daughter best of all when she was throwing well-deserved barbs.

What Heather didn't understand was there was nothing she could say to Mariella, no harsh aside or sarcastic comment that could compare to the relentless internal dialogue of judgment Mariella dished out to herself on a daily basis.

"You've been reading too many of the comments on my social media pages. I'm glad for it, though." She looked over her shoulder and nodded at Heather, whose face had gone beet red.

The girl wasn't quite the master grief-giver she fancied herself to be. She didn't have the cutthroat drive for it. Another point in the nurture versus nature column.

"Let me be a cautionary tale if nothing else. Make better choices, Heather. Choices that don't include trying to get into the local bar with a fake ID."

"How did you know about that?"

Alex flipped on his blinker as he glanced at Mariella and then back at the road. "Yeah. How would you know about that? Is that true since you've been in Magnolia?" he asked Heather in a concerned voice. "Because it's a horrible idea."

Mariella shrugged. "I know people," she told them both. "You could get into real trouble, Heather, and not just the kind where you wind up in a cast."

"I wasn't going to drink," the girl answered grumpily. "But everybody at the office goes to Champions bar for Tuesday night karaoke. They're always talking about it the next morning, and I feel like a big loser because I can't take part. The one stupid activity I did do, I wound up with a broken arm. I don't need to be of legal age to sing along with some dumb pop song."

Mariella heard the pain in the girl's voice. She knew it probably had more to do with insecurity than some casual office bonding. She'd looked up high-IQ kids on the internet. Other teenagers who were in the same situation as Heather in graduating early from high school.

It made a difference to be younger than classmates for most of their lives. There was a lot of social awkwardness that went with it.

"Hey." She unfastened her seat belt when Alex parked in the dirt lot of the recreation area outside of town. "Doogie Howser managed it okay, and you will, too."

Heather gave her a what-the-hell look. "That was a television show."

"A really good one," Mariella countered.

Alex turned as well. "We can organize some staff bonding activities that don't involve bars or rappelling lines on the side of a rock wall. I'm sure we can come up with something."

Heather looked unconvinced. "It doesn't matter. It's not going to change anything. I'm a lot younger than most of those people, and they're not even old like you."

"Ouch."

Mariella snickered.

"You know we're the same age," he reminded her.

"It's still funny." They all got out of the SUV, and Heather headed for the restroom while Alex pulled the fishing gear from the back.

"We'll meet you down by the lake," Mariella told him.

"Are you sure that's a good idea?"

"I want a minute with her."

He nodded. "I'm guessing she wanted a minute with you, too, which is why she's here."

That thought helped settle the nerves that bounced around Mariella's stomach. She waited outside the building for her daughter to emerge.

"You could try volunteering at the local rescue or joining some other organization for young people in town. That might be a way to meet people."

"Kids my age don't want to hang out with me," Heather said, tucking a strand of hair behind her ear. "People like me are freaks to normal teenagers."

"You are a normal teenager," Mariella answered. "You're moody and emotional."

Heather blinked. "Is this supposed to be a pep talk?"

"I've told you before I don't want to replace your mother. I think it's clear to both of us that I'd have no skill in that area anyway. Maybe we can try to be friends?"

She felt hot pricks of anxiety rise in her when Heather just looked at her. "I thought that maybe you coming back to Magnolia meant..."

"I guess friends would be okay," Heather said. "Although

it probably makes me even more pathetic that I have to have a friend who's…like…a real adult."

Mariella flashed a grin. "If it makes you feel any better, I'm known for my immaturity."

Heather laughed and seemed to relax a bit. "Yeah, I got that."

They walked toward the water together, joy warming Mariella from the inside. It never ceased to amaze her how life continued to take unexpected turns. Sometimes even for the better.

# CHAPTER SIXTEEN

HEATHER GOT OUT of the car in front of her tiny house a few hours later. "Enjoy managing those porta-potties," she said to Mariella with a satisfied cackle. "Here's hoping it's not a hot weekend."

"You are enjoying this way too much." Mariella groaned. "It was pure luck that you got that last one. I had a huge fish on the hook."

"But you couldn't reel it in." Heather held up her casted arm. "Even one-handed, I beat you."

"Fine," Mariella conceded. "You beat me. You are an expert fisherperson. Your dad would be proud."

Heather's features went soft. "I think he would be, too." She looked past Mariella to Alex in the driver's seat. "Thanks for dinner. I'll see you tomorrow and don't worry about what I talked about earlier with fitting in or friends at the office. I'll get rid of the fake ID, and I'll be fine."

"I know you will," he told the girl. She seemed to appreciate that as well, and there was a definite spring in her step as she headed toward the building.

"She doesn't hate me anymore," Mariella said, nodding. "I guess that's a start."

"I don't think she ever hated you. She only wanted to hate you."

"I'm not sure the difference matters, but I'll take it. Tonight was fun. Thank you for helping me make it okay with her. Once again, I owe you."

Alex blew out a breath. He'd had fun, and having Heather along had taken his mind off the actual reason he'd invited Mariella out with him in the first place.

Now that reason came crashing back.

"Would you like to come back to my place for a minute?"

"I need to get home."

Frustration stabbed through him. He didn't want the night to end. "Sure. That's fine."

He started in the direction of Mariella's house.

"It's Millie," she said as he drove.

"Have I met Millie?"

She shook her head. "I didn't think to introduce you the other night. She's my goldfish."

He kept his eyes on the road. "Oh." That was an answer he hadn't expected, and he felt his lips twitch.

"Don't laugh at me," she warned. "Millie gets lonely if I'm gone for too long. The store was busy, so I didn't have a chance to run home and check on her over the lunch hour."

He processed that. "You check on your fish?"

"Just because we had a good night together doesn't mean I won't kick your butt if you start giving me attitude about my pet."

"No 'tude," he promised. "I'm impressed that you keep an animal alive. It's more than I've committed to."

"Do you want to meet her?"

"Yes." He parked in her driveway, and they walked up the front steps in companionable silence. "Why didn't I see your fish the last time I was here?"

Mariella's forehead puckered. "I moved her to the guest bedroom while I was sleeping in there. I needed the company."

A feeling he didn't dare put a name on stuttered through his chest at the vulnerability of that explanation. "Makes sense," he said, keeping his tone measured. He didn't want to push her away by making a big deal of it.

"Hey, sweet girl." Mariella moved into the kitchen and gestured to the glass bowl on the counter. "Did you have a good day?"

Alex grinned. "You're talking to a fish." He couldn't say why he was so immensely charmed by this situation, but he had the sudden urge to wrap Mariella in a tight hug. He had a feeling she'd bristle if he tried it, much like attempting to snuggle a feral cat. Yet the look of adoration in her gaze when she smiled at the bobbing fish in the tank couldn't be denied. She was a closet softie despite all of her prickly edges.

"Did you hear about Amber?" Mariella asked and the moment was over.

Maybe she'd done it on purpose because he was getting too close. He nodded. "It was actually why I texted you about getting together in the first place."

Disappointment flashed in her eyes for a moment before she schooled her gaze again. Damn. He hadn't meant to upset her. "Also, I wanted to hang out with you," he added.

"Nice recovery."

He didn't correct her assumption at this point, even though finding out about Amber coming to town had been more of an excuse than anything. It was a conversation they needed to have nonetheless. "You're okay with her being here?"

Mariella shrugged. "My issue wasn't as much with your ex-fiancée as with mine. Do I appreciate the way she trashed me in the tabloids and on social? No. Did I deserve it for the way I made a horrible scene at your wedding? Yes."

There it was again—her unwavering conviction that she'd earned every bad thing that came to her because of mistakes she'd made.

"Jacques wasn't the first man Amber had cheated with," Alex said, keeping his gaze trained on the fish. There was merit to the theory of fish as a calming presence.

Even though he'd just revealed one of the most humiliating secrets of his life, he felt an overriding sense of calm. He didn't know whether to attribute that to Mariella or Millie but figured he could give them each credit.

"You knew and you were going to marry her anyway?"

He shook his head. "I'm not that big of a putz. I found out after. Some guy approached me in a bar and said he'd been with her after the Met Gala the previous year. She'd flown him to a movie set in Thailand for a two-week fling."

"Maybe he was lying. Maybe he wanted to claim America's sweetheart as one of his conquests."

"There were details he shared with me, things only someone who knew her well could know. Intimate details."

"I'm sorry."

"For all I know this is her pattern. There could have been more guys. There would have been if I'd married her."

"America's sweetheart certainly has some spice in her." Mariella handed him a bottle of water from the refrigerator. "I suppose that makes you want her here all the less."

"I don't want her here at all," Alex agreed. If he never saw his ex-fiancée again, it would be too soon but…he waited for Mariella's reaction.

Avery had explained to him how much this opportunity with Drake—that unfortunately also involved Amber—

would mean to the town. Specifically, to the owners of the Wildflower Inn.

He appreciated that Avery had come to him in the first place. They didn't need his buy-in to make the appearance happen.

"It's fine," Mariella said after a moment. "Emma and Angi feel the same as you. They don't want her anywhere near the town."

"But you're okay with it?" He wanted to draw out her feelings because they mattered to him. She mattered to him.

"I behaved badly, but so did Amber. Her appearance would help my friends and our business. This is my life now, and I'm not going to sabotage it out of bitterness. I've spent enough time on self-sabotage. I'm going to say yes to Amber coming to Magnolia for the event."

Mariella stared at him as if he'd just grown a unicorn horn out of his forehead.

"I didn't expect you to say yes."

He frowned. "Did you want me to refuse so you wouldn't have to say no?"

"No." She shook her head. "I promise I don't care if Amber comes to Magnolia. I don't even care if she trashes me all over town. Okay, I would care if she did that, but I can't stop her. She hurt you. She cheated on you. You didn't deserve that."

"I'm not disagreeing with you."

"Then you also have to know there is no possible way she's going to take personal responsibility for any of it."

"Also agreed."

"Which means you're in danger. Danger, Will Robinson. Do you understand?"

"She doesn't hold power over me. She never really did."

"She holds all the power. If you see her, she is going to try to make you think that her cheating was your fault."

"It wasn't my fault. I know that. You know that. Remember how we talked about faith? Maybe you should have a little in me." He could almost see the wheels spinning in her complicated brain as she processed that one.

"I don't want you to be hurt again," she said after a moment.

Should he reveal that she was the one who had the power to hurt him at this point? Nope. He wasn't ready to deal with that, even in his own secret heart. He certainly wasn't going to share it with her.

"It's closure," he said, "for both of us."

"I don't like it." He'd moved nearer as they were speaking and now reached for her. She turned to look at her fish as he held her but didn't pull away. "I don't like it at all."

"I find your concern sexy," he said, brushing a kiss against the corner of her mouth.

"This isn't funny, Alex."

"I'm not joking, Mariella. Amber can come to Magnolia if she wants."

"And you told Avery this?"

"Not yet."

"Aha." She jabbed a finger into the air. "Because you're not certain about it. You're not sure."

"Because I wanted to be certain you were okay with it. If you don't want Amber here, and you need me to stop it, I will."

"Don't do that."

He tried to read her expression, but as usual, she was a mystery to him. A fascinating, wonderful, infuriating mystery. Alex had never been the addictive type. He did everything in measured outcomes, but this woman was different.

It was as if she was the hot rush of a drug into his veins. No matter how much he got, he wanted more.

"Do what?" he asked.

"Be a nice guy."

"Would it be better if I was a jerk?"

She started to pull away then grabbed his shoulders like she couldn't stand to let him go. "Yes, it would be better if you were a jerk. Instead you're good and honorable and I don't know what to do with that. I wasn't built to deal with honorable. Now I'm surrounded by good friends and a daughter who doesn't hate me and you. You are the worst of all. I don't know how to handle somebody who isn't a jerk. Jerks I can manage. It gives me permission to be a jerk in return."

"You're not a jerk."

"I spent a lot of my life being a jerk. It's what I know."

"You're someone different here."

He liked how undone and discombobulated she seemed. When her walls came down and he witnessed the real Mariella—the one she hid from most people. He liked that he brought down her walls even when she didn't want him to.

"Do you want me to go?"

"I want you to stay."

"Why?" He shouldn't ask the question. Don't look a gift horse in the mouth, as the saying went. He should stay with her and not ask for more, but he couldn't help himself.

For a moment, he thought she might kick him to the curb for the audacity of expecting her to open to him.

"Because when I'm with you," she said, her voice whisper-soft, "I feel like I can handle anything. Whatever storm life throws at me, you seem to be the calm in the center of it. I've only ever lived in the destruction. I never realized how powerful the peace could be."

Satisfaction bloomed inside him, swift and sure. Their mouths joined, and it wasn't the same as before. It wasn't him kissing her or her kissing him. It was the two of them together and it meant more to him than anything.

When she led him to her bedroom minutes later, he couldn't imagine ever wanting to leave.

MARIELLA ATTENDED A festival planning meeting later that week at Sunnyside. She found it hard to concentrate when her thoughts kept straying to Alex. There was no need to try to define what was between them, although it felt like everyone around her wanted to put a label on it.

Word traveled fast in a small town. By the time she'd seen her friends for coffee the morning after having dinner with Alex and Heather, they'd been more than mildly curious. She'd managed to play it off by using Heather as an excuse. She didn't think she was fooling either Angi or Emma.

Things were only going to get worse as far as talk went because Alex had invited her to join him at the town's weekly farmers market tonight and then have dinner after with Dylan and Carrie Scott.

Dylan was the local real estate developer who'd sold Alex the building and they'd become friends. Carrie was a native to the town, the daughter of famed artist Niall Reed, and part of the trio that had set Magnolia on the course for revitalization.

If Magnolia had movers and shakers, the Scotts were it. Mariella had met them on a couple of occasions. They'd been polite, but they were Alex's friends. She knew from experience that friends often weren't as forgiving when someone they cared about had been wronged.

She told herself not to get too worked up. Her habit of

worrying about the past and the future ensured that she didn't enjoy the present the way she should. She very much wanted to enjoy her time with Alex.

A woman in a trendy floral-print dress and flowing honey-colored hair approached their group as they got up from the table, the meeting finished. As often happened when they met at the bakery, Mary Ellen had been called away to handle some low-level emergency.

"You're Heather, right?" the woman asked with a sweet smile.

Mariella guessed she was in her late twenties, unfortunately too old to be a potential new bestie for her daughter. She was determined to find people for Heather to hang out with over the summer. Her maternal instinct might be rusty, but she could handle the basics like supporting Heather in making a friend or two.

"I'm Taylor," the woman said. "We spoke on the phone."

Heather offered Taylor a genuine smile. "Dylan's assistant?"

"Exactly. I was hoping you could tell Alex how sad I am that tonight wouldn't work."

Mariella's ears pricked up at that. Heather wasn't fazed by it.

"I hope we can reschedule," Taylor said.

"Yeah. I'll tell him. It's all good."

Heather didn't seem to notice that anything was wrong, like the fact that Mariella was having a minor panic attack on the inside. She could tell Luann sensed something based on the way the older woman stared at her.

Mariella ignored it. She could pretend with the best of them.

They walked past the woman and out into the bright May sunlight. When it was just the three of them again, Mariella put a hand on Heather's arm. "So Alex was supposed to go on a date with that chick?"

Heather shrugged and took a final drink of her coffee before throwing it into a nearby trash bin. "I don't know. I lose track."

"Of the women he dates?" Was the thread of panic in Mariella's voice obvious?

"Of the women who try to date him," Heather corrected then grimaced. "Wait. You and Alex are just friends. You're not…like…upset about this or anything?"

"Not one bit. We are friends."

"Just friends," Luann echoed.

"Okay, good." Heather nodded. "Because that would be weird. My boss and my…well, you and Alex dating would be weird."

"Super weird," Mariella echoed.

The girl gave her a tiny hug that made her heart skip a beat, said goodbye and headed down the street to her car.

Mariella could feel Luann still studying her. "Don't say anything," she warned.

"I wasn't going to. I know when something isn't my business."

Mariella didn't believe that for a second. She felt like she was in a standoff with some sort of wild predator. She needed to not make eye contact. That would defuse the situation or so she hoped. "Great. Good to know. Nothing to see here anyway. I'm heading—"

"To the store? I'll go with you."

Mariella started down the sidewalk. "I have an appointment with a bride at the inn. We're doing a final fitting for her gown."

"Even better," Luann said. "I've always loved that moment when a woman sees herself in a beautiful new dress."

"How about if I text you a picture? I don't think it's appropriate for you to join me at the fitting. A private moment and all that."

"Nonsense. I'm in the business. Mine is a perfect second opinion. I'm sure the bride won't mind."

Mariella stopped at the edge of the sidewalk in front of her car. "Does it matter to you that I mind?"

Luann shook her head. "Not really. Unless the reason you mind is that you don't want to talk to me about how Alex Ralsten is your secret boyfriend."

Mariella gritted her teeth. "He is not my secret boyfriend."

"Your nose is growing."

Mariella started to lift a hand to her face then gripped it at her side. "Stop that."

They stared at each other for a few weighted moments before Mariella looked away. She'd gone soft since coming to Magnolia. "Fine. Get in the car as long as you don't bring up anything about Alex Ralsten. You heard what Heather said. It would be weird."

"She's a kid and it's like her parents are dating."

"No, it is not." Mariella yanked the seat belt across her body then pulled away from the curb only to have another car beep at her.

"You're supposed to look before you pull out," Luann advised. "It's hard when you're used to driving in the city. It's a free-for-all there."

"I didn't drive in the city. I took cabs or the subway."

Luann snickered. "There is no way you took the subway."

Mariella wasn't sure what the other woman was insinuating with that comment, but she didn't like it.

"Are you going to be like this the entire time? Because I will pull over and push you out."

Luann let out a throaty laugh. "I need your answer about taking over my role, and we need to confirm it with Alex. Like I said, I want to make the announcement when we introduce the fall line at the Magnolia Blossom Festival."

"You have my answer," Mariella told her. "It's no."

"I need a different answer. This is important."

"I understand, which is why I'm saying no. Alex doesn't want to work with me, and I would be a terrible brand spokesperson."

"I spoke with Kiki Rogers."

Mariella jerked on the wheel then quickly straightened it. "Tell me that's a joke."

"It's not."

"You committed to this, Luann. You can't back out now, and you certainly can't think to bring in somebody like Kiki." The former model had recently dipped her toe in the waters of fashion design with less than stellar results.

"She could learn about the brand," Luann insisted but it didn't sound convincing. "She works out a lot."

"Then hire her for an ad campaign, not to run the creative side of the company."

"I'm trying to hire you," Luann reminded her. "You said how much you've liked doing the design for these brides again. The Fit Collective can be like that on a larger scale. Alex is a good guy. This is personal for him. I don't want to let him down."

"Did he tell you his family wants him to move back to New York?"

Luann's head snapped up in surprise. "He forgot to mention that. He's not considering it, I'm sure."

"I think he is. So your business partner is getting ready

to cut and run and you're getting ready to cut and run and where does this leave the company and the town?"

"Hopefully, in your capable hands."

Mariella growled in frustration as she parked on the west side of the inn near the cottage. "Why won't you take no for an answer?"

"Because it's not the answer I want."

Mariella got out of the car and stomped around the front until she stood face-to-face with Luann. "I will consider your job offer."

She wasn't sure what possessed her to say that other than the fact that Luann was right when she guessed Mariella missed designing. Owning A Second Chance was fun and she enjoyed the customers but it wasn't her passion. Slowly but surely, she was beginning to believe that she deserved the happiness she'd denied herself for so long.

Whatever form that took.

# CHAPTER SEVENTEEN

MARIELLA WAS WAITING on one of the wrought-iron benches outside the shop when Alex approached that evening.

He'd clearly come straight from the office because he was wearing a pale blue button-down that had probably once been crisp but now looked rumpled, along with khaki-colored trousers. He could have been a Magnolia local. All surface Southern charm and easy swagger.

She knew she still didn't look like she fit in. She could wear all the Reese Witherspoon–inspired fashion she wanted, but Mariella was a city girl at heart, and it showed.

It shouldn't matter. She had her friends here and a good life. It also shouldn't matter that Alex might have invited her to go out with him tonight because sweet-as-peach-pie Taylor wasn't available. Maybe there'd been others he'd asked before her if Heather was right about the long list of women interested in dating one of the town's most eligible bachelors. Mariella had no reason not to believe the girl. Alex would be a catch in any setting.

She squared her shoulders although she had no claim on him or any right to feel the way she did. Peevish wasn't a pretty stance on anyone, and she'd been the one who asked to keep their association on the down-low. She'd only agreed to tonight because so many locals went to the farmers market each week that it would be easy to appear as if they were simply together with friends.

Friends felt like a pale endeavor based on what she truly wanted from Alex. She had only herself to blame, which irritated her all the more.

"You look lovely," he said as he drew closer. Damn her stupid heart and the way it reacted to his words and the smile he gave her. The one he seemed to save for her.

"I do okay for sloppy seconds," she said.

He frowned.

She hadn't used the term in the right way, but he should be able to follow along.

"Am I supposed to know what you're talking about? Does this have something to do with Amber?"

Mariella wished she could blame her current agitation on Amber. A story was easier to tell with a clear villain. She should know. She'd played that role often enough.

Taylor seemed like a nice person. A young woman who wanted to go on a date with a handsome, successful man. Somebody who might be worthy of dating a man like Alex.

"I met Taylor this morning," she said as she stood, brushing invisible lint from the front of her dress. She'd chosen a striped dress in a fabric close to seersucker in its weight and drape. A nod to Southern fashion, although she'd paired it with a chunky statement necklace and Valentino gladiator sandals in black patent leather. Southern with an edge she could handle. She'd stand out like a sore thumb at a small-town farmers market, which hadn't been her intention but fit her current mood to a tee.

Maybe she and Alex both needed the reminder that she wasn't a complement to the life he wanted to create.

It seemed to take a few seconds to place the woman's name. "Dylan's assistant," he said with a nod. "She's a nice girl."

"She's real sad she had to cancel her date with you." Look at that. A bit of a Southern drawl had found its way into Mariella's tone. She had a glimpse into how and why decades of steel magnolias had perfected the art of wielding their soft words like knives.

His brows drew together. "I didn't have a date planned with Taylor."

"It's fine." Now Mariella felt like a fool for bringing it up in the first place. "It's not like we're actually dating or anything."

"Yes. No. I mean this is…" He jammed his hands into the pockets of his khaki pants, and she had the distinct impression he was trying to stop himself from reaching for her. Quite possibly to wring her throat.

"This is a date," he continued, the quiet words delivered with a force that would have made a Southern matron proud. "I asked you out on a date tonight, Mariella. I'm picking you up here because you just got off work. We're going to go to the farmers market and then to dinner with my friends. After, I'm going to drive you home. At the very least I'm going to walk you to your front door and kiss the heck out of you."

"I told you I don't want a big public spectacle. Your chivalry is wasted on me." Her thundering heart told a different story. Her heart was all about chivalry.

"I don't know another way to be, and I haven't even started wooing you. Your expectations need some work, sweetheart. I get that you have a history with men who don't treat you well. I'm not one of them. Don't put me into that category."

She bit down on her lower lip, hating that he'd called her out and the truth of his words. She was being unfair. "Taylor said you were supposed to go on a date with her."

A blush colored his cheeks, utterly charming her. "This might sound conceited but there have been a lot of women since I've moved to Magnolia who want to date me."

"Hashtag facts," she muttered.

"I haven't gone out with most of them. I haven't cared about going out with anyone until you. Which is bizarre, but I'm getting used to it."

"Well, that just gives me a warm and fuzzy feeling all over. You're getting used to me."

"I think I'm doing better at it than you."

She smiled despite herself. "I'm an emotional train wreck."

"Then it's a good thing you pulled into my station."

"Oh, no. You pulled into my station. I was here first."

"Now we're both here, and make no mistake about it, you are the person I want to be with. Not just behind closed doors. So if you want to argue about something real—"

"Fine. I'll stop arguing about the legions of women in this town who would throw themselves at your feet. Your ego doesn't need any help from me."

He clutched a hand to his chest in mock surprise. "I'm not sure I'd recognize you if you weren't being contrary."

She thought about telling him that she'd agreed to consider Luann's job offer as a real option for the future. They'd need his approval, and she couldn't imagine a world where he'd give that. Or how she could spin his refusal into something that didn't feel like rejection.

As much as she enjoyed sparring with Alex, she wanted more of the peace she often felt when she was with him. Mariella was still becoming accustomed to enjoying calm in her life instead of the spinning madness she'd grown so used to.

"You just don't want to admit that you like me most of all," she said then sucked in a breath at the thought he might like her less than she did him. Which was barreling quickly past most of all and morphing from like into a far more powerful emotion.

She should have known better. Alex wasn't one for playing games. He drew her closer and brushed a tender kiss over her mouth. "I'm happy to admit that to anyone who will listen."

He made her feel like a cat in a bowl of cream, luxuriating in the rich warmth of him.

When a car drove by and honked, she quickly pulled away. "But no one can know," she said.

He frowned. "You said you didn't want a billboard in town but—"

"No one can know there's anything more than friendship between us. Heather said it would be weird."

His frown returned, but he fell into step next to her as she started toward the town square.

"What does Heather have to do with you and me?"

"I don't want to upset her."

"You think lying is a good idea?"

"It's not a big deal." She nudged him playfully. "It's the modern times. We don't need labels anyway and neither of us is going to post cringey selfies on social media."

"I don't like it."

She wanted to take his hand, but that would defeat the purpose of what she'd just asked him to do. "Please, Alex. I'll talk to her but for now can we keep this between us? I just got to the point where things feel okay with her. I don't want to mess it up."

He didn't say anything for several moments. It didn't speak well of her, but she couldn't jeopardize her connection with Heather. She had to hope Alex would find a way to understand.

"Okay," he answered finally, his mouth set in a hard line. He really was a good guy. "But I don't like it."

Her breath felt bottled up in her chest. She reached out and squeezed his hand before releasing it again. "Trust me. I'll make it worth your while."

"It sounds like you're talking about trading sexual favors for my complicity. I should probably feel taken advantage of."

"Just appreciated," she clarified.

That seemed to soothe him and the tension eased like dandelion fluff floating away on the breeze. The situation wasn't perfect, but Mariella would make this work. She was close to attaining things she hadn't even allowed herself to want before now, and she would make sure she didn't sabotage any of it. She forced herself to ignore her doubts and allowed joy to infuse her like warm sunshine as they stopped by the first booth at the market.

"ARE YOU SURE you want that one?"

Meredith Ventner watched Alex with a funny look on her face as he lifted the cat carrier into his arms to peer inside. A swipe of claws against the cage door rewarded his effort, followed by several rounds of intense purring.

The cat inside was orange, almost the exact color of a basketball, but with the personality of an angry tiger. Her yellow eyes shone in the shadows and the front paw that had taken a swipe at him was encircled in a white stripe.

The Furever Friends booth was located on the edge of the market, with a colorful banner and several wire pens where available canines lounged, played and generally charmed potential families who came by to look. There were also a few plastic carriers on a long table, an adult cat looking for its new owner in each one.

Meredith was like the Pied Piper of adopters with her chin-length bob, denim overalls and effusive energy. People drifted past then stopped as if they couldn't help but choose one of her animals to make their own.

Alex had sensed this about the rescue's sprite-sized owner from the start, which is why he'd given her a wide berth until now.

"I thought you came over here to look at dogs," she said as the cat inside let out an outraged squawk.

Alex hadn't known cats could squawk. He was charmed even though he knew the cat meant it as a warning. Alex wasn't the best at picking up on cautionary cues given by indomitable women. "Turns out I want this cat. Is there a problem with that?"

"Well…"

Ryan Sorensen, an ER doctor Alex had met the night of Heather's accident, who also happened to be Meredith's fiancé and Emma's brother, sidled up next to her. "The problem is that the feisty kitty you're holding was on track to be Meredith's latest foster fail."

Meredith gave Ryan a not-so-gentle elbow to the ribs when he tried to put his arm around her shoulder, which didn't deter him in the least. There was a sophisticated air that clung to the man even though he'd made Magnolia his permanent home. Despite his big-city experience, Ryan seemed right at home in the role of animal-adoption support person for Meredith.

"What's a foster fail?" Alex asked, trying to follow along.

Ryan dropped a gentle kiss on the top of Meredith's

head. "She takes in the animals that are the hardest to love and keeps them for her own. It usually starts as a temporary foster situation, but she has a special place in her heart for the biggest challenges."

Meredith gave a little snort but didn't deny it. "And look at how well that turned out with you," she told Ryan with an eye roll. The affection between these two seemingly opposite people was palpable, and Alex had to look away for a moment to hide the unjustified envy he felt.

"To qualify as an adopter for this cat, I want you to sign up for a shy-cat training session and commit to at least three follow-up home visits where we can review her progress."

"Is that the typical process?"

"She makes it up as she goes along," Ryan revealed.

"I do not. It's typical in a situation like this. You've already said you don't have a lot of experience with cats and Bex is special."

"Where does the name Bex come from? Should I keep it?"

"I named her after Bellatrix Lestrange in the *Harry Potter* books. She was my favorite character."

"Despite being a murderous villain," Ryan added with a chuckle.

"Minor detail." Meredith looked past Alex for a moment. If he wasn't mistaken, something akin to understanding dawned in her light gray eyes. "Bex is special, but I think you can handle her."

He wasn't surprised when Mariella came to stand next to him a moment later. "What's this?" She gestured toward the cat carrier, which had gone remarkably silent for the moment.

"I'm adopting a cat."

Mariella stared at him then into the carrier, earning a throaty growl from Bex. "I thought you were a dog person."

"I'm a dog person. I'm also a cat person. I'm a person who's ready to make a commitment, and this animal needs a home." Stating the words out loud gave him a rush of adrenaline.

Mariella's eyes narrowed, but Meredith gave him an approving grin.

"You might only need one home visit," she told him. "We'll see how you do with her."

"That's big," Ryan confirmed. "She must have a lot of faith in you."

Alex glanced toward Mariella, who'd crossed her arms over her chest like a protective barrier. "I hope Meredith isn't the only one." Mariella looked like she was ready to either scream or hug him.

He couldn't understand why it bothered her so much that he was adopting this cat, but she didn't approve. Did that say more about him or the animal?

"I'll keep her at the booth until y'all are finished at the market. When you pick her up, we can go over the rest of the care instructions and fill out the paperwork."

Alex nodded while Mariella continued to frown. "Sounds good. We're supposed to go to dinner with Dylan and Carrie. I can cancel if you think I should be at home with Bex."

"She'll be fine. Time on her own to acclimate will be good for her." Meredith's smile went soft at the edges. "Carrie won't last late anyway. She's about to pop. She is so fat right now."

Ryan squeezed Meredith's shoulder. "I don't think that's the best way to describe it."

"She's orca-whale fat." Meredith doubled down on her original assessment. "And she's happy about it so I don't think she'd care about me calling her out. She's fat and happy."

"I guess you're next," Ryan told her with a teasing glint in his eye.

For an instant, Meredith's eyes went wide and she clawed at her throat like she was having trouble breathing. "Alex," she said on a croak, "you can leave the carrier under the table. I've got to go..." She looked around at the bustling booth without focusing on any one person. "Do something."

"I like to freak her out," Ryan said with an affectionate smirk as Meredith hurried off to talk to a family that surrounded one of the far pens. "We're not exactly nearing the place Carrie and Dylan are, but we're in negotiations. She's going to make a great mom even though it terrifies her."

"I have no doubt based on how she mothers her rescues," Alex agreed.

He placed Bex's carrier under the table as Ryan went to placate his fiancée.

"Anything else you want to see or booths we need to visit?" he asked Mariella as he straightened.

She was staring at him. "You can't just do that."

"Do what...adopt an animal? People do it all the time."

"You said you weren't ready for a commitment." The words were spoken through clenched teeth and sounded like an accusation. "You told me that."

"Things change. I saw Bex, and I knew I wanted her."

"Do you know how old she is or her history? She could live a long time. People make emotional decisions without realizing what they're signing up for—the good and the bad and years of either."

"I'm aware. She's also had a rough go of it. Meredith and I went through the details. I'll be good for her, and I think she'll be good for me."

"You can't bring her to my house. She looks like the type of cat who would knock Millie's bowl off the counter for access to a fresh snack."

"I'll remember not to ask you to cat-sit," he said as he led her away from the booth. A little distance from Bex might be in order at the moment.

Mariella jerked away from him when he put a hand on the small of her back. "Why are you so calm?" she demanded.

"Why are you so worked up?"

She looked like she didn't know how to answer that. "I wasn't joking," she finally said, "about being an emotional train wreck."

"Trust me." He nodded and brushed a finger against her wrist, subtle so no one watching would even notice. "I picked up on that."

"Doesn't it worry you?" They were walking down the farmers market's center aisle. Several people waved or called out greetings, as many to Mariella as to him. She might not realize it, but she belonged here.

"A lot of things scare me. Most of them I can't control, so I try not to worry too much."

"It's annoying how wise you are," she said and he laughed.

"You like annoying."

She squeezed his hand for a precious moment. Not an outright hand-holding because of the stupid business of keeping things secret but enough for Alex to know it was special and her way of reminding both of them of the connection they shared.

Satisfaction tingled along his nerve endings and made his heart full.

"I like you," she said softly, the emotion in her voice lending a magnitude to the simple words.

He tightened his grip on her fingers in response. "Good. Because I like you, too."

That and so much more.

## CHAPTER EIGHTEEN

As HE LET himself into his quiet house the following week, Alex had to admit that Mariella might have been right to doubt whether he could live up to the responsibility Bex needed.

What had possessed him to adopt the cat the night of the farmers market? Mariella had called him wise but more accurately he should be shoved in the corner with an emotional-IQ dunce cap on his head. His thoughts and feeling had been a tumultuous muddle thanks to the conversation on the way there with Mariella.

Even without Heather's disapproval, it was smart to keep their burgeoning relationship under wraps for a while. There'd already been enough speculation in town and with Drake and Amber on the books to arrive for their movie shoot and the Magnolia Blossom Festival, he didn't want to feed the gossip mill. The town was abuzz with excitement at the idea of two A-list stars potentially rubbing elbows with the locals.

Alex could have told people they weren't missing much with Amber, but he knew she'd turn on the charm, especially if it meant his neighbors would be more receptive to her version of their breakup.

The spotlight would be on him even more brightly. He wouldn't choose the attention, but there was no way around it. The best thing for both him and Mariella would be a low profile until the Hollywood types were gone. He might be wise, but she'd been right.

His mind and heart were consumed with Mariella, a woman who wasn't willing to publicly claim him, and Bex, a cat that acted as interested in clawing his eyes out as snuggling up to him.

The animal had spent the first several days in his home holed up under the sofa in the bedroom he'd converted to an office. She didn't make a peep during daylight hours, but as soon as he turned out the lights for bed, she began a seemingly endless chorus of meows, feline chirps and full-blown howls.

Alex had closed the door to the office, but that encouraged her to complain more loudly. He'd tried talking to her and offering a variety of treats and toys for stimulation, but none of that had made a difference.

Last night, he'd finally resorted to sleeping on the sofa with the hope that she'd be soothed by his presence but not tempted to go for his throat while his defenses were down. He'd woken close to 4:00 a.m., roused by the rhythmic purr in his ear. At some point during the night, the cat had curled up next to his head, her relaxed body pressed against him.

Assuming she'd be more receptive to his attention in a drowsy state, he'd reached up a hand to pet her white belly and managed one long stroke before she'd nipped at his wrist. Then she'd jumped from the couch to retreat under the sofa.

The damn cat reminded him far too much of Mariella, although she probably wouldn't appreciate the comparison.

The first night they'd stayed together, Mariella had curled around him, draping an arm across his chest, only to pull away as soon as she woke.

But Alex wasn't going to quit on Bex—or Mariella for

that matter. There was a difference between quitting and pivoting in order to view a challenge through a new lens.

He'd spoken with Meredith at length earlier that morning and had Heather cancel his afternoon appointments. He'd stopped at the rescue before his early return home and felt prepared to make some real headway with at least one of the women in his life.

"Hello," he called as he entered the house like he expected the cat to respond. A flash of orange fur darted around the corner of the hallway.

It had to be a good sign that Bex was willing to explore the house on her own. He hoped she'd returned to the office and followed her in, leaving the door open so the cat didn't feel trapped.

He sank onto the carpet in front of the sofa and ripped open the tube of lickable treats that Meredith had given him. He squeezed a dollop of chicken-flavored puree on the tip of his finger and lowered his hand to the floor.

Alex had no faith in this experiment but also very little to lose.

Meredith had called the treat tube "cat crack," but Alex had a feeling his new pet wouldn't be enticed so easily. To his shock, it only took a minute before he heard a rustling from underneath the sofa.

"That a girl," he said quietly, looking straight ahead so he didn't spook her. He tried to stay relaxed and completely still at the same time. A moment later, he felt the sensation of a rough cat tongue against his finger. Bex eagerly licked the dab of treat he'd put there, purring all the while. "You are so smart. It really is cat crack."

He leaned forward ever-so-slightly to watch her. She didn't make eye contact but continued to lick his finger like a queen deigning to enjoy her master pastry chef's prized creation. When his finger was empty, she butted his hand with her soft head.

"Was that a thank-you?" he asked as much to himself as the cat. "Look at you and your good manners."

To his utter amazement, the cat climbed into his lap and turned a quick circle then curled into a ball. He didn't dare move as he listened to her gentle rumble begin again. A smile split his face and a feeling of deep satisfaction filled his chest.

One fiercely independent woman wooed, he told himself, and one to go.

BY THE TIME he got to the office the next morning, that feeling of contentment was a thing of the past.

He'd sat with Bex for nearly an hour before lifting her onto the cat bed he'd put on the sofa in the office. The animal stayed relaxed while being moved, but she must have held it against him because he'd awoke to find that she'd pooped on the floor of his shower overnight.

He'd cleaned it up and, just to show there were no hard feelings, brought in the treat tube to give her a little something for the morning. All he got in return was a few new angry marks on the back of his hand.

His mood did not brighten when Heather informed him Luann was waiting in his office.

"I resign as creative director," she announced before he'd even shut the door.

"I don't accept it," he'd countered, his head throbbing harder than the wounds on his hand.

"Accept it or not, it's happening. We'll still be partners in the business, but I'm no longer going to work here." She pointed to the top of his desk. "I brought you a couple of donuts from Sunnyside to ease the sting."

He eyed the bag but didn't reach for a donut.

"I don't understand why you are doing this right now. You made a commitment," he reminded her, then glanced at his watch. "We have a marketing meeting in fifteen minutes to finalize the PR plan. Things are going to get rolling even more after the festival launches the collection. It's a calculated risk to take this local spin on things. We need to show a united front."

She shook her head. "No."

He could deal with off-color or temperamental or snotty Luann, but this quietly resolved version of her didn't sit well. It felt like he was treading water in a calm sea—calm other than the dark dorsal fin that circled him. "Does this have anything to do with Mariella?"

"Unfortunately, no. I think she wants to come on board, Alex, but she's afraid of your reaction. Specifically, of your rejection. Kiki is ready whenever we make her a formal offer."

"We aren't giving Kiki a job at the Fit Collective. And Mariella isn't afraid of me. If anything, you've got the roles reversed there. The woman terrifies me at every turn."

Luann flashed the hint of a knowing smile. He didn't dare ask what she thought she knew based on his comment. "Either way…" She sighed. "My decision is made. I'm flying to Nebraska tonight."

"What are you talking about? What's in Nebraska?"

"My son, his wife and my grandbaby. I'm going to spend the summer with them. I rented a house on the lake and I'm going to be Nana for a couple of months."

"Do you even like kids?"

"You know me too well. I'm going to learn to like kids. I'm going to learn to be a normal person and a good mother.

Or if it's too late for that, I'm going to be a fantastic grand-mother."

She held up a hand when he would have argued. "I appreciate your faith in me, Alex. You gave me a chance when nobody else would, and I probably didn't deserve one."

"This is how you repay me," he muttered, running a hand through his hair.

"You can't see it now, but I'm doing you a favor. The fashion world isn't for me anymore. I've been trying to tell you for weeks. I don't know how to be politically correct."

"That's an excuse. You could figure it out if you wanted to. You are brilliant."

"Once again, I appreciate your faith in me, but the truth is I don't want to figure it out. I want to walk away on my terms. Maybe that's what I wanted all along. I know what I'm doing to you isn't fair. Hiring Mariella as a replacement was as much to ease my conscience as to help the company. I wouldn't blame you for hating me."

Alex drew in a breath and studied the scratches—both fresh and fading—that covered his hands and arms. What the hell was wrong with him that he put his faith in people who didn't want or deserve it?

Maybe he should do the same thing. He had the offer from his stepfather. It was probably time to stop pretending he could be the one to lead this company to success. It was impossible to be a leader when he could barely en-list followers.

"Don't walk away," Luann said.

"I think you've forfeited your right to give me advice, business or otherwise."

"Be that as it may, I'm giving it anyway. My tenacity is one of the things you love best about me."

He shook his head. "Right now, there isn't anything I

love best about you. I'm sorry," he said almost immediately. "I'm frustrated. I thought you and I were a team."

Luann walked toward him where he'd taken a stand in front of his desk so he wouldn't have to look at her resignation letter or the guilt pastries. She reached out a hand to pat his cheek much like a mother would.

Not his mother specifically, but he could imagine it happening in other families.

"You're a sweet young man," she told him. "But too kind for your own good. It's okay to be mad, Alex. Your feelings are valid."

"I know that," he mumbled although the way his stomach clenched told a different story. He hadn't been allowed to express his feelings for most of his life—not the difficult ones anyway.

He suspected it came from being left with a single mom who was emotionally fragile after being humiliated and discarded by his father. When she'd met his stepdad and remarried, Alex had gotten the clear impression that he was extra baggage along for the ride. And the ride was a lot smoother when he wasn't making waves.

He hadn't realized until this moment how often he shut down his feelings to make the people around him happy or more comfortable or because it was easier.

With Amber, it had been simple enough to convince himself that, as the artist, she was more entitled to displays of emotion than him. His role was as her steady rock, and he took it seriously. Fat lot of good that had done him.

"Then you should know I'm pissed as hell." He stepped away from Luann's touch. "You've put everything we worked for—I worked for—in jeopardy. The media is going to have a field day with this kind of organizational change."

Luann glanced toward the window as if drawing courage

from the bright morning then back to him again. "Not if we manage to convince Mariella to step in. It's not too late."

He didn't argue because what was the point? It was tempting to invite Mariella to join the company. Her talent was undeniable and the thought of working with her on a daily basis held a strange appeal.

Without a creative director on the eve of launching their first collection, things could fizzle out before they even got started. So what if the early reviews had been great? Would retailers and the general public get behind the brand if they didn't think it had staying power?

There had been enough bad press to overcome due to Luann's personal history, and people might be happy to see the Fit Collective fail rather than succeed. His stepfather would be among the former group.

"I'll call her and…" Luann began, but he shook his head.

"Go," he told her, plucking the letter of resignation from the desk. "We're not your problem anymore."

"I still want to support you." She sounded as apologetic and sincere as he'd ever heard.

Now that Alex had loosened the reins on his feelings, he had no desire to pull them back again. "I don't want or need your help."

She frowned. "I'm still your financial partner."

"Go to Nebraska and be a grandma or whatever it is you decide to do next. I'll talk to the board to come up with a plan to buy you out."

"Now you're talking like a real businessman," she said with a huff of laughter. "I'm not sure I like it."

"Like it or not, this is what your actions have brought us to. This is the me who's here now."

She studied him for a long moment. "I'm sorry, Alex. I wish you nothing but the best. You deserve it."

He stepped behind his desk and sat in the plush leather chair, wondering if he agreed with her. In his world, the ones who got their way were people like Luann and his stepfather. They took what they wanted even if their choices hurt other people.

Was that what he had to do? He thought about Amber coming to town and Mariella insisting they keep their relationship a secret. Everyone around him was looking after themselves.

Alex wondered if the adage was true in this case. If he couldn't beat them, maybe his best choice was to join them.

MARIELLA CAUGHT SIGHT of a flash of pale blond hair early Saturday morning as she jogged past downtown's central grassy park.

She checked her watch then glanced up at the robin's-egg-blue sky like the cloudless swath of color might offer an answer to her silent question.

The bride getting married today at the Wildflower Inn had singular pale blond hair. She was an ethereal beauty with big green eyes and a penchant for sighing when overwhelmed. She would have made a lovely sister to one of Jane Austen's heroines.

From what Mariella could tell, Theresa Marshall, the bride in question, seemed to be frequently vanquished by her emotions. Mariella slowed then stepped onto the thick grass, still moist with dawn dew.

There was no reason to panic, she told herself. Theresa hadn't given any indication she might be having second thoughts or in the market to add herself to the Wildflower's list of brides with cold feet.

She certainly seemed happy enough two days earlier when they'd met for the final fitting for her gown. Theresa had chosen a simple peasant-style dress with tiny daisies embroidered along the bodice.

It was a departure from the gowns Mariella normally created, even since she'd reinvented herself as a custom wedding-gown designer for Wildflower brides. She loved catering to what her customer wanted without needless worry over her brand.

Wiping away the sweat from her forehead with the hem of her athletic tank top, she slowly approached the park bench where Theresa sat, as if the woman might bolt at any second. "Are you contemplating your last few hours as a free woman?" she asked then wanted to smack herself upside the head.

If the bride was considering running, the last thing she needed was a reminder about giving up her freedom, whatever that might mean to her.

Mariella also knew that if the woman wanted to back out of the wedding, she'd find a way to help her.

At the end of the day, it didn't matter if the situation meant more bad press for the inn. Mariella wanted the people she worked with to be happy no matter how that looked for them. Emma and Angi would feel the same.

"I'm going to be truly free when I am finally married," Theresa said with a tragic smile.

"Those are happy words spoken in the saddest tone I've ever heard. I haven't met your soon-to-be husband but I hope he's a man who makes you happy."

Theresa dashed a hand across her cheeks, brushing away tears and the remnants of smudged mascara. "Charly makes me so happy. My life hasn't been the easiest. He's taking on a lot with me."

Mariella sat cross-legged on the grass in front of the

woman, who seemed to need a little extra physical space for herself. "We all have baggage."

Theresa shook her head. "Not like mine. Let's just say my uncle wasn't a good man. He was a very, very bad man. I don't want to give voice to the things he did. The things people who said they loved me ignored. Not today. Today is about my next chapter with Charly."

Mariella forced down the sick feeling rising in her gut at what this sweet woman left unsaid. "It sounds like you're having trouble releasing the past. Sometimes it's difficult to step into the future or even appreciate the present moment when what came before looms so large in your mind and heart."

Mariella could be giving that advice to herself as much as to the anxious bride. She still harbored guilt from the mistakes she'd made years ago, unable to truly claim the life she wanted because of her inability to let go.

Yet it was easier to be a cheerleader for someone she barely knew than take a hard look at her own life.

"That's why I came out here this morning," Theresa told her. "It's not that I don't want to marry Charly or I'm having second thoughts. If he's willing to marry me with everything he knows, I'd be a fool not to. But I don't know how to move forward without allowing the past to retain its power over me. I don't want to give my family the satisfaction of that."

"Are they coming to the wedding?" Mariella almost hated to ask the question. "I realize we never got into that during your fitting. I'm sorry for not being more of a support to you. You were quiet, and I didn't want to overstep. I let the client take the lead on how much she wants to share."

"You were right," Theresa said sweetly. "I didn't want to talk about it. Maybe I should have because I've been a nervous wreck. My family isn't coming. No one but my cousin. She's the only one who believed me when I revealed what was happening." Her rosebud mouth thinned. "I wish our uncle wouldn't have given her a reason to know that I was telling the truth."

Mariella felt like her heart would break in two for this girl. "You are here, Theresa. You survived. Charly loves you for that. I bet if I asked him, he'd say he was just as lucky to be marrying you. Don't let the past keep its hold on you. It won't be easy and I'm sure there are people you can talk to who will help way more than I ever could. Just know that I don't see you as a victim. I see you as the woman you are now, ready to claim her own happiness. You can do this. I believe in you."

Mariella took the woman's hand—which was about ten paces outside her comfort zone—as Theresa cried for a few more minutes. After releasing Mariella, she wiped her face again and rose from the bench.

"I'm glad you stopped to talk to me, although I promise I wasn't in jeopardy of being one of your runaway brides."

"That's a relief," Mariella said quietly. "But we want what's best for you."

"What's best for me is marrying Charly and having a happy life. Isn't that the best revenge against the people who did you wrong? Finding happiness despite what you had to go through to get it."

"I think you're right." Mariella dabbed at the corner of one eye, telling herself it was just an errant bead of sweat. "I think you've helped me more than I've helped you."

Theresa offered a genuine smile then glanced at her watch. "I should get back before they notice I left. I don't want anyone to worry, especially not Charly. He only needs to know there's no place that I'd rather be than at his side for the rest of our lives."

Theresa hugged Mariella tightly—which Mariella took more comfort in than she'd admit—then headed toward a hatchback parked on the other side of the town square.

Mariella drew in a shaky breath as she headed toward the street again. She hadn't finished her run for the day but her knees felt too weak for jogging.

She headed toward the bakery, unsurprised to find Heather and Alex at a table together, poring over some sort of work stuff on the girl's laptop.

Everyone was working overtime to get ready before the festival next weekend.

"You look pasty for somebody who's been exercising," Heather said when she noticed Mariella walking toward their table.

"The usual?" Mary Ellen called from behind the counter.

"Nothing this morning." Mariella waved to the bakery owner as she continued to approach the table where Alex and Heather sat.

She didn't stop until she was so close that her hip brushed the side of his arm. Instead of looking at him, she kept her gaze trained on her daughter.

"Alex and I are dating."

The girl's mouth dropped open, and Mariella heard several audible gasps from the surrounding tables. She wouldn't let fear or anxiety or the thought of how people might judge either one of them stop her.

Heather shook her head. "You told me—"

"I'm sorry," she interrupted, nerves dancing across her stomach. Her breath was coming out in shallow puffs, and she struggled to string together coherent sentences. "It's new. I didn't want to upset you. Neither of us did. I like him." She allowed herself to meet Alex's gaze, searching for the approval she hoped she'd find there.

"I like you, too," Alex said, reaching up to link their fingers, the touch calming her in ways she couldn't explain. A small smile played around the corners of his full mouth.

It wasn't exactly a surprise. He'd said the words previously but not so publicly. Even if he hadn't, Alex wasn't the type to be intimate with a woman if there wasn't some affection behind it.

In fact, it was his inherent honorability that both attracted and terrified her.

Heather looked between the two of them. Mariella couldn't interpret the girl's expression. "I also like you," she told her daughter.

Heather lifted a brow.

"Obviously not in the same way I like him," Mariella plodded on.

Alex patted her arm with a laugh. "You're killing it here."

She pretended to swat at him.

"I want a relationship with you, Heather. However you're willing to let me in. I was wrong not to tell you about Alex and to ask him to pretend. Things will work better if we're honest."

Heather slowly nodded, and Mariella noticed that all eyes in the bakery were upon them. She couldn't blame people for their curiosity but the details of her connection to Heather belonged to the girl. Mariella would respect whatever her daughter decided going forward. "I guess I can't complain about honesty. Although if I have to see the two of you making out, I'm going to throw up."

"Nobody's going to be making out," Mariella assured her.

"At least in public," Alex added.

"That's disappointing." Josie Trumbull, who owned the dance studio and had just gotten engaged to the local bookstore owner, leaned over from the table next to them. "If I were twenty years younger and wasn't already blissfully in love…" She wagged a finger in Mariella's face. "I'd give you a run for your money."

Alex shrugged as he grinned up at Mariella. "Not sure you'd stand a chance, sweetheart."

His veiled compliment made Josie so happy that Mariella couldn't help but laugh.

Alex stood and planted a gentle kiss on her lips. "This doesn't count as making out," he said against her mouth. "No tongue."

"Gross," Heather said, but she didn't sound upset.

Mariella barely registered her daughter's good-natured complaint.

The happiness coursing through her felt fizzy like champagne and overwhelming like the best high she'd ever experienced. It was better than anything she'd felt before because it came from inside her. This feeling of happiness was real and true, which made it all the more powerful. She wasn't sure how long it would last, but she wanted to ride this wave as far as it would take them.

# CHAPTER NINETEEN

"WHAT MADE YOU think declaring your intentions for Alex Ralsten in the middle of Sunnyside was a good idea?"

Mariella groaned as she watched the video Angi played on her phone later that night. It showed her declaring her affection for Alex in front of Heather and the rest of the bakery patrons.

"Your bride made me think it," Mariella answered as she nibbled on a bite of leftover wedding cake.

"She's our bride," Emma corrected. "They are all ours because we're a team. Theresa was radiant and happy so whatever conversation you had with her clearly helped."

Angi nodded and pointed her fork in Mariella's direction. "It helped both of you based on how fast you marched over to the bakery after talking with her. I think it's adorable."

"Theresa didn't have cold feet," Mariella assured them. "Don't think that talking brides out of running away is going to be a regular occurrence around here. She would have come back even if I hadn't talked to her."

Mariella didn't attend every event at the Wildflower Inn. Most of her work was done in the pre-planning stages, but sometimes a couple would inspire her to be more involved or to witness their happy union. She could blame her softening attitude toward love on that.

It was difficult to spend so much time watching people

pledge their troths and not want to believe in the promise of happily-ever-after.

Not for her, though. She and Alex weren't headed in that direction. For sure. Although the way he looked at her when she made her stand in the bakery caused warmth to permeate her veins even now. She didn't think any man had ever looked at her like that.

It was one thing to be embarrassed in front of customers at the bakery. She gave a sharp shake of her head. "I just hope that video doesn't get out. Not when Amber is coming with whatever press follows her here."

"It isn't as if Josie posted it to the town's Facebook page or anything."

"You're sure?"

Emma nodded. "I called her as soon as she sent it, which was right after the big event."

"Speaking of…" Angi grinned. "What happens next?"

"I'm not sure," Mariella admitted. "Dating a man who is a decent human being is new for me. I wonder how long it can last before I find a way to screw it up?"

"Don't say that," Emma told her. "There's no guarantee you're going to screw it up."

"Yeah," Angi agreed. "Maybe he'll screw it up."

Emma shook her head. "Or maybe it will just be good."

Mariella appreciated her friend's optimism, although Emma didn't sound completely confident in that matter.

Why would she? Mariella had no track record when it came to successful relationships. Her history with Alex made it even less likely they could go anywhere.

It didn't change the fact that she wanted to try. Finding the guts to tell him made something tight in her heart relax ever so slightly.

She also appreciated that Heather had accepted her pronouncement. The girl, who'd babysat Isabella today while Jasmin worked, spent some time in the store while the baby was napping. She'd helped with inventory and hung out with Mariella and Jasmin like it was the most normal thing in the world.

Maybe there was something to making good choices despite her fear. Maybe Mariella truly had put her penchant for self-sabotage in the past. She wished she had as much faith in herself as the people around her seemed to. All she could do was her best to live up to the faith they'd placed in her.

MAYBE IT WAS fate conspiring to tell Mariella she'd gone too far with her declaration, but it felt as though the moment she had publicly outed her and Alex, life became so busy she didn't have a moment to even consider going on a real date.

The only consolation was that his world seemed equally chaotic, especially with Luann off to Nebraska. Although it wasn't textbook romantic, she and Alex worked together every day, both on the final plans for the festival as well as the Fit Collective collection launch.

They hadn't talked about her formally joining the company in Luann's absence, nor was she ready for that. But Alex needed help so Mariella stepped in. Heather had actually been the one to insist that Mariella's experience could benefit them. They'd each expressed their gratitude at having her input with meetings and pulling together details of the collection.

From her years in the fashion industry, Mariella knew that designing clothes was only the first step. So much of the work involved marketing the collection and cultivating a client base who bought into the story of the brand.

Mariella loved telling stories with fashion, whether it

was the tale of a woman about to embark on the next chapter of her life with the partner she'd chosen or someone trying to reclaim her health and vitality or appreciate the strength of her body in whatever shape it took.

To that end, the first thing Mariella had suggested was to cancel the company's contract with the New York City modeling agency. She'd convinced a dumbfounded Alex that the best way to communicate the positivity his brand embodied was forgoing professionals for local models. Real women from the community to represent the Fit Collective and showcase its place in Magnolia.

Already the tactic had worked. Whether or not the press and the fashion industry appreciated what they were doing, the people in town did.

Women from Josie at the dance studio to Lily who owned the hardware store to Mary Ellen were modeling the clothes. Even Meredith from Furever Friends had agreed to model at the Magnolia Blossom Festival. Meredith had quite the soft spot for Alex since he'd adopted Bex.

It didn't compare to the soft spot growing inside Mariella where he was concerned. That spot was quickly engulfing her whole chest, which made it difficult to draw a full breath when he was around.

Even though they hadn't been on a formal date since her declaration, he'd made it clear in a myriad of tiny ways that he cared for her. Whether finding little excuses to touch her as they worked together stringing lights and putting up decorations for the festival or bringing her coffee or a boxed salad when he thought she was working too much.

His thoughtfulness never wavered. And she couldn't complain that she was truly losing herself to him. Although when it came to Alex, it didn't feel like a loss or falling or anything scary. It felt like finally being confident in her place in the world and having a person who made her fit without having to be anything but herself.

She wanted to tell him how she felt but something stopped her. Fear mostly.

What if this was just who he was? A good person. The type of man who cared about the people around him. She'd seen him drop off coffee to Heather and bring in little treats for people who worked in the office. He was intrinsically thoughtful. Maybe Mariella was fooling herself into thinking that she was someone special to him. But, oh, how he made her feel special.

Or maybe that's what normal well-adjusted people did. Before Magnolia, Mariella had met so few of them in her life. She'd seen and heard about plenty of romantic overtures as she worked with brides at Belle Vie leading up to their big day, but she hadn't trusted it.

She knew how easy it was to get caught up in the fantasy. That's how a good portion of her adult life had been spent after all, pretending that things were perfect while ignoring the hairline cracks in the foundation of her life. Now she wanted something real and solid. Although she still didn't trust herself not to mess it up with Alex, she knew they would have no chance if she didn't try as much as he did.

With that in mind, she forced herself to leave the store in Jasmin's capable hands for the remainder of the day. After delegating a few of the more time-sensitive tasks for the festival, she made a stop by the grocery store, and then the pet aisle at the hardware store. She texted Alex to ask if he would join her for dinner that night then headed home to get ready.

Millie watched her with unblinking fish eyes as Mariella bustled around the kitchen chopping vegetables and sautéing them, then she started on the sauce by heating olive oil—the extra virgin kind.

But she couldn't quite stem the tide of nerves rolling through her, like the waves crashing against the shoreline after a storm.

She told herself that cooking for a man she was dating did not mean anything. It didn't have to mean anything. She was just doing something nice for him. The way he did nice things for her all the time. But the more minutes that ticked by, the more the knots tightened in her stomach until she was almost nauseous from them. She was so distracted that she burned the first pot of sauce she made, the acrid smell of charred cream filling her kitchen with a disgusting scent.

She glanced at the clock, realizing she was running out of time, and hurried to start over.

"Millie, why can't you have opposable thumbs?" she demanded of the fish, who stared back at her without an answer.

"It's no kind of grand gesture if I feed him cereal for dinner," she said to the goldfish. Millie darted into her little castle as if understanding her human mom's predicament.

Mariella didn't care what anyone said, that fish understood her when she talked. Millie understood her more than most creatures who possessed opposable thumbs.

She had just started slicing through a second round of onions when the doorbell rang. The knife slipped from her hand, and she felt the sharp blade cut through the tip of her finger.

Oh, no. No bleeding damsel in distress action.

She grabbed the dish towel from the counter and pressed it to her finger as she stepped toward the door. "Rain check," she called out. "Something's come up. I need to take a rain check. So sorry. I'll Venmo you money so dinner's still on me."

She felt as much as heard his deep chuckle. "Open the door, Mariella."

"Can't."

"I am not leaving."

He wasn't leaving because he could sense that she was, once again, in train-wreck mode. Alex was a person who fixed things that were broken.

She didn't want to be broken. She didn't want to need fixing. She didn't want to need him.

She balled up the towel in her fist and tucked that hand behind her back as she cracked the door a few inches. "See, I'm fine. I'm sorry. It's emergency festival-planning business. Everything else is peachy keen."

He nodded in agreement, but they both knew she was lying. "I just left Heather. She told me everything was good with the planning. She told me I could turn off my phone tonight if I need to."

"Did you tell her you were coming here? Because—"

"She knows. She's okay with it."

The girl had told Mariella she was okay with it, but Mariella hadn't been sure whether to believe her.

"Well, this doesn't have anything to do with Heather. It's Wildflower Inn business."

He nodded again. "Let me in. And show me your hand."

There was no way he could know or potentially even guess that something was wrong. She refused to believe that she was so easy to read. "I'm sorry I wasted your time. I really would appreciate taking a rain check."

He continued to stand in her doorway, seemingly undeterred.

"Fine. You're like some kind of modern-day Sherlock

Holmes determined to uncover every one of my secrets, even the most innocuous ones."

"I want to know every secret you have," he confirmed. His eyes took on an intensity that made it hard for Mariella to breathe.

She opened the door wider and took a step back. Then she whipped her towel-wrapped hand around and held it up for his inspection. "I don't have any big secrets other than I'm a klutz and no good in the kitchen. I cut myself chopping an onion. You rang the doorbell and it scared me so, in essence, it's your fault."

He stepped inside and took her bandaged hand in his. "Want me to kiss it and make it better?"

"I'm fine, but thank you for the kind offer."

"What are you cooking? It smells singular."

She narrowed her eyes, feeling at once amused and exposed by him. "Apparently, I'm cooking cereal because that's what I'm good at."

"Cereal is a highly underrated dinner food," he told her.

She laughed even as she shook her head. "Don't do that. Don't be nice. I'm plenty capable of cooking a decent meal. I'm capable of a lot of things that normal girlfriends do."

"Have I ever given you the impression that I want or expect you to be regular?"

"I know it's what you want. You're a white-picket fences/minivan type of guy."

"Minivans are also underrated." He smirked but went serious at the look of distress that she clearly wasn't doing a great job of hiding. "Mariella, I don't care if you cook for me. I'm not looking for you to change who you are."

Wasn't that just the problem? He was making her want to change without even asking. Just by his goodness. A shiny halo seemed to glow around him. "Now you're making me sound pathetic and it's pissing me off."

"I don't mind pissing you off."

"Of course not." Because he was damn near perfect. He could handle her moods and her insecurities and he made her feel like she might be able to handle them, too. Even though she knew that wasn't true. Eventually they would pull her down like they always did. If he got too close, they would pull him along with her. There'd be nothing either of them could do to stop it.

She took a breath and reminded herself that they weren't at that point yet. She was borrowing trouble that didn't belong to her. She had plenty enough to deal with in the here and now.

"I have eggs," she blurted.

Alex nodded. "I don't like fried eggs or runny scrambled eggs."

For some reason, this bit of choosiness on his behalf delighted her.

"You're picky about your eggs."

"I'm selective," he conceded then added, "I do have opinions, you know. I'm not a doormat or a man who can be easily manipulated."

"Not when it comes to eggs, anyway," she said, trying to hide the giggle in her voice but not a lot.

"This entertains you?"

She nodded. "Very much so."

"You are definitely not regular," he confirmed. This time she didn't take offense because he spoke the words with too much affection.

"How do you feel about omelets?"

The corners of his mouth pulled down. "I feel like you can't make them without runny insides."

"A frittata then."

"That sounds delicious. What can I do to help?"

In the end, working side by side with him in the kitchen was more enjoyable than cooking on her own. He turned on music, and she got to witness another thing that made Alex seem truly human. He was a horrible dancer. Endearingly so because he didn't care.

She wasn't sure she'd ever met a man more comfortable in his skin and she appreciated it more than she could tell him.

They ate at the table and then cleaned the kitchen together, the same way they prepared the food. Well, the cleaning took a bit more effort because there were still the remnants of her disastrous sauce episode to manage.

When they were finished, Mariella would have invited him to watch TV. Before she could speak, Alex drew her into his arms.

"I've missed you," he told her.

"You've seen me every day this week."

"I've missed this." He buried his face in the crook of her neck then left a trail of fire as he drew his mouth along the sensitive skin of her throat and collar bone. "It's all I've been thinking about—you warm and willing."

She leaned away so she could look into his eyes before he kissed her so senseless that she forgot even her own name. "You think of me as warm and willing?"

"It's a fact."

"Do you ever wonder if I'm just going through the motions?"

Alex frowned, and she wondered if she'd gone too far with the question.

They had great sex. No doubt about it. The best of her life. But she still felt insecure—not that she didn't know what to do or how to do it—but maybe she wasn't as open as she should be.

"What's this about? And don't tell me that you're still thinking about Jacques. I can handle a lot, but I'd rather eat a week of runny eggs than hear you're worried about your ex-boyfriend while I'm kissing you."

"No. I'm thinking I don't want to disappoint you. I'm happy right now." She laughed, studying the color of his shirt. "That makes me nervous. I don't trust happy."

"You can trust me," he said. It wasn't the first time he'd told her that.

"I know. It's not you that I'm worried about, Alex. It's me."

"You've got this," he assured her. "Remember my faith in you."

That still didn't feel natural, but it was the whole reason she'd invited him over. She wanted to prove she could handle the normal parts. The good parts. She could handle being happy.

"Can you stay the night?" she asked. "We might not have much quiet time together until after this weekend and…"

"I'd love to stay," Alex said and then kissed her again. They moved into her bedroom where the light from the street cast a warm glow over her bed.

She liked her bed better when Alex was in it. She liked herself better with him. Now she just needed to work on her belief in faith, especially in what they had together. That it was more than burnt sauce and a change in dinner plans. When she looked in Alex's eyes, anything seemed possible, including a future.

# CHAPTER TWENTY

WITH THE WEEKEND of the Magnolia Blossom Festival upon them, Mariella seriously considered going dark or at least trying to avoid Amber.

Facing the woman who had set out to destroy Mariella's career after taking her fiancé to bed had been easier in theory than reality.

She could have managed any variety of festival details and made it look like she was busy and not in stealth avoidance mode. But Mariella would have known. Alex would have realized what she was doing. Amber would have loved it. And there was no way Mariella would give that woman the satisfaction of knowing how much her short stint in Mariella's life had left its mark.

Which is how Mariella ended up in the formal sitting room of the Wildflower Inn, flanked on either side by Angi and Emma, as Avery Atwell went through the list of activities and events Drake and Amber were each scheduled to attend. The crew was busy setting up for the scene they'd film today in one of the upstairs bedrooms.

The film producers had rented out the entire inn, which made Emma happy, although neither of the stars was staying on property. Mariella figured Drake and Amber needed more than one paltry room each, no matter how tastefully decorated.

It had been awkward seeing the bride whose wedding

she'd crashed, although Mariella couldn't summon any of the bitterness she'd once held toward Amber.

She nearly—but not quite—felt sorry for the woman, whose narcissism wouldn't allow her to admit what a mistake she'd made by treating Alex so badly.

Amber had been pleasant to Emma and Angi in the way Mariella imagined visiting monarchs would be when shaking hands with someone they deemed worlds beneath them.

She was as camera-ready gorgeous as Mariella remembered. Her glossy chestnut hair fell in perfect waves around her shoulders and she wore a silk wrap dress that hugged her willowy frame. For all of Amber's famed skill with acting, she hadn't been able to hide the flash of loathing in her expertly made-up eyes when Mariella had entered the room.

Drake had been all dumb-jock swagger and Hollywood charm. He was shorter than Mariella would have guessed, not quite her height although he wore boots with a thick heel and gained at least an inch from his expertly pomaded honey-blond hair. She wondered how often film crews had employed tricks to make him look taller than his costars. Amber was tiny so it wouldn't be an issue for this pairing.

Maybe that contributed to Amber's casting because the costars had zero off-screen chemistry. She'd heard of actors who made demands about the physical traits of their castmates.

Everyone involved with the movie must know her history with Amber, so either Drake was a better actor than she gave him credit for or he put the details out of his mind. He greeted every person, including Mariella, with the same sort of golden-retriever enthusiasm.

Mariella appreciated his sincerity. She'd dealt with enough rich and famous people to consider herself a good judge of character. Drake didn't strike her as the sharpest knife in the drawer, but he was nice.

Avery finished her spiel about the festival activities and Emma stepped forward to offer whatever help she could to the crew during their time at the inn. They'd already left goodie baskets with locally made bath products and snacks in each room.

Drake gave her a thumbs-up while Amber flashed a smile that didn't reach her eyes. Her assistant, a girl who looked like she was barely older than Heather, scuttled over to Amber's side. The poor thing was so pale that Mariella wondered if Amber kept her chained in the basement when she wasn't working. She already had a notebook flipped open as if she could sense Amber's impending need.

She wasn't the same woman who'd worked for Amber when Mariella had been designing her wedding gown, but she figured assistants cycled through Hollywood on a regular basis.

Avery blew out a breath as she came to stand with Emma, Angi and Mariella. "I think that went well."

"Famous people are just like you and me," Mariella said with a nod.

"Only with millions of followers on Instagram," Avery clarified, looking less like the unflappable town ambassador Mariella had grown used to and more like a starstruck fan.

"Excuse me?"

They all turned toward Amber's mousy assistant. "Ms. Turner had a question about the fashion show listed on the schedule." She addressed the question to Avery, but Mariella felt a palpable ripple of tension make its way through the group at the mention of the Fit Collective's event.

"What's the question?" Avery asked, all traces of nervousness gone in an instant. She drew back her shoulders and looked down her nose at the girl, clearly unwilling to engage in any sort of trifling where Alex was concerned, millions of Instagram followers be damned.

Mariella could see Amber watching them from where she stood with Drake and a few other cast members. She understood without Amber's assistant saying another word that this would be where Amber made her play.

Mariella should have known this was how it would go. She was low-hanging fruit as far as Amber was concerned. Alex was the real prize in Magnolia.

"We heard that the show is utilizing local modeling talent."

"Community members," Avery agreed with a nod.

"Real people," Mariella added. "It's part of the branding strategy."

"Ms. Turner would like to volunteer." The assistant spoke the words as if she were bestowing a great honor on them.

Hell, no. Mariella rolled her lips together to keep from saying out loud the words that wanted to escape her mouth.

"That's a generous offer," Avery conceded, "but I'm not sure—"

"I'm a real person," Amber said with a trilling laugh as she sashayed forward to join their group.

"Of course you are." Avery inclined her head. "But we don't want to overburden you this weekend. You're already doing so much for the festival."

A diplomatic approach. Mariella appreciated it but knew it wouldn't fly with Amber.

"I'm certain I could handle it." Amber pouted as she fiddled with the two-carat diamond pendant hanging on a delicate gold chain around her neck.

Was Mariella mistaken or had the woman affected a subtle Southern drawl? Avery was beginning to look a little wild-eyed. Mariella understood the woman's predicament of balancing her loyalty to Alex with the need to keep the talent happy.

Luckily, Mariella only had herself to consider. And Alex.

"It's not a good idea, Amber," she said firmly. "The focus should be on the collection. If you are part of the show then it becomes about your past relationship with Alex."

Amber's coral-tipped fingers stilled. "What makes you such an expert on his company?"

Mariella froze like a deer caught in the crosshairs of a hunter's rifle. She'd tried to keep the work she was doing for Alex behind the scenes, but she had a feeling Amber knew. Amber also clearly didn't like the idea of two people she'd left as debris in her wake finding their way to each other and creating something new.

"Did you think I wasn't aware of your involvement with Alex and his company?" Amber's words landed like shards of glass against Mariella's skin. "I saw him just last night when we got to town." Her smile turned benevolent. "Of course I rang him right away. We were so close once upon a time, and there are no hard feelings between us. Or secrets. I'm sure not everyone can say that about a former lover."

Mariella felt Angi surge forward and put up a hand to block her. She wouldn't jeopardize anything about this weekend, no matter how much she wanted to punch Amber right in her creamy throat.

"Did you mention to Alex that you wanted to be a part of the fashion show? It's his company."

"I've had so much on my mind," Amber said with a practiced hair toss, "and we focused on catching up on a personal level." She wrinkled her pert nose. "That's how it goes with the ones you never forget. Time fades away in an instant. I'm sure you know what I mean."

"I don't know what you mean," Emma said stiffly. "Perhaps you could explain in exactly what context you and Alex had your little tete-a-tete last night?" Amber's eyes narrowed slightly. In the circles in which she traveled, no one would dare question or challenge her in any way.

Mariella loved her friends, and in her truest heart, she knew Alex wouldn't have spoken badly about her to Amber. She believed without a doubt that he wasn't pining for his lost love.

He'd told Mariella he liked her. He'd shown her in a hundred other ways that his feelings went far deeper, but they never talked about anything more than "like" or discussed the time frame beyond the generic "being together."

He hadn't asked her to think about considering Luann's position now that the older woman was well and truly gone. Maybe he didn't want her that involved in his life. Maybe he was still holding a part of himself back.

She wouldn't blame him. In some ways, she'd been doing the same thing. So why did her heart ache?

"Ultimately," she told Amber, "the decision rests with Alex."

"Then I'm as good as the star of the show." The director called her over at that point, and she practically skipped away, her work done for the moment.

"Who should I contact about the pieces Ms. Turner will wear for the fashion show?" the assistant asked, her words landing with all the finesse of a fart in Sunday service.

"You should not…this is ridiculous," Angi muttered.

"I'll handle it," Mariella told the assistant. "Give me your phone, and I'll put in my contact information. It doesn't look like Amber's measurements have changed since I fitted her for a wedding gown. I should be able to come up with something for her."

The girl looked chagrined as she handed over her phone to Mariella but said in a calm voice, "She's going to want to be the star."

That wasn't a joke. "I understand," Mariella agreed, also certain the weekend would be more difficult than she could have imagined.

ALEX WATCHED MARIELLA stride toward him across the town square and his heart gave an extra thump inside his chest.

In truth, it was more than a thump. Each time he saw her, his chest felt as though it was filled with a herd of thundering mustangs. Ever since she'd made her public declaration, his walls had been coming down swift and sure.

He could put a name on what he felt for her even if he hadn't shared it yet.

*Love.*

He was in love with Mariella Jacob, the head-over-heels kind of all-encompassing emotion. But he wanted to wait until after this weekend to tell her. The festival would be over. Amber and the rest of the Hollywood crew gone from Magnolia and, hopefully, out of his life for good.

That's when he would tell Mariella he loved her. She'd need some time to adjust. It would freak her out, but he was a patient man. He'd wait as long as she needed to wrap her mind and heart around the idea that he wanted to be with her. Only her.

She'd accused him of being a white-picket-fence type of man. Maybe he was, but only if that fence had her waiting on the other side. He didn't care about the details. They could figure those out as they went along as long as they were on the journey together—forever if she'd have him.

He smiled as she drew closer but his smile faded as he noticed the tightness around her mouth and the corners of her brilliant blue eyes. She'd had a meeting with the cast and crew from the movie at the inn today. If Amber had done something to mess with Mariella, Alex was going to have a word with his former fiancée.

"How was it?" he asked when she was almost directly in front of him. He didn't want to assume things had gone badly at the inn. Maybe she'd been stuck behind a slow-moving tractor on the way into town. He knew she loved to drive fast.

"Where were you last night?" she demanded, not bothering to answer his question.

"You know where I was." He studied her, trying to unwrap the puzzle in her gaze. "I spent some time with Bex and then came to your house late after she'd settled for the night."

They'd had plenty of time working together recently, but it had felt important to spend one last night with her before the craziness of the festival weekend started.

Mariella crossed her arms over her chest. "Is there a woman you're leaving out of the equation?"

"I don't think…" He started to shake his head no then paused. "Amber," he murmured.

"Amber," Mariella repeated. "You were with Amber before coming to me. She said it was quite cozy with the two of you playing catch-up."

Alex mentally cursed his former fiancée. "There was nothing cozy about it. I was down here with a few guys helping to put together the bleachers and stage. She stopped by with somebody from the movie who was looking for additional shooting locations. A producer or location scout.

I don't know his official role. The guy spoke with Mayor Mal for a while so Amber and I talked."

"But you didn't think to mention that to me?" Accusation dripped from her tone.

"It was after eleven when I got to your house." He leaned toward her. "If you remember, you answered the door in a silk robe with nothing underneath. So, no. I wasn't thinking about Amber. My brain cells took the fast train south at the sight of you."

He tucked a loose strand of hair behind her ear, relieved when she didn't pull away. "Which is a compliment by the way."

"She wants to model in the Fit Collective show." Mariella looked at the ground like she couldn't quite make eye contact with him. "I told her I'd work it out with you."

"No."

"You can't say no."

"I just did."

Her hands were fisted at her sides. He covered them with his until she relaxed enough to let him link their fingers.

"This is important, Alex." At last she met his gaze, and he realized how upset she was.

"You are important. She's doing this to get to you, sweetheart. I won't let her."

"It could be huge for sales."

"I don't care about—"

She lifted a finger to cover his lips. "You have to care. It's your company. I'm okay. She shocked me when she said she'd spent time with you and I didn't know about it."

"I'm sorry. It was a passing conversation. I promise. She doesn't mean anything to me. You know that, right?"

She sighed. "Yeah, and now I'm annoyed that I let her win the first battle."

He didn't want to think of this weekend as a war or love as a battlefield or enlist any other clichéd negative imagery right now.

Should he tell Mariella about his feelings? Would she gather strength from knowing he loved her? Maybe then whatever happened this weekend with Amber wouldn't matter as much because together they could weather any storm.

But something stopped him. Most likely the fear that he'd send her running in the other direction.

"It will be fine," he promised, hoping she could read between the lameness of his lines to understand how committed he was. She had to know, right? Even without those three little words, she would know she was important.

"Fine," she said but didn't sound at all convinced. "And we're going to put her in the show."

Alex winced. "That sounds like a horrible idea."

Mariella arched one delicate brow. "It will be fine." The words sounded even lamer when she said them. "How's the rest of the setup going?" She looked around the bustling lawn. Heather was on the far side of the square helping Josie wrangle a troupe of young dancers.

"My kid is awesome," she murmured.

"She's going to run the world one day," Alex agreed.

Mariela shifted closer to him. "When does her mother arrive?"

Once again, he wished he could take some of Mariella's emotional burden. There were so many people she supported with little regard for her own well-being. Heather's adoptive mother was coming to town for the weekend. He knew the girl had talked to Mariella about it and asked her to give them as much space as possible.

It wasn't as if Mariella could hide out in her house again,

but she'd do whatever she could to make the weekend easier for Heather. He hoped Kay Garrison appreciated the effort and that the passing of time might give her a little perspective on Heather's relationship with Mariella.

The two of them were alike in so many ways, particularly in how much they wanted to pretend nothing bothered them when they each felt things deeply.

His phone rang and he pulled it out of his pocket to glance at the screen before sending the call to voice mail and shoving it back in.

"Your stepfather again?"

"He doesn't like to be told no."

"But you won't change your mind, right?" As Mariella searched his face, he had the urge to turn the conversation back to her again. That was easier than allowing his issues to be the topic of conversation.

"I told him my focus is on the Fit Collective. I owe it to myself to give the company a real shot."

She nodded. "You have something special here."

He lifted her hand to his mouth and brushed a delicate kiss across her knuckles. "Oh, I know it."

She rolled her eyes but that didn't stop a blush from staining her cheeks. "I'm talking about the company."

"Me, too." He squeezed her hand. "When this weekend's over, we need to talk about your role going forward."

She sucked in a small breath. "I'm just helping you out as a friend. You don't need me for—"

"I do," he interrupted. "I need you."

She looked away and bit down on her lower lip. "I started following Kiki Taylor on social media. She's stepping up her game."

"Luann mentioned her just to get a rise out of you. Kiki isn't right for what we're trying to build with the company."

"You don't think that I am either. We've covered this."

Things change. He'd changed and was pretty sure she had as well, but now wasn't the right time to discuss it. To share everything written across his heart. "I think we've done okay together so far."

That made her laugh, which he hoped was a good thing.

"So far," she agreed and leaned in to give him a quick kiss.

"It's a couple of days of Amber. I heard Mary Ellen and Josie going on about Drake Simpson earlier. You can distract yourself from thinking about her by mooning over him."

"I got a pretty good look at Drake this morning." She wagged a finger in front of his face. "So we're clear, you are the only guy I'm mooning over."

"Good to know, 'cause it would have been embarrassing for a Hollywood heartthrob to have his butt kicked by me."

She grinned and kissed him again. "This weekend is going to be awesome, and I already can't wait until it's over."

"Me, too, sweetheart."

The strain he'd sensed in her earlier had eased. Alex wasn't going to let anything or anyone—not Amber or Drake or the dang queen of England—come between them. At the end of the Magnolia Blossom Festival, he was going to profess his love to Mariella, and he had to believe that love would be enough.

## CHAPTER TWENTY-ONE

MARIELLA WAS TEXTING Angi as she left the shop that evening which was to blame for her nearly running over someone as she walked around the building's corner.

"So sorry," she said as she automatically reached out a hand to steady the other person. And found herself looking into Kay Garrison's shocked face.

"I'm sorry," she repeated, thinking about the numerous reasons she had to apologize to Heather's adoptive mother.

"It's okay." Kay offered a tentative smile.

Did Mariella imagine the way the other woman's features had gentled? At the very least, Kay didn't appear nearly as inclined to shank Mariella as she had that morning in the store's office.

They stood together as an awkward silence descended around them before Mariella started to move around Kay. She'd had no intention of provoking Heather's mom by engaging in conversation when she could accomplish that just by her existence.

"Wait."

She turned.

"I was coming to see you." Kay's voice barely registered above a whisper.

"I can reopen the store if you need something," Mariella offered. "A candle? Jasmin is probably upstairs if you're more comfortable—"

"I was coming to see you."

Mariella nodded at the same time she had the overwhelming urge to take off running down the street in the other direction. What was it about conflict that sparked her fight-or-flight response?

She should be used to it by now—the way opportunities to demonstrate emotional maturity followed her through the streets of Magnolia like a teenage girl trailing after her high school crush.

Mariella hadn't asked for the chance to behave like a grown-up. She'd managed to build a wildly successful career behaving with the maturity of a toddler coming down from a sugar rush. But Magnolia was different, and she couldn't deny that she liked the changes the town had inspired in her.

Making her way through the sometimes choppy waters of a relationship with the daughter she'd given up was one of the recent successes she was most proud of. Because of Heather, she trusted herself at this point. No matter how Kay treated her or what she wanted to discuss, Mariella would find a way to be all right with it. She might run home to toss her cookies after, but she'd get through it now.

"Very few people know about my connection to Heather, and I trust the ones who do. You don't have to worry about that changing while you're in town." She grimaced as she thought about Josie recording her in the bakery that morning when she laid claim to Alex and talked almost openly to Heather. "That might not be exactly true. A lot of people probably guess but we're far enough south here that politeness dictates they don't come right out and ask. I haven't even had anyone bless my heart that I can remember for months."

Kat blinked. "Do you always talk this fast?"

"Only when I'm so nervous my palms are sweaty and I can actually hear my knees knocking together. I'm trying hard not to stress puke."

"I came here to thank you," Kay said in a voice as soothing as that of any artificial intelligence digital assistant. Look out, Siri and Alexa. Kay Garrison might be coming for you.

"From what Heather says, you've let her take the lead in setting the pace of your relationship with her."

"Can you say that one part again?" Mariella asked as she tried to contain the smile tugging at the edges of her mouth.

"The part where I thanked you?"

"No, the part where you said I have a relationship with Heather."

"You don't agree?" Confusion colored Kay's tone.

"I do. I feel like we have a relationship. I desperately want a relationship with her. More than anything I've ever wanted." Mariella made a face. "And after giving up alcohol, drugs and binge-eating Ben & Jerry's all at the same time, that's saying something."

Kay swallowed audibly. "I suppose it is."

"Long time ago." Mariella waved away her revelation with the flourish of her hand. "I'm not trying to scare you."

"Everything about you scares me," Kay said with a staccato bark of laughter. "But we have something precious in common, Mariella. I've come to realize that she might mean as much to you as she does to me."

Mariella nodded. "Possibly more."

"Don't push your luck." Kay let a thread of steel permeate her soothing voice.

"Understood."

"I'm not sure you and I are meant to be friends, but we are destined to be a part of each other's lives going forward." Kay adjusted the collar on her drop-waist button-up dress. It was made out of some sort of stretchy fabric that could best be termed athleisurewear, just like Alex was selling in his company.

Mariella calmed the emotions rioting through her by re-designing Kay's rather frumpy weekender dress into something that was both stylish and practical. She didn't think women needed to sport a designer logo to be trendy or adopt a younger generation's fashion sense to have style.

A bit of tucked stitching through the waist would lead to a more flattering silhouette, even on a woman whose body had gone through the changes brought by age and experience. The color might be improved upon, too. The blue was a bit garish, but if she toned it down and muted the color—maybe adding in some violet undertones—the shade could be flattering on a wide array of skin tones.

"What do you think?" Kay snapped a finger in front of Mariella's face.

Right. They were in the middle of talking about Heather, and Mariella had spaced out on a design tangent. Her feet might not have moved, but she'd run away just the same. Emotional maturity. Focus on what she could handle at this moment.

"I think I owe you a huge debt of gratitude," she said to Kay, forcing herself to be vulnerable. "For becoming my daughter's mother. I think she's incredible, and I think you're incredible. And you're beautiful. Although you should never wear that color blue."

Kay's mouth dropped open before she shut it again. She inclined her head. "I asked if you wanted to have dinner with Heather and me at the Italian place in town?" She smoothed a hand over her dress. "Do you really think this is an awful color on me?"

"Yes...on dinner," Mariela clarified. "You could do better with the dress." She glanced over her shoulder toward her darkened storefront. "I'm pretty sure I have one that would look stunning on you in the shop right now. One of my Raleigh clients brought in a whole load of consignments for this weekend. She's a bit of a shopaholic, which benefits me and my customers. And you, if you're interested?"

"We're going to freak out our daughter in a massive way," Kay said.

"But in a good way," Mariella added.

Kay flashed a bright smile. "A good way. Why don't you show me that dress?"

OF ALL THE contingency plans swimming through Mariella's mind, the one she'd least expected to employ was how to deal with a monsoon rainstorm that coincided with the timing of the fashion show.

Avery didn't seem fazed by the dark clouds that swirled high overhead on the festival's second afternoon. The day before had gone off without issue. According to Avery, this year's Magnolia Blossom Festival was on track to be the most successful event in town history.

As expected, legions of people from around the area had shown up for the chance to see Drake Simpson and Amber Turner in person. Mariella had taken a bit of satisfaction in the fact that most of the visitors were interested in Drake.

While Amber had enough adoring fans to keep her satisfied, the charming leading man was the real star at this show. The cast and crew had finished filming at the inn, and Emma was nearly giddy with excitement at the social media shout-outs the Wildflower was receiving. One of the supporting actors had even booked a weekend to celebrate his parents' thirtieth wedding anniversary later that summer.

Reservations and inquiries about the property had started to tick up after the first Instagram mention by Drake. Even Mariella had to admit Amber had done her part, posting a few vibey shots of herself around the property.

By silent agreement, she and Mariella were avoiding each other. Heather had been charged with managing Amber's involvement in the fashion show. The girl grumbled and complained about including the starlet with the other local models, mostly because she knew Mariella was trying to pretend like Amber's presence didn't bother her. Mariella had a lousy poker face.

But Mariella was concentrating on the things she could handle and the positive parts of the weekend outweighed the challenges. Dinner with Heather and Kay had started awkward. Eventually, the three of them had settled into a rhythm of conversation and asking questions without prying.

It was worth forming a bond with her daughter's other mother—something that would last even after Kay went home and Heather moved to Chapel Hill. She had never thought that she would be friends of a sort with the woman who'd raised her baby, but once Heather got over her shock, it had been clear the girl liked having her two moms together.

Mariella groaned as a distant rumble of thunder reverberated through the tent behind the festival's main stage.

"We're prepared for this," Avery reminded her as she handed out matching umbrellas to the models gathered in clusters around the tent. This was the final event of the festival. The rain had held out so far, and Mariella prayed they could eke out another dry hour before the skies opened up.

"I wasn't thinking about the potential for rain," she told Avery. "The forecast said sun in the morning and cloudy skies for the afternoon. Clouds are not rain."

"Clouds bring rain," Avery observed.

Mariella snorted. "Thank you, Al Roker."

That earned a laugh from Avery. Very little ruffled the woman as far as Mariella could tell. Avery patted Mariella's Fit Collective sweatshirt-clad arm. "Afternoon showers are typical this time of year. It's going to be okay."

Mariella wished she could be so sure. A feeling of unease had plagued her all day. She should be used to pre-show jitters, but this felt different as if her body was taking its cues from the charged air around them. The hair on the back of her neck stood on end, and her stomach refused to settle.

She peeked between the curtains to where Alex sat in the front row, flanked by reporters on either side. Several Fit Collective investors had also come to town for the weekend, although she'd refused to meet them in any sort of official capacity. She was still nervous about the future.

Like Avery, Alex seemed so sure things would work out for the best. It was that faith he relied on and expected her to trust as well. She wanted to trust. But faith didn't come easy to a chronic non-believer.

Mariella had relied too heavily on her resilience and stubbornness to plow through life's challenges. Magnolia gentled her spirit, but it was tough to enact lasting change, especially in moments that meant as much as this one.

Alex seemed to sense her gaze on him because he glanced over and gave her a private smile and a nod. Some of the nerves fluttering through her settled. As she'd told him before, he was her calm in any storm.

She pointed toward the sky, which continued to appear ominous. He shrugged and saluted her with his umbrella.

They would be okay, even if the skies opened mid-fashion show. If nothing else right now, she had faith in him and his belief in her. The tightness in her chest eased.

Alex was more than the calm in a storm. He was her person. She loved him more than she wanted to because allowing herself to be vulnerable meant opening up to the potential of being hurt.

From a young age, Mariella had been disappointed and discarded by the people she'd loved. She'd closed her heart because that had been the best option for keeping it safe.

Alex had slipped past her walls in big and small ways. His innate kindness and the fact that he treated everyone he met with respect and honor. Plus, he didn't take her crap or allow her to manipulate or scare him off. He seemed to like her just as she was, heaven help them both.

So she loved him, and after the festival, she planned to tell him. He saw goodness in her that she hadn't recognized and his faith had given her the freedom to discover her own.

Maybe she would agree to work with him at the Fit Collective. It might be fun to spar and create and spend every day together. But if that was too much...if she was too much...that would be okay, too.

They would find a way to make it work. Her faith, at least in her willingness to try, was unwavering.

A commotion at the far end of the tent caught her attention. Amber waved her arms in front of her while Heather and one of the junior designers looked on.

Heather's expression was one of pure annoyance while the other woman looked vaguely terrified. No matter how her future with Alex's company turned out, Mariella wouldn't let some spoiled starlet intimidate his employees or hijack his first show. She would deal with Amber.

"Do you want me to handle it?" Avery was already moving toward the scene.

"I've got it," Mariella told her. She'd spent long enough avoiding Amber and paid her dues for the public scene she'd created—a pound of flesh and then some. Although Amber hadn't suffered any consequences that Mariella could see for her role in that unfortunate situation, Mariella didn't care anymore.

The longer Amber was in town, the less sway she held. When Mariella came to stand in front of Amber now, she barely felt anything and certainly not the level of upset she had at the start of the weekend.

"Is everything okay?" She smiled and felt the serenity in it.

Amber must have noticed it, too, because her eyes narrowed even as she flapped her arms wildly in front of her. "Are these clothes lined with burlap?" she demanded. "My whole body itches."

Mariella gestured to the other models standing in curious clusters around them. "No burlap and you seem to be the only one having trouble. The clothes are made from sustainable fabrics. No one should react to them."

Amber's face was starting to turn an alarming shade of red. "I'm having a reaction. Look at me. I can't go out there like this." She scratched her chest and arms like a kid who'd wandered into a patch of poison ivy at summer camp.

Mariella felt the first trace of real alarm trickle down her spine. "You don't look good," she told Amber.

The woman continued to scratch at herself. Her gaze cut to her put-upon assistant. "Do something. Make it stop."

The dark-haired girl reached out and scratched between Amber's shoulder blades. "Does that help?"

"No, you fool."

The girl snatched her hand away.

"But don't stop," Amber whined.

"It's time for the show to start," Heather said as if they weren't witnessing a Hollywood A-lister have a complete meltdown. A bigger crowd was gathering in front of Amber, but Heather didn't seem to be the least bit concerned.

She was the only one who appeared calm which made Mariella suspicious. She grabbed the girl's elbow and yanked her out of earshot of the larger group. "Do you know why Amber is struggling right now?"

Heather wouldn't make eye contact. "I don't think so. Maybe she's reacting to something she ate. I couldn't say."

Mariella squeezed her arm. "You're not convincing me."

"I guess she might not be able to participate in the fashion show." Heather tapped a finger on her chin. "Oh, darn."

"Maybe it's lice or scabies," she suggested as she turned back to Amber.

Mariella suppressed a sharp snort. There was a reporter from some paper Mariella didn't know the name of hovering around the edges of the still-expanding crowd.

At Heather's offhand suggestion, the bespectacled man's eyes widened. He began to tap furiously into his phone as he hurried out of the tent, likely trying to get better reception to call his editor with the potential story of America's sweetheart plagued by lice.

Mariella had a feeling Amber was more accurately plagued with Heather's misguided attempt to put the actress in her place.

"The crowd is getting restless," Mary Ellen called in a stage whisper as she turned from looking out into the audience. "The thunder sounds closer, so we should start while it's still dry."

"You can't start the show without the star of it," Amber said, clawing at her neck so hard Mariella worried she might draw blood.

She fully faced Heather, blocking the girl from Amber's view. "What did you do?"

Heather's eyes went wide before she dropped her gaze to the ground. "Nothing. I can't believe you would think—"

"Tell me. I don't know if it's an allergic reaction or she's at risk for going into anaphylactic shock, but we can't have this. The story of the Fit Collective's first fashion show isn't going to be a Hollywood star being hospitalized after wearing the clothes. Do you understand?"

Heather's expression turned mulish. "It's called Tickle Terror."

"Excuse me?"

"Itching powder. Next-day delivery."

"Oh, no."

Heather looked around Mariella with a frown. "I wanted to make sure it affected her, so I used a lot."

"Why?" Mariella whispered.

"Because she's awful and was mean to you and…" Tears filled the girl's eyes. "You're my mom. One of my moms. I didn't want her to do anything during the fashion show that made you feel bad or caused you and Alex to fight. I just…"

"It's okay." Mariella hugged the girl. Her stomach was rolling and pitching as she scrambled for a way to handle the situation without incurring Amber's wrath.

The starlet was practically sobbing now.

"Somebody find an EMT or a doctor," the assistant shouted.

"Ryan's in the audience," Meredith announced. "I'll bring him back."

"What the hell is going on?" a familiar voice demanded, and Mariella forced herself to take in rhythmic gulps of air so she wouldn't throw up. She released Heather as Alex stalked toward them.

"I'm dying," Amber wailed as the crowd parted to let Alex through. "Your clothes are killing me."

"Calm down," he said, his confused gaze switching between Amber and Mariella like she could give some insight into this complete nightmare scenario.

"I've done such a bad thing," Heather whispered.

"Don't say a word," Mariella told the girl.

"Amber." Alex's voice was lethally sharp. All conversation stopped at his commanding tone. "Is this real or are you faking it for attention?"

"Faking it?" Amber continued to fidget and scratch up and down her body. At least her face hadn't gotten any more mottled. It seemed like she could breathe okay, so whatever reaction she was having to the powder didn't seem life-threatening.

Mariella's heart sank even considering that as a possibility.

"My skin is burning and it feels like I just dove into a swimming pool filled with poison ivy." Amber's face crumpled. "This is real, Alex, and it's bad."

"We'll take care of you," he said, his voice gentler. He spun in a quick circle. "We need everyone out of the tent to start. Amber should have privacy while we figure this out."

The crowd began to slowly disperse.

"What about the fashion show?" someone asked.

"Canceled," Alex immediately answered.

"No," Heather said. "You can't do that."

"Of course he can," Amber countered. "No stupid line of clothes is more important than me."

Now Mariella felt the urge to puke for an entirely different reason.

Amber's assistant stepped forward. "You all should continue with the fashion show while we take care of Ms. Turner."

"Lucy, no," Amber protested.

"You don't want to be photographed the way you look now," Lucy said quietly. "If the show goes on, it will be a good distraction. They can explain that you were called away for an emergency. Trust me, Amber. No one should see you right now."

"Fine." Amber groaned as she raked her nails up the back of her leg. "Someone get all these lookie-loos away from me."

Mariella placed a hand on her daughter's shoulder. "Heather, take the models outside the tent."

"It's starting to rain."

"Then make it quick." Mariella raised two fingers to her lips and let out a shrill whistle. "Everyone is going to follow Heather. New plan...you'll all take the stage at the same time. Bring your umbrellas. Keep smiling as Heather describes the story behind the collection. No one talks to the press. Got it?"

Her friends and neighbors nodded and dutifully headed for the tent's side opening. She could hear raindrops starting to pelt the roof and prayed that the worst of the storm would hold off just a few minutes longer.

Ryan and Meredith rushed in as the rest of the models were leaving. "I'm Dr. Sorensen. Can you tell me what's going on?"

"I'm dying," Amber wailed again.

Alex moved closer to Mariella, a look of quiet desperation etched onto his features. She wanted to reach for his hand but didn't dare. Not with what she knew she had to do.

"She's itchy and burning," Lucy clarified. "It doesn't seem to be as bad as it was a few minutes ago."

"Let's get you out of those clothes," Ryan said. "The first thing we need to do is figure out the cause of—"

"I'm the cause." Mariella cleared her throat when her voice broke. It was more than her voice. Her heart felt as though it were breaking in two.

# CHAPTER TWENTY-TWO

ALEX LISTENED TO Mariella's words through the tunnel of sound in his head. White noise that he hoped could block out the soul-crushing reality of what she was saying.

"I told you she was a nightmare," Amber said, scratching with one hand as she jammed the wide-brimmed hat her assistant handed her low on her head with the other.

"Ms. Turner," Ryan said in a tone Alex imagined he used to placate agitated patients in the hospital. "You should head back to your house and shower. I'll call in a prescription for topical cream in case you have any lingering issues. Your assistant has my cell phone number. Don't hesitate to call if things aren't improving."

Amber sighed. "I already feel better knowing that my injuries—" she clutched a hand to her chest "—won't be fatal."

Alex heard Meredith snort while Mariella's features remained expressionless. What the hell had she been thinking? What in the world was she thinking now?

"Yes," Ryan agreed with a frown. "Your reaction to itch powder is uncomfortable but not potentially life-threatening."

"Will I have any lasting nerve damage, Doctor?" Amber had gone full-on Academy Award mode.

Ryan shook his head. "No."

"That's a relief after being the victim of some lunatic

woman with a vendetta against me." She wagged a finger in Mariella's direction. "You should be ashamed of yourself, and you can bet that I'm going to—"

"You aren't going to say a word," Alex told his former fiancée. He hated that Mariella had done this and, even more, that she didn't try to defend herself against Amber's verbal assault.

He wanted her to say something. Anything that might explain why she'd been reckless and foolish when they were so close to the end of the weekend.

Everything he wanted had been within his grasp, but in the span of a few cracks of thunder, it was gone.

Even so, he wasn't going to let Amber hurt Mariella more than she'd already done to herself. They didn't need Amber Turner's punishment when Mariella could take care of that all on her own.

"Why shouldn't I expose her for the psychopath she is?" Amber demanded.

"Things have changed since our wedding day," he said calmly. "I've changed. Right after you and Jacques went on your little love tour, I talked to a number of your former conquests. I don't think you want me to get into the sordid details now." He inclined his head toward Meredith and Ryan, who looked as uncomfortable as he felt. "But if one word of this situation is breathed in the press or social media, I will blow you up, Amber."

"After what she's done, you're going to take her side?" Amber sounded shocked and disgusted.

Alex was fairly shocked as well. He had no idea why he still had the urge to protect Mariella. She'd told him she was an emotional train wreck. He'd been warned, and yet had no real understanding of how deep her penchant for self-destruction ran.

"Have her people call me," he told Lucy, "if they want details, but don't let her breathe a word of this."

Amber appeared ready to lay into Mariella again, but Ryan stepped between them. "Ms. Turner, I must insist that you go now. The sooner you rinse off, the better you'll feel."

Amber threw up her hands then turned on her heel and stalked off. She was about to exit the tent when she turned back to Alex. "I hope you're happy. I also hope that Kate Hudson's clothing line outsells yours tenfold. Maybe I'll call her about a collab. So there."

And with that bizarre parting shot, she was gone.

Alex heard a thunderous round of applause followed by a few enthusiastic cheers. He glanced out the front of the tent and noticed the glimmer of sun-dappled light breaking through the clouds.

The rain had held off although his life was as black as the night sky.

Meredith and Ryan glanced between Mariella and Alex. For once, even sassy Meredith seemed at a loss for words. "Sounds like the show was a success even without your big star," she said after a moment. The words echoed in the awkward quiet of the moment.

"I never wanted her to be a part of it," Alex said through gritted teeth. He turned to Mariella. "You were the one who thought this would be a good idea."

"We're going to head out now." Meredith tugged Ryan toward the nearest tent flap.

"I'll check on Amber later tonight," Ryan called.

Alex nodded. "Thank you."

"There's no way to keep this quiet." Mariella sounded as hopeless as he felt. "Amber won't be able to help herself."

"She will," Alex said, feeling certain. He hadn't shared with anyone the specifics he'd uncovered about his former fiancée. It embarrassed him that he'd cared enough to try to vindicate himself after their breakup.

The anger, humiliation and betrayal he'd experienced then had seemed all-consuming but those feelings were nothing in comparison to the bottomless chasm of heartbreak he faced now.

He'd let Mariella into his heart and he couldn't conceive of a way to cut her out. Except she'd given him no choice.

"Why, Mariella?" He'd asked her to have faith in him—in them—and she'd wholly employed her practice of ruining things when they got too good.

Maybe he should take it as a compliment. She must be petrified of what she felt for him if she'd blown up their future with the force of a nuclear explosion.

"I can't tell you why," she said quietly.

Of course not. She didn't even have a reason for her behavior. It was inherent to her character.

"It doesn't matter," he told her with a sigh.

Her gaze took on a starkness he hadn't imagined ever seeing there.

She shook her head. In an instant, the look in her eyes changed. Their blue depths went from being filled with sorrow and regret to reflecting the crystalline turquoise of a glacier—frozen solid without an ounce of heat.

"I tried to warn you." She threw the words at him like a grenade. "I told you I was a train wreck, and you said it didn't matter."

"I thought we were strong enough to get through it. I thought our faith in each other would be enough."

"It was," she whispered, so softly he barely heard the words.

They couldn't be true because otherwise she never would have taken the risk that she had with Amber.

"Pranking her was so ridiculously stupid it didn't even begin to touch funny."

"Do you think it was meant to be funny?"

"Was this about Amber or about us?" he asked, unable to stop himself. "Was hurting her a way to wreck us before we even had a chance?"

"You believe I would do that?"

His heart felt like a lead weight inside his chest. "I don't know what to believe at this point."

"I should go. Before everyone comes back. The wreckage that seems to follow me everywhere feels like too much for you right now."

She had no idea what he'd be willing to handle if given the chance. But he wasn't going to beg.

He watched her slip out of the tent's back flap and disappear, wondering if she was gone for the moment or for good.

He wanted to call her back and tell her that none of it mattered. She could destroy every good thing in his life and he'd still want her. He'd come back for more. But he didn't. He let her go.

Heather rushed in, her face flushed and eyes glistening with excitement. "They loved it. And there's no rain yet. We actually saw a rainbow above the stage. Like it was meant to be. It's meant to be, Alex."

She glanced around the empty tent. "Where is Mariella? What happened with Amber? Tell me it's okay."

"It will be okay," he said, not wanting to upset the girl in this moment. They'd worked too hard.

He knew he should feel happy as he left the tent and climbed onto the stage. This moment was everything he'd wanted. Even Luann had sent a text earlier wishing him luck.

But it felt flat without Mariella next to him. He couldn't

imagine how anything would feel exciting again if she wasn't a part of it.

He smiled and hugged the friends who'd helped him by modeling the debut collection. He shook the hands of his investors who were none the wiser about Amber's absence. Drake Simpson showed up and happily posed for pictures with the women of Magnolia. It was publicity gold, and Alex couldn't muster any excitement.

He put on his best professional demeanor and suffered through the next fifteen minutes of shaking hands and making plans for what would come next with the company. The clouds gathered again, and gratitude poured through him in an intensity that matched the deluge of rain pummeling down when the sky finally opened.

He'd gifted each woman the clothes she modeled as a way of saying thank-you, so most people had already left the square in advance of the impending storm. He ducked back into the tent, not ready to go home.

Leaving felt like a surrender. As if he were truly taking the first step in moving on when he hadn't even told Mariella he loved her. Would that have made a difference?

If she'd felt confident in his devotion to her, would that have changed what she'd done? He sank onto the grass and lowered his head into his hands.

What happened next? He had no idea where to go from there. All he knew was that he couldn't imagine anywhere that would feel like home without her.

A few minutes—or maybe it was a few hours later—two sets of rain boots appeared in his line of sight. Two of the boots were a classic navy hue and the other set a leopard-print pattern. He didn't have to look up to know who they belonged to.

"Where is she?" Angi demanded, nudging his knee with her leopard-print toe.

"We've been to her house," Emma added, her tone softer. "She's not there."

"I don't know. She left after a failed attempt to derail the fashion show with a stupid prank gone horribly wrong. She didn't even bother with an apology."

"It doesn't make sense," Emma said. "Josie told us how bad of shape Amber was in before the show. Why would Mariella do that to her?"

"Revenge?"

Angi let out a derisive sniff. "That doesn't make sense either. Mariella's pattern is hurting herself, not other people. Granted, you were caught in the cross fire of that meltdown at your wedding but it wasn't premeditated."

"And she's in a better place," Emma said as she crouched down in front of him. "This is her home. She doesn't have to engage with somebody like Amber. She has us. Plus you and Heather. She's part of this community. Why would she jeopardize that with some sort of childish prank?"

"I don't know," he admitted, yanking on his hair in frustration. "The worst part is I don't care. I love her anyway. I love her in spite of the fact that she did it and because she's not perfect. Maybe that makes me a world-class fool."

Emma patted his knee. "A fool for love is the best kind."

"And our girl is worth it," Angi added.

"I know that. I'm trying to figure out a way to convince her of it while ensuring she doesn't blow up the whole town in the process."

Angi snorted. "When the going gets tough, Mariella starts lobbing bombs. She and I have that in common."

He gave a humorless laugh. "I would love to resolve

this without any other casualties, but easy or hard, I'm in for all of it."

"You have to find Mariella and tell her that," Emma said as she straightened. She and Angi each offered him a hand.

Alex certainly could have stood on his own, but he let the women help him. It wasn't a bad idea to save his strength because getting through to Mariella might be the battle of his life.

"She didn't do it," a shaky voice called out. The three of them turned. Heather stood soaking-wet just inside the tent. She looked like she was waiting at the gates of hell.

Kay had an arm around the girl's shoulder, and Alex realized it wasn't rainwater running down her cheeks. Heather was quietly crying.

"What's going on?" he asked as his heart flipped over in his chest.

"Mariella was protecting me," Heather said. "I'm the one who put itching powder in Amber's clothes. All of this is my fault. I'm so sorry."

Emma and Angi gave twin gasps of surprise, but Alex couldn't even manage that. The breath whooshed out of his lungs like he'd been sucker-punched.

He thought about Mariella's unwillingness to explain or defend herself or even to apologize. None of it had made sense, but this explanation did except....

"Why?" he asked Heather. "Why pull a prank on Amber?"

"It wasn't supposed to be that bad." Heather wrung her hands in front of her Fit Collective logo sweatshirt. "I saw a video online. It was just supposed to irritate her and keep her from participating in the fashion show. That way she couldn't do something to make Mariella mad or upset you. I didn't want anybody else bothered by her. I care about you guys too much to let some stupid, spoiled starlet mess everything up."

Alex forced his lungs to pump air in and out. Kay shot him a beseeching look. "She didn't realize the consequences," the mom explained. "I'm not excusing the behavior, but her intentions were good."

"Why didn't you admit to it from the start?" Alex asked.

"Mariella told me to stay quiet. We didn't know what Amber was going to do in retaliation. I'm sorry. It was stupid and selfish. I thought she could ruin my acceptance at UNC or post something that went viral and the whole world would hate me."

She scrubbed a hand across her face. "I should've just said it then. Because now I hate myself and that's even worse. Mariella is gone and you guys don't know where she is. What if she doesn't come back?"

"We'll find her," Alex said. His heart settled just as quickly as it had flooded with panic.

Mariella hadn't tried to destroy what was between them. She should have told him, but he understood why she felt like she had to make the choice she did. It was her chance to be a mom to the daughter she loved with her whole heart. He loved her even more for her misguided loyalty.

Angi elbowed him hard. "You have to find her."

He held up his hands. "I'd like to. I just wish I knew where to start loo—"

A crack of thunder split the air. In that instant, he knew where she would have gone, and it made his heart tighten with panic all over again. "I've got it," he whispered, more to himself than anyone else.

"Then go," Emma said with a gentle shove. "Bring her home."

Alex nodded but in his soul, he knew he just needed to get to her because when he found Mariella, he'd find his home.

MARIELLA NEEDED TO go home—if only because Millie would be waiting for her evening fish flakes.

Well, that and the fact that Mariella no longer had feeling in her toes.

She wrapped her arms more tightly around her knees as if that would help keep her extremities warm after sitting on the beach in the rain for the past hour.

At least it had stopped thundering and lightning. The rain now came down in a steady stream, but Mariella was already soaked from her head to frozen toes.

It had been stupid to be on the beach in a thunderstorm, but the jolt of terror she'd felt at each booming clap had allowed her to feel something.

Something other than the crushing heartache of walking away from Alex.

She'd done the right thing for Heather. The girl had too much riding on her future for Mariella to have allowed her to risk Amber's wrath. She still wasn't sure they could trust that Alex's threat would keep Amber silent. Even if she had a guarantee, she would have made the same choice.

It had taken eighteen years, but she'd been given an opportunity to act like the mom she'd always wanted to be— sacrificing for her daughter wasn't a difficult choice other than having to hurt Alex as part of it.

She hated the pain she'd seen in his dark gaze and knowing she'd put it there. It was the right decision, but she'd damaged him. Shouldn't that prove she had no choice but to walk away?

Mariella hurt the people she loved. She was like a scorpion who had no choice but to sting. The plan when she'd come to Magnolia had been to hold onto her heart, to protect it and keep it safe.

Instead, she'd opened and let people in—her friends in town, Heather and Alex. She was protecting them by walking away.

That didn't seem to stop the turbulent emotions causing her heart to burn with sorrow.

How could her whole body feel icy cold other than the one part she wanted not to feel?

Shadows played across the wet sand as evening crept along the horizon. The waves pounded into the shore, churned up by the storm. The whitecaps and crashing roar mesmerized her, but she didn't approach.

There was low and then there was the emotional state she'd been in that night she'd walked into the water in Mexico. She wasn't there.

As bad as things were now, she'd find a way to get through it. The journey would be made a lot easier if she could ever manage to cut out her heart and abandon her love for Alex.

Something caught her eye, and she turned to find Alex stalking toward her like she'd conjured him with her need.

She tried to scramble to her feet, but her limbs were numb and not working the way they should and she pitched forward so that when he got to her, Mariella was on her knees.

This man had brought her to her knees.

She deserved it and did her best to swallow back her tears. What did it matter? The rain washed them away as soon as they fell.

But somehow Alex knew.

He dropped to his knees and gathered her into his arms. She didn't have the strength to fight him and allowed herself to be scooped into his lap. He kissed her forehead and her cheeks, trailed his mouth along her jaw.

"I love you," he said into her ear, his warm breath making goose bumps prick her skin. "And you should have told me it was Heather."

"I couldn't," she said on a ragged breath. "I needed to do it that way for my daughter. You have your priorities and I have mine. Your company—"

"You are my priority, Mariella. I'm sorry I didn't tell you before. I'm sorry if you doubted it for one single second."

"It wasn't you that I doubted," she told him, figuring if there was a time for honesty, that time was now. "I have all the faith in the world in you, Alex. Not so much in myself."

"Can my faith in you be enough?" he asked.

She thought about that, wondered if it could be true. "I wanted to come to you whole."

"Oh, sweetheart, none of us is completely whole at this point. Don't you see?" He placed a hand on either side of her face, the warmth of him heating some of the icy places inside her. "My broken pieces fit with yours. We're only whole together, Mariella. We're better together."

"I don't want to lose you," she said, biting down on the inside of her cheek to keep from breaking down into embarrassing sobs.

"You could never lose me. You will never lose me. Even if you go on a self-destructive rampage for the ages, Mariella, I'll be the one to follow in your wreckage. It would be my great honor. I promise I won't let you go. You are my home."

"That's a big promise." She smiled through her tears, her heart thumping in a new and brilliant rhythm. "But I don't want the rampage. I want to have courage, Alex. You've helped me begin to find it. I'm a work in progress."

"We both are," he assured her.

"And I want to do the work with you." She brushed her lips across his, hers tingling at the contact. "I love you," she said as her chest swelled with emotion.

Alex deepened the kiss and it was like finding the other half that she'd been missing, the certainty of knowing that together they truly were whole.

When he pulled away, his wet hair stuck to his head and raindrops glistened on the tips of his eyelashes. "Mariella?"

"Mmmm," she murmured, ready to nuzzle into him again.

"Can we go home and get warm?" He nipped at her bottom lip. "Preferably naked and in bed."

She let him help her to her feet, a deep-rooted sense of peace settling over as he drew her close. She joined their fingers together. "There is no place I'd rather be."

# *EPILOGUE*

NERVES QUIVERED UP and down Mariella's spine like the tickle of a caterpillar's legs.

"What if they hate each other?" she asked, her tone hushed so as not to distract from the magnitude of the moment. "It's important they don't hate each other."

Alex wrapped an arm around her shoulder. "It's important to me that Bex doesn't eat Millie."

"Don't even suggest that." Mariella clasped a hand over his mouth and he kissed her open palm.

"I'm joking," he said after peeling her hand away from his lips. "Bex will love her."

"Just as long as it's not with her mouth."

He pulled her closer. "We've got this, sweetheart."

Mariella nodded. It had been a month since the Magnolia Blossom Festival, and this weekend Alex had moved into her house so they were introducing Bex to Millie, and she desperately hoped they would do okay together. Otherwise, Millie would be moving to the office at A Second Chance.

She was working on having faith. Right now faith that his not-quite-feral cat wasn't going to try to snack on her beloved goldfish.

His house was already under contract, which spoke to how Magnolia was growing. They would be hosting a going-away party for Heather, who'd be moving to Chapel Hill at the end of the month.

The girl had insisted on admitting the truth to Amber before the actress left town. Mariella and Kay had taken Heather to the starlet's rented house. To Mariella's surprise, Amber had actually been sympathetic to Heather. Far more than she'd been when she thought Mariella was to blame. Turned out, Amber had been adopted and never had the chance to meet her birth mother.

Mariella had seen a different side of Amber. Not that the two of them were destined to become besties, but Mariella had finally found a true feeling of serenity with regards to her past.

Maybe that's what had made her so ready to embrace the future. And she'd take every step of it with Alex at her side.

"Look at that," Alex said against her hair. "Bex likes Millie."

A smile tugged at Mariella's mouth. The cat gently nudged her head against the glass bowl while Millie darted from one side to the other. Bex looked over her shoulder toward Alex like she was seeking his approval.

"You're a good girl," he crooned. The cat yipped then hopped off the counter to explore other parts of the house.

"That was remarkably uneventful," Mariella said, her grin widening.

"Let's keep Millie's bowl out of reach until we're sure Bex isn't interested," Alex suggested. "So far, it feels promising."

"Lots of promises," Mariella murmured, holding up her hand to display the third finger on her left hand. A week earlier during a picnic at the beach, Alex had gotten down on one knee to propose.

They'd met Emma and Cam plus Angi and Gabe for a celebratory dinner in town. Surrounded by her friends, Mariella had been almost bewildered by the joy she'd found in Magnolia and with the life she'd created there. The life she and Alex were creating. It would be the two of them forever, and she was happier than she ever imagined.

\* \* \* \* \*

# SPRINGTIME
# IN CAROLINA

# CHAPTER ONE

JOSIE TRUMBELL PLACED a gentle hand on the head of the young girl at the barre. "Spread your arms, Lucy. Elbows high."

The girl dutifully tried to follow the directions. The tip of her pink tongue poked out from one corner of her mouth as she concentrated. "Am I a beautiful butterfly, Miss Josie?"

Josie felt some of the melancholy that had gripped her in recent days ease at the girl's innocent question. "Yes, you are, sweetheart. A beautiful butterfly ready to spread your lovely wings."

They were working on a routine for the early spring dance recital, which was to take place in two weeks. She liked to think the annual event at Josie's School of Dance heralded the change of seasons for both current students as well as families who'd previously sent their children to Josie. But this year, the recital would mean more. Josie's former mentor and dance master, Jennifer Plowman, was coming to watch; perhaps to judge all the ways Josie hadn't lived up to her potential.

Still, tradition was important. She had a place in that for Magnolia, North Carolina. That counted for something. She would leave a legacy, even if it wasn't on the scale she'd once imagined.

She glanced at the clock on the wall at the fireside of

the dance studio. "It's time to get packed up now," she said. "Your mom will be here any minute."

Lucy released her pose, shoulders slumping in relief as though she'd been in position for hours instead of seconds. The girl was adorable with her dark braids, big melted-chocolate eyes and fair skin. She reminded Josie of herself as a child. Perhaps if Josie'd had a daughter of her own, she would have looked like Lucy.

"Thanks for letting me come in and make up the class." Lucy scrunched up her pert nose. "If I get behind in class, Megan Miller will tell me I have to stand in the back."

"Megan doesn't get to choose where people stand," Josie reminded the girl.

"She thinks she's the boss of me. But you're the boss here."

Josie reached for a smile but couldn't quite grasp it. The dance studio she'd owned for the past fifteen years was indeed her kingdom. She was the benevolent ruler of this space, although sometimes she doubted her ability to lead even this corner of the world.

Lucy toed off her soft ballet slippers and traded them for scuffed Crocs decorated with colorful buttons. Josie adjusted a couple of pictures that lined the wall above the hooks and shelves where students placed their personal belongings. Photos of her when she'd been younger and a professional dancer. Back when she had thought everything in life would go her way with hard work and dedication.

Before life had taught her differently.

"You used to be beautiful," Lucy told her, stating the words as fact rather than an opinion.

Josie heard an audible gasp behind her even as her heart clenched.

"Lucy Louise, apologize for your rudeness." Brandie, the girl's mom, looked aghast. "Miss Josie is still beautiful."

"Old people aren't beautiful, Mommy. They are classic and respectable. That's what Memaw says."

"Like a well-maintained Model T," Josie added with a laugh that sounded only a tiny bit hysterical.

"Your grandmother should learn to keep her mouth shut." Brandie offered Josie an apologetic smile. "I don't think my mom would have said exactly that."

Josie flashed a tight smile. They both knew her mother would have said that and more. And it was true. Josie wasn't beautiful in the way she had once been. She was in her late forties and changes were upon her body. Big and small shifts she couldn't control and certainly wouldn't choose if she had her druthers.

Things like crow's feet and crepey skin and an extra layer of padding on her hips. Sagging in places where her body had once been firm and supple.

She told herself it didn't matter. Her body still functioned the way it was supposed to for the most part. At least she hadn't started with the night sweats or growing random facial hair the way some of her friends lamented. She was downright lucky.

"It's all good," she told Brandie. "There are worse things to be than classic. Lucy, practice your arabesques so you're ready for next week's class. It will be the final rehearsal before our recital."

The chimes above the front door of the dance studio jingled, and a rush of cool air blew in along with the girls for her next class.

They were a group of beginner students between the ages of six and seven with energy and enthusiasm to spare. She rolled her shoulders and mentally prepared herself for an hour of giggles and distracting questions as the girls worked on their basic positions.

Each of the children wore a pink or black leotard with pale pink tights. Josie had settled on the standard ballet uniform from the moment she'd opened her dance studio. She loved the rich history of it and the nod to classical ballet even if most of these girls were with her so their frazzled parents or after-school babysitters could get a break for an hour.

It was silly to focus on her vanity or let regret chase away the joy she found working with young students. There were just so many happy couples finding love in Magnolia lately. It made her feel nostalgic about the choices she'd made and the path her life had taken.

She heard the whispers that went through the usual group of mothers and didn't need to turn to know what had caused the change.

She turned anyway. She was only human after all. Brandon Johnson, single father and recent Magnolia transplant, stood at the studio's entrance, eyeing the gaggle of thirsty moms like a rabbit might gaze at a nearby coyote pack.

Morgan, Brandon's bright-eyed and boisterous daughter, grabbed her backpack from her father's arms and skipped over to join her new friends in the lobby.

The poor guy looked down at his empty hands like he wasn't sure where his unicorn-emblazoned shield had gone.

"Come in," Josie told him, offering what she hoped was a calming smile. Brandon had recently moved to town to work at the Fit Collective, a clothing company specializing in fashionable athletic wear for women. She wasn't sure what he did for the company—his title was brand ambassador or something equally hip and nebulous.

But she liked him. If she'd been ten years younger, she

might have really liked him. It had been almost that long since she'd had a boyfriend. The term sounded so juvenile when she thought about it.

It made her feel old.

He gave an almost imperceptible shake of his head. "Can I speak to you outside for a moment?" he asked, his vowels clipped. He'd grown up in Chicago or Milwaukee or someplace with a brutal winter. He spoke differently than the men around Magnolia with their lazy vowels and the drawn-out Southern cadence she'd come to appreciate.

"Of course." She turned to the girls. "Everyone at the barre to stretch. I'll join you in a moment." She met the gaze of one of her best friends, whose bonus baby, eight years younger than her closest sibling, was a part of the class. "Helen, would you supervise the class for me?"

"Take your time," Helen said with a wink.

Josie rolled her eyes but felt a blush creep up her cheeks as she followed Brandon into the brisk afternoon.

"I can't go in there," he announced as soon as the door closed behind her.

"The moms around here aren't as ravenous as they first appear." She moved to pat his arm then pulled her hand away at the last moment. Josie liked touching people. She was a hugger by nature, but it felt weird with this man. Like it could send a message she wasn't ready to give.

Brandon's verdant green eyes widened. "Morgan and I moved here six weeks ago, and I have enough casseroles in my freezer to keep us fed through a zombie apocalypse."

He was an exceptionally handsome man by any standard. Nearly six feet with a chiseled jaw and movie-star features that included those brilliantly colored eyes, an aristocratic-looking nose and lips so full they'd make a Kardashian sister jealous.

She'd heard one of the women say that he'd been a model when he was younger, and Josie could believe it. He was the closest thing she'd seen to physical perfection in a long time, and there were plenty of handsome men in town.

"One of the South's strongest love languages is food. They want you to feel welcome."

"Oh, I got the message loud and clear." He glanced past her toward the door. "I know that most of the parents stick around to watch class and visit. I'm not sure I want to get close enough for more."

Josie clasped a hand to her mouth when a giggle burst from her throat. She was not prone to tittering like a schoolgirl and reminded herself that she was a classic. That put a damper on her humor in an instant.

"Understood. I doubt Morgan will mind if you aren't..."

Her voice trailed off as she watched Stuart Madison, her once—and hopefully future—best friend approach from the direction of Carrie Scott's art gallery.

He was in his mid-fifties, running the local bookstore, Off the Shelf, for the past ten years since his grandfather passed away.

Before returning to Magnolia, Stuart had lived in Atlanta. He'd been a high-powered attorney but had given up his career and marriage to take over the family business in their quiet coastal town.

They'd become friends right away, although for several years, Stuart had wanted more. His crush on Josie had become a bit of a joke around town, and she'd always appreciated that he didn't seem to care.

It was as if the role of pining suitor fit him, some sort of modern-day Heathcliff without all the drama and death, which was a plus. Not to mention there were no moors for him to stalk across in Magnolia, although the blustery look on his face as he noticed her and Brandon standing together would have done any brooding hero proud.

"Hey, Stuart," she called, momentarily forgetting about the handsome single dad standing at her side.

Stuart was attractive in his own way. Tall and broad and dark like a pirate from the olden days. Taken separately, his features didn't seem to be anything special. Gentle hazel eyes set slightly too far apart framed by obscenely long eyelashes and heavy brows that made him appear serious even when he laughed.

His nose was a tad too big, and his mouth the slightest bit too wide. His upper lip was thin but his lower one full in a bee-stung pout.

She'd once been perusing the new release section of his store and overheard a group of women clearly in town on a girls' trip describe his mouth as kissable. Specifically, one of the women had commented that she'd like to see if a mouth like that could do the wicked things it brought to mind.

Josie had at once been horrified, offended on his behalf and shockingly aroused by the images those illicit words created in conjunction with a man she was determined to see in only a platonic light. She had experience with love, and every time it had turned out badly.

The moment she'd decided that Stuart was steadfast and dependable—the kind of man she wanted in her life for years to come—had been the instant she'd ruled him out as a romantic partner. No way would she take the chance of ruining their friendship.

But something was destroying it anyway. Or at least it felt that way to her. Stuart was still kind, and they shared their weekly movie nights and went on long hikes the way they had for years, but he'd changed. Or his feelings for her had changed.

Maybe they'd finally muted into nothing more than restrained affection. What kind of horrible person did it make Josie that she wanted more?

She wanted him to look at her the way he had for years. The way that made her feel special even when the men she casually dated managed to live down to her expectations and disappoint or hurt her. Stuart had always been there to pick up the pieces, but she had a feeling he wasn't willing to do that any longer.

"How's Carrie doing?" She shifted to include Brandon in the conversation. "One of our friends is having a baby in the next few weeks."

"That's great," Brandon said with his gleaming smile. Seriously, the man was a walking billboard for whitening strips. "Babies are cool."

Stuart's jaw tensed, although Brandon didn't seem to notice. "Babies are a miracle," he said.

"That, too," Brandon agreed, still affable.

"I brought Carrie some books," Stuart said to Josie. "The kid needs a good library from the start."

She tried and failed to draw in a full breath around the ache in her chest. Stuart had lost his only daughter to an aggressive form of childhood cancer. She knew the books he'd taken to Carrie had likely been the ones that had belonged to his own child.

"That's really great," Josie said, realizing how silly the words sounded when she knew what the gesture truly meant.

Brandon gave Stuart a friendly thumbs-up. "Well done, man. It feels like kids start on the electronics right out of the cradle. Way to be a good influence. Solid."

"That's me." Stuart started to walk around them. "Solid."

Josie wanted to say something more. She wanted to call him back and ask what had happened between them. Why couldn't they go back to how it had been? But that wasn't fair.

She didn't blame him for moving on with his feelings but wished she didn't have to lose his friendship in the process.

"I should get back to class," she told Brandon. "Morgan will be fine. Don't worry about not watching, although you're welcome at any time."

He offered another brilliant smile. "Appreciate that. I was also wondering if you might like to get dinner at some point?"

Josie's gaze tracked to Stuart. Brandon had the kind of voice that carried, so she couldn't imagine her friend hadn't heard, but he kept walking and disappeared into the bookstore like the thought of her going on a date with another man meant nothing.

"That's a nice offer." She couldn't quite believe it possible that this man, who was physical perfection and likely ten years younger than her, would be asking her on an actual date. "Things are busy as we get ready for the spring recital, but maybe some time."

He looked disappointed. Probably didn't hear the word *no* often, especially with all of those casseroles crowding his freezer. Maybe he was into classics.

She was undoubtedly honored but that didn't seem like the right feeling for the moment. Her feelings had been such a jumble lately.

"I've got to go," she said into the awkward silence and hurried back into the dance studio. Needing the safety of her tiny kingdom now more than ever.

## CHAPTER TWO

THE FOLLOWING MORNING, Stuart stopped into Sunnyside Bakery for a coffee and a bear claw because that was his Wednesday routine. He knew the young baristas who worked in Mary Ellen Winkler's establishment in the years since he'd moved to Magnolia thought he was an eccentric stick-in-the-mud. Maybe that was the truth.

But when his daughter had died at age ten and his marriage and career imploded, threatening to take him down in the process, routine had saved him. Perhaps his dependence on habit was what made it so hard to give up Josie and accept what everybody had been telling him for the better part of a decade.

She didn't like him like that. He was strictly in the friend zone.

From the moment he'd met her at a town council meeting all those years ago, she'd captured his heart with her innate kindness and the way she cared about not only her students, but their families and everyone in this town.

He knew she'd had disappointments and been knocked down by life a time or two, just as he had. But he also recognized that she could still live in the light, despite the shadows that sometimes crowded her gentle brown eyes.

They'd also been friends long enough for him to know she had horrible taste in men. If there was a guy who'd treat her poorly within a hundred-mile radius of Magnolia, she'd find a way to fall for him.

Stuart didn't know the beefcake dude she'd been talking to yesterday, but there were lots of new people moving into Magnolia thanks to the town's recent resurgence. It was good for his business, but Stuart liked things the same.

He didn't want to wait in line for his coffee or have trouble finding a parking space if he needed something at the hardware store. Some things couldn't be helped, though, and at this point progress was one of them.

He suppressed a groan as he noticed the line of people already snaking around the coffee shop's gleaming front case.

Mary Ellen spotted him and waved a hand, gesturing him to follow her into the kitchen. Stuart's stomach rumbled in anticipation. He hoped it meant what he thought it did.

"Fresh bear claws," she said with a wink. "I saved one for my best customer."

"Now I'm worried you want something." Stuart took the pastry she offered on a Fiesta-ware plate and noticed a steaming cup of coffee on the stainless-steel countertop. "Coffee, too? You must really want something."

Mary Ellen, a round woman with a kind smile and ruddy cheeks, rolled her eyes. "So suspicious," she accused. "Can't I offer a special treat to a friend?"

"What is it?"

She sighed. "I don't want anything from you," she clarified. "I want something for you. I want you to be happy."

"I'm happy," he retorted without hesitation, then took a bite of the bear claw. "Especially at the moment. More so if we don't have to talk about my happiness."

"What's going on with you and Josie?"

All that sweet, melty goodness turned to cardboard in

his mouth. "Nothing, as you well know. Everyone knows. I overheard her being asked out on a date yesterday by some new guy."

"I heard," Mary Ellen said gently. "We had book club last night. She said no to the new guy, by the way."

"Not my business."

"It should be." Mary Ellen wiped a crumb from the counter. "You love her."

"We're friends."

"You want more, Stuart. Don't bother denying it. We all know you want—"

He'd placed the plate with the half-eaten pastry on the counter with more force than necessary. "I want people to leave me alone."

He wiped his hand on a kitchen towel and gulped down half the coffee she'd poured. He'd always taken his coffee black, and the bitterness stung his tongue with the sugary residue of the bear claw still in his mouth.

He welcomed the bite and grimaced as he swallowed. "You and I are both well aware that my feelings for Josie have made me a laughingstock in this town for years. I didn't care what anyone thought. All that mattered was Josie because she's amazing."

Mary Ellen's smile softened. "Yes, she is."

"But she doesn't want me."

"She doesn't think she deserves you," the baker clarified. "That's different."

"Language nuances don't make much of a difference when the result is the same." He placed his coffee on the counter when he realized his fingers were starting to shake.

Stuart was a private man, but he knew Mary Ellen meant well. Most people in Magnolia did, which was why he loved this community. It had helped heal him when he needed it most. His friendship with Josie was part of that, but they'd gone from healing to hurt, and it needed to stop. He needed to stop it. "My daughter died ten years ago next month."

"I'm sorry," Mary Ellen said.

"Me, too. Every day. What I've finally come to understand—and I'm not the sharpest knife in the drawer with regards to insight—is that I haven't been honoring her life or her memory by playing small. I took over my family's bookstore because I needed a do-over on life, and she loved it here. She loved going home with a new bag of books that my grandfather chose for her."

He picked up the bear claw then placed it on the plate again, unable to muster any enthusiasm for his favorite breakfast treat. "I'm not going to register with a dating app or try some random hookup, but I can't be open to what life might send my way when I'm hung up on Josie. I need to release her as much for her benefit as for mine."

"What if she doesn't want you to let her go? What if she's come to depend on you but has gotten complacent with the status quo? What if she wants more, Stuart?"

His heart seemed to skip a beat inside his chest before it settled into the familiar ache that was his unwelcome affection for a woman who didn't return it.

"I think this is for the best," he said, not sure whether he believed it. "Josie and I missed our moment. Now I need to get to the store and open up."

"Let me wrap up that bear claw for you." Mary Ellen's voice was as gentle as he'd ever heard.

He shook his head. "Thanks, but it's not necessary. I've lost my appetite," he said as he turned to walk away.

# CHAPTER THREE

"MISSED OUR MOMENT? We haven't even had a moment." Josie threw up her hands in disbelief as she paced from one end of the dance studio to the other the following night.

"Is that such a bad thing?" Carrie Scott asked from where she sat at a large folding table, adding the last bit of detail to the backdrop for the spring recital.

Carrie was the daughter of famed painter Niall Reed and an accomplished artist in her own right, but she still made time every year to help with the scenery and decorations for the spring recital.

This year's theme was "Watch Us Grow" with songs and costumes celebrating a season of renewal and transformation. All Josie could think about was Stuart transforming from her best friend to a man ready to cut her out of his life.

Her rational mind understood she was being unfair. But she'd come to depend on Stuart. He was her safe place, and she didn't know how to move forward without that. It wasn't as if she'd never considered having a relationship with him.

He was attractive in a big, brooding, bookworm sort of way. She'd had to tamp down her body's tingling at his touch on numerous occasions over the years. But it was for the best. It was for both of their benefits. She'd held back because she had a terrible track record with romance.

She didn't expect him to pine after her for years, although she liked knowing he was always there to support her when things went badly with the men she dated.

"How can it be good if he pulls away?" She hadn't meant to eavesdrop on his conversation with Mary Ellen. She routinely headed to the back of the bakery in the morning to visit with her matronly neighbor and hadn't been able to force herself to walk away when she'd heard Stuart's assessment of their relationship even though it hurt. "He's my person."

"I think he wants to find somebody willing to be his person in return." With her willowy frame and delicate features, Carrie was one of the kindest people Josie knew, but her quiet words felt like a slap in the face.

Josie couldn't disagree. But she also didn't like what it said about her. She didn't like herself at all at the moment.

"Do you want to be Stuart's person?" Carrie asked.

Josie stopped pacing and turned to face the mirror that ran the length of her studio room. Her dark hair remained pulled back in the bun she wore for teaching, and she yanked out the hair tie. Recently, she'd had to start coloring her roots, a concession to vanity but one she wasn't willing to give up.

She'd come to Magnolia after a career-ending back injury and the breakup of her relationship with the temperamental company director she'd loved and idolized in equal measure. At that time, being independent and able to support herself without help from anyone—any man specifically—had been essential to her healing, both physically and emotionally.

That was her mental space when she and Stuart became friends, and she'd never quite let him out of the friend-zone box. Now that he'd kicked away the walls on his own, she didn't know where that left her. There were things she hadn't been willing to admit over the years, even to herself. Her feelings for her steadfast friend topped that list.

"Yes," she whispered as panic shot through her.

It was terrifying to consider what she might be risking if she tried. "I don't even know if he wants me in that way at this point, and what if things don't work out? Things never work out for me with romance."

She shook her head. "Forget I said anything. It's a stupid idea. What if we're together and I get too needy or he wants more than I'm willing to give? What happens when things go badly and we're work neighbors who live in the same town and I lose my best friend? Just forget it."

Josie startled as Carrie took her hand. She hadn't realized the other woman had stood to approach her. "So you've just had an entire relationship in your head. It took twenty seconds from start to finish."

Josie blew out a sigh. "Which feels longer than a few of the relationships I've had."

"Don't you think you should give Stuart a chance if this is how you feel?"

"I should have given him a chance years ago. It's probably too late now. He said as much."

"You won't know unless you try."

"I made a choice not to fall in love because love hurts."

"Sometimes letting a chance slip away hurts just as badly."

Josie tugged on the ends of her hair. "I think love is for young people. People who aren't so bruised and battered or set in their ways. You know I'm not easy to get along with."

"Josie, everyone in this town loves you."

"They love me as the eccentric dance teacher who is kind to their kids. They don't know me. Or who I was before. Or who I might want to be in the future. Sometimes I'm not sure I know me."

"Whose fault is that? Is that because of them or because of you?"

Josie held up a finger. "You are more than a decade younger than me. You're not allowed to be so wise."

"You've helped so many people in Magnolia. You've always taken care of us, Josie. Maybe it's time to take care of you."

Josie's heart pinched as she mustered a smile. "I'm not sure I remember how."

# *CHAPTER FOUR*

STUART FOLLOWED MAGGIE, his twelve-year-old black Lab, into the front yard the following evening. According to the vet, his sweet girl had hip issues and was primarily deaf plus blind in one eye, but she still wagged her tail and ate like a champ. She loved their evening walks through the neighborhood. He didn't bother with the leash because she wasn't prone to wandering and her days of chasing squirrels were long behind her.

They never made it more than a few blocks before turning around, but he would assure her that she was a good, strong girl and had walked at least nine miles uphill both ways.

As he turned, he noticed Josie's Subaru hatchback parked at the curb. Fear sizzled through him as he noticed her slumped over the steering wheel.

He rushed toward her car as Maggie lumbered over to do her business in the flower bed.

"Josie," he screamed. Her head snapped up and she looked around like he'd scared the crap out of her.

Appropriate because she'd just scared the crap out of him.

"Are you okay?" he demanded as he got to her car and yanked open the door. He wanted to pull her out of it. To put his hands on her and make sure there was nothing seriously wrong.

She gathered her thick fall of mahogany-hued hair in one hand and draped it over her shoulder as she straightened, her posture reflecting the prima ballerina she'd once been.

"I'm fine," she said as if this were an ordinary occurrence. As if anything about this was normal. "I wanted to talk to you."

"Did you pass out? Did you hit your head? Have you eaten dinner?" He fired off the questions in a staccato rhythm. She had to hear the panic threading through his words.

She bit her lower lip and unbuckled her seat belt. "I just needed a moment to think before I got out of the car."

Stuart stepped back and gave her room to exit. He didn't want to give her space right now. He wanted to crowd her because something wasn't right. She never looked like this with him—unsure and vulnerable.

Yes, he'd put up a necessary distance between them lately, but for the most part, she seemed blithely unaware of it.

"Is this about that new young guy you're dating? Did he do something to you?" He shook his head. "It's none of my business. Never mind. Don't answer."

"I'm not dating Brandon." She got out of the car and shut the door, using the motion to move a few paces away from him. She wore a tank top under faded chambray overalls with a chunky sweater made of soft grey wool overtop. She'd had those overalls for as long as he'd known her, probably much longer.

They looked like a holdover from her days as a dancer in New York City, the type of comfortable and quirky outfit she would have worn while she'd been living her best life in Manhattan. He wished he'd known her then if only to catch glimpses of the woman she was going to become.

The one who was his best friend, even if being close to her broke his heart.

"I'm not dating him," she repeated with more force than necessary.

"I mean it, Josie. Your dating life is not my business."

Maggie nudged Josie's leg, looking for some attention from one of her favorite people.

"Hey, sweet girl." Josie crouched down to take the dog's giant muzzle between her hands. "You are looking gorgeous tonight." Maggie snuffled, accepting the praise like it was her due, then turned and started down the sidewalk without looking back.

"Do you want to walk with us?" Stuart asked.

"Yes."

They fell in step together, although the strain between them was palpable.

"Just so we're on the same page, you came over to talk about something that couldn't be shared during the workday? Then you had to gird your loins at the curb until you got the nerve to come in."

"I'm not girding anything," Josie countered with a derisive sniff. "I was thinking."

Stuart waved to one of his neighbors. "What were you thinking about?"

"I think you and I should have sex."

He stumbled but righted himself before he landed face-first on the sidewalk. "Are you sure you didn't hit your head?" His voice trembled, and he cleared his throat.

"That's not the reaction I was hoping for."

He did his best to come up with a coherent response, but it felt as though all of his brain cells had migrated south. They were currently hollering at him to stop arguing, grab his dog and his woman, march back to the house, and take her up on this wild-hair suggestion.

The thing he'd dreamed about more times than he could say because it would be too embarrassing to admit how often he'd imagined it.

They continued to walk as the tension pulsing between them grew to hurricane intensity. And damn if he didn't want to head straight into the storm. No, he reminded himself. He'd made a decision. A choice that would keep him safe and sane.

"Where is this coming from?"

"I don't want to lose you," she said. The physical desire pulsing through him sagged like a week-old helium balloon.

"So you're offering me friend-zone pity sex?"

"No," she said, sounding both hurt and embarrassed.

*Welcome to the club.*

"Josie, I know you don't feel that way about me. I'm not your type. I've accepted that, but you have to know I'm not the type for casual sex."

She glanced at him out of the corner of her eye, folding her arms over her chest like she was the one who needed protecting. "Do you think it would be casual between us?"

"No," he whispered, which was all the more reason to deny himself the thing he wanted most in the world at this moment.

"I'm messing this up." She ran a jittery hand through her hair.

He didn't know what was happening. Normally he could read Josie. He knew what made her laugh and the types of things that irritated her. He was well aware that she did not like to be spoken to until she'd had at least one cup of coffee—if not more—and that two drinks were her limit or else she'd end up with a horrible hangover the next day.

"I haven't had sex in seven years," she blurted.

Well, there was a detail he hadn't known.

Her shoulders slouched. "Men don't really want to have sex with women in their forties."

"That is not true," he ground out, unable to hold in his denial.

"Most men don't. So I haven't. I dated men, and stuff happened. Sexy-times stuff."

He put his hands over his ears and started to hum.

"Come on, Stuart." She tugged at his arm.

Maggie had made it to the small open space situated at the end of the block and was enthusiastically sniffing the trunk of a nearby tree.

Josie faced him. Her chest rose and fell as she drew in a shaky breath. Her whiskey-hued eyes were wide, like a deer caught in headlights. She licked her lips and nodded, more to herself than him. "This isn't how I planned the conversation to go in my head. I shouldn't have started with sex. Sex doesn't even matter."

He lifted a brow. "It matters, Josie."

"Right. Well, it's not the most important thing. I've been on such a dry spell, I might have forgotten how it works. But I'd like to remember. With you. Not casually, Stuart." She stopped and shook her head like she was having as much trouble following her words as he was. "The point I'm trying to make—badly—is that I would like to date you."

It was precisely what he'd wanted to hear from her for almost a decade, so he couldn't quite believe the word that popped out of his mouth in response.

"No."

# CHAPTER FIVE

JOSIE STOOD IN the Sunnyside Bakery kitchen the following morning as Mary Ellen stared at her in disbelief.

"You must have misunderstood him."

"Stuart is well and truly over me," Josie lamented, trying not to sound pathetic. "I waited too long. I was too scared or dumb to realize I had a wonderful man right in front of me. I took him for granted. I took advantage of his friendship, and now I have to move."

"Move?" Mary Ellen dropped the rolling pin she was using to press out dough. "You're talking nonsense. Stuart is talking nonsense. You should go out with that younger single dad. Make Stuart jealous."

"I don't want to play games." Josie took a deep swig of coffee, her second cup of the morning. "And I'm not wasting time going out with a guy I don't care about."

"Maybe you could care a little," Mary Ellen suggested with a grimace. "At least long enough to break the dry spell. Seven years is a long time, Josie-girl." She gestured toward Josie's lower body. "Is everything working okay? They don't have a little blue pill for us ladies, but there are things—"

"It all works," Josie said, choking slightly. "My body might not be as tight and toned as it once was, but things work. It's been a solo job for a while, but that's okay, right?

Like Annie Lennox once said, sisters are doing it for themselves."

"Did Annie have a man like Stuart available when she sang that?"

"I don't know. She doesn't live in Magnolia. That's not the point of the song."

"Honey, you might have frightened the poor man."

"I frightened a man by telling him I want to date him? Horrible thought."

"Or did you do it on purpose?" Mary Ellen picked up the rolling pin again and pointed it in Josie's direction.

Josie frowned. "What is that supposed to mean?"

"It means that sometimes when we're scared, we mess up what would be good for us because it's easier than taking a chance."

"You think I'm doing that with Stuart?"

"You don't want to lose him, but a real relationship is..." She sighed. "It's a lot harder than the one-sided adoration that's been going on for too long. You have to be in it. When was the last time you tried that hard?"

Regret rolled through Josie along with a healthy dose of frustration. "It wasn't as if I expected to end up alone in my late forties. I wanted to get married and have a family. It just never happened. Eventually, I got used to it."

"Because it was safer," the older woman suggested.

Josie's mom had died when she was in her late twenties, and she appreciated Mary Ellen's sage advice, even if she didn't always want to hear it.

"In some ways."

"Safe only gets you so far."

"But he said no. How is this still my problem when he said no?"

"He carried a torch for a long time. There's also a certain

safety in one-sided love. You both have to take risks. Are you going to give up because there's a roadblock in the way of what you want or are you going to dig in and try harder?"

"I'm afraid," Josie admitted after a long moment. "You were married once, so I don't think you can understand. I didn't get to this age being single on purpose, which might be why I've been ignoring my feelings for Stuart. Somewhere along the line, being independent became part of my nature. I don't know how to do anything else."

"Stop making excuses."

Josie rolled her shoulders. She was receiving doses of tough love left and right from her friends and actually appreciated it. She needed it. "You're right." She took a final drink of coffee and nodded. "I'm done with excuses. I'm going to get through the recital, then I'm going to talk to Stuart and make it really work. At least give it my best shot."

"That's all you can do."

"I just hope it will be enough."

"We're here for you. You and Stuart. Seeing two of our favorite people together would make everyone happy."

With a new sense of anticipation and resolve, Josie said goodbye and went about her day.

She leased her studio space to a yoga instructor and a local Zumba class during the mornings. Around lunchtime, she started her own schedule of classes to teach: an adult ballet class with a lovely group of women, then onto her beloved youth classes.

The hours flew by with her regular schedule plus preparations for the spring recital. She always loved the week leading up to a big event, and this one held even more promise because of her plans.

By the end of the day, a mix of excitement and nerves

coursed through her, and she knew the best way to calm herself again would be to burn off the excess energy. She sometimes went months without dancing for her pleasure, but the joy of it came back to her quickly.

She turned on her favorite music, took a deep breath and let her body move with the beat. She'd been trained as a classical ballerina but sometimes, like today, she just wanted to feel the music. It was simple to forget her worries and concerns when the music took over.

She danced until her muscles ached and sweat rolled down between her shoulder blades. Her lungs drew air in and out in ragged puffs. She'd been trained to push her body and, in the process, had learned to find serenity in the soul of a song.

When the music finally ended, she slumped forward, exhausted but with a sense of peace that had alluded her far too long. She was never more herself than when she danced. Somehow it came as no surprise to look up and find Stuart watching her from the doorway to the studio, like she'd summoned him there.

"I'm sorry to interrupt," he said, his voice pitched low. "Forget that. I'm not sorry at all. The back door was unlocked. I came in and you couldn't have paid me to walk away. You are incredible."

Maybe Josie should feel like her privacy had been violated or be embarrassed over the abandon with which she'd been moving. Her form wasn't what it had been during her younger years. Her body wasn't what it had been either. When a person relies so much on physical appearance, it's hard to deal with the changes that came with the passing of time.

Yet she wasn't embarrassed or angry. Instead, she was grateful. Because if there was a chance she could make him understand what she felt, it was through the way her body moved.

She swiped a hand over her forehead, which was damp with sweat. "I was thinking of you," she told him, knowing those words were the most honest thing she could say. "As I danced, I thought of you, Stuart. How I feel about you and what I want from you. What I want for us."

He moved toward her, his long legs eating up the distance like a starving man approaching his favorite meal. The intensity in his eyes stole her breath. It was different than how he'd looked at her in the past—with gentle affection or starry-eyed adoration. Raw hunger lit his kind eyes.

He looked at her like a man looks at a woman he wants to do wicked things with. Oh, how Josie wanted those things, too.

He reached her and cupped her face in his hands, fusing his mouth to hers in a way that was somehow both demanding and infinitely tender.

She'd imagined kissing Stuart, but it was better than anything she could have dreamed. Sweeter, more erotic and completely perfect. She never wanted this moment to end.

# CHAPTER SIX

STUART HADN'T EXACTLY planned to kiss her. He wanted to kiss Josie. He'd wanted to kiss her every day for the past ten years.

He knew he'd hurt her by saying no when she'd showed up at his house, but it had felt wrong. The wrong time and the wrong order. How could he be certain she was the right woman for him and then when he finally got a chance with her, it felt wrong?

He didn't trust himself. Josie was smart and funny and lit up every room she walked into. He was grumpy and easily annoyed. He wanted to be a better person for her but wasn't sure he knew how.

What if he actually didn't deserve her?

He was like a moth drawn to a flame when it came to this woman. He'd stopped in when he saw a light and heard music on the way to his car.

He knew the extra hours she spent working before each recital. Even though she mostly taught kids, and their parents would think they were stars no matter what happened during the performance, Josie did her best to make every moment perfect.

When he'd come to the studio door and saw her dancing with so much passion and wild abandon, Stuart had been awestruck.

And when she'd said she'd been thinking of him, every

doubt and fear he'd had disappeared, at least for the moment. Because when she looked at him with that kind of ferocity, all he could remember was that she belonged with him. His heart belonged to her for as long as she would have it.

Her skin was warm and their mouths melded like they were made for each other.

This wasn't like a normal first kiss. This was the kiss of two people who knew what they were doing. Who understood what it meant to give themselves to another person.

She wrapped her arms around his neck, and he groaned as he pulled her flush against him. Her curves fit into the hard planes of his body like a puzzle coming together.

Even though desire battered him from all directions like a windswept summer storm, he forced himself to go slow. Josie deserved to be cherished and savored.

If she let him, he would spend the rest of his life doing just that.

Eventually, she pulled away, gazing up at him with hazy eyes. He put that dreamy expression on her face, and he'd never felt prouder.

"I didn't know you could kiss like that," she said as she touched her lips with her fingertips. "I didn't know it would be like that."

"I did." He dropped a gentle kiss on her forehead. "I knew it would be like that and better."

One corner of her mouth tipped up. "Are bookworms supposed to be cocky?"

"We are an underestimated breed." He shrugged. "Avid readers are shown to be more imaginative and have immense attention to detail." He ran a finger from her chin down the elegant column of her throat to the top edge of her leotard. "Those characteristics give us an advantage in life, which includes the bedroom."

She closed her eyes for a moment as if she was considering it. "But you said no," she whispered after a moment. "I asked you to have sex with me. I asked you to go on a date. You said no."

"I meant it, Josie. I don't want to be a man you date or have a quick turn with in the sheets so you can get me out of your system. I want more from you. I want more for you. I want everything. Your crusty mornings before coffee and the late nights when you need someone to rub your feet plus all the in-between moments. I'll accept that I might never be the man for you, but I'm here to tell you that I won't settle for anything less."

He could see when she truly understood what he was saying. Panic flashed in her eyes. He was shocked she didn't pull away, and maybe that was a good sign. He claimed her mouth again, searching his brain for the strength to walk away from her if she didn't want what he did. She'd ruined him for any other woman.

There would never be anyone for him but this beautiful, confounding, spirited dancer. But he would not settle. He'd done that for too long.

He forced himself to release her and took a step back. "I'm not asking for an answer now. We both know I'm a patient man. If you say yes to me, it's a yes to all of it—the good and bad, the happy moments and the times of sorrow."

Stuart cleared his throat and said the words he'd thought in his own head a million times before. "I love you, Josie. I choose you. Who you are now."

He gestured to the frames that lined this studio wall. "Not the girl in those photos. She was talented and radiant, but she can't hold a candle to the woman you are today. You are the woman I want."

His heart was flinging itself against his rib cage so hard, he thought she must be able to hear it. Maybe he was messing everything up. She'd offered him more than he'd imagined receiving from her, and he'd told her it wasn't enough. But he couldn't accept less than everything. She meant too much to him.

"Okay," she said, her voice husky. She swallowed as if unsure of what came next. "That was quite a declaration, Stuart. Have you been holed up in the romance section of the bookstore lately?"

He grinned. "I've been waiting a long time to say those things to you. No matter what you decide, it won't change my feelings."

She gave a shaky nod.

"I'll see you at the recital. Your former dance teacher is going to be proud of what you've created here."

"I wish I could believe that." She glanced at the photos he'd just mentioned. "I don't think this is the future she expected for me."

"At our age, most people aren't living the lives they expected when they were younger. But if this life makes you happy, it's the right one. You have instilled a love of dance in hundreds of children in this community. If Jennifer Plowman is as dedicated as you believe, she'll appreciate that."

"How do you always know the right thing to say to me?"

"I'm not sure that's true." This conversation would change everything if she decided she didn't want him the way he wanted her. "As much as I love books, I'm not always great with words. You know that. But I'm telling you the truth, and I hope you can believe it. Good night, Josie," he said, and forced himself to turn for the door.

# CHAPTER SEVEN

THE NIGHT BEFORE the recital, Josie stood in the studio, alone again. She wasn't dancing like she had earlier that week when Stuart found her.

Instead, she held a hammer in one hand and the final framed shot of her as a young dancer she'd removed from the wall in the other.

A knock sounded on the front door. She was shocked to come around the corner and see Jennifer Plowman, her former dance instructor and one of the most well-respected ballerinas to grace the American stage, standing on the sidewalk.

Jennifer had risen to prominence between the eras of Martha Graham and Misty Copeland. Josie remembered feeling both grateful for and terrified of working under the demanding teacher's tutelage.

Jennifer was in her mid-seventies now, and unlike Josie, hadn't allowed the years to soften her dancer's slim figure. Her hair was drawn into a severe bun as she stood in regal splendor, like a queen waiting to be shown into the parlor.

Josie hurriedly opened the door. "I thought you were arriving tomorrow," she said as she watched a black luxury sedan pull away from the curb.

Jennifer sniffed and dabbed at her trademark red lips. "It's supposed to storm in New York tomorrow. I didn't want to take a chance on my flight being delayed. It isn't every day that I get to be a special guest at my former star pupil's dance academy recital."

Josie laughed softly and picked up Jennifer's monogrammed luggage to bring it into the studio. "Dance academy might be a stretch. It's a sweet little operation but not impressive on a grand scale."

"Do not make yourself small," Jennifer said in her subtle British accent. She'd come to America in the late sixties after a working-class upbringing outside of London. It was rumored that George Harrison had written a song about her. Jennifer was the kind of woman to inspire men in that way. Her confidence and charisma were legendary.

Even before the back injury that ended Josie's career, she knew she would never reach the heights her mentor had. She had the talent but not the chutzpah for fame.

Gazing around her studio as she gave Jennifer a tour made her realize she didn't much care. It was as Stuart had said. She'd created a good life in Magnolia. A life that made her happy.

"You're right. I'm proud of my studio and the dancers I've taught. Each one of them has meant something to me."

Jennifer took her hand and studied her. "You always had a heart as big as your talent, my dear. But I sense something has changed."

"Well, yes." Josie looked toward the wall of photos she'd just finished mounting. Had her former dance master seen pictures online of the way the studio had looked before? "I took down the photos of myself as a young dancer because they are the past and this space is about my present life and the future."

"The photos of you with the children are lovely, but that's not the change to which I'm referring." Jennifer inclined her head. "The last time we spoke, there was an edge to your voice. The joy I'd come to rely on was not there. Now it is. What brought it back?" She indicated the painted backdrops against the far wall. "Is it the anticipation of the recital?"

Josie's heart fluttered at the thought that she could be read so easily, although Jennifer knew her better than most. "It's embarrassing to admit at my age," she said as she tugged her hand away. "But it's love. I'm in love."

"With your bookstore owner," Jennifer said, as if it were obvious.

"Wait. How could you know that? I didn't even realize it until very recently."

"I've heard you talk about him over the years. It was obvious. I simply thought you were living out your own version of a Merchant Ivory film complete with repressed feelings, misguided regrets and a healthy dose of melancholy."

Josie huffed out a laugh. "That sounds rather awful."

"I might have lived in America for most of my life," Jennifer said, lifting her chin. "But I'm still British to the core. We appreciate unrequited love the same way we do a perfect cuppa."

Josie placed a hand to her chest to try to quell the rising tide of emotion there as she understood she'd loved Stuart for far longer than she'd realized.

"He told me he loves me, and I didn't say the words in return," she admitted in a hushed tone.

"Why?"

"I'm still afraid of being hurt."

"How does it feel to think of losing this man?"

"It hurts almost more than I can bear. He told me he doesn't want to date me. He wants more. Everything. And that he needs to know I want that, too."

"So you must tell him," Jennifer said as if it were that simple.

Josie sighed. "I've been on my own for a long time. Most of my life at this point. I'm at peace with who I am. I've stopped feeling like the passing years are a roll call of the things I've missed. I'm afraid of being hurt, but I'm also terrified of giving up my independence."

"My dear, loving the right man is about adding to your life. Adding the ability to give and receive love. Stuart is this man's name, yes?"

Josie nodded.

"He's a good person?"

"Yes."

"He cherishes and adores you?"

A sound somewhere between a sob and a laugh bubbled up in Josie's throat. "He cherishes and adores me. When you say it like that…"

"It's your responsibility to allow him to cherish and adore you. This does not negate your independence. You can be a strong woman with a protective, supportive partner."

"But you were never with a man in that way."

Jennifer's smile turned wistful. "True, but I like to think I would have welcomed love into my heart if given a chance. You have such a big heart, Josie. Open it. Otherwise, you are going to regret it and that's a difficult way to live."

Suddenly, the fears that had held Josie in thrall for so long seemed to loosen their grip. They didn't disappear entirely, but she knew she could overcome them and that Stuart was worth taking the risk.

He'd put his heart on the line for her and deserved the

same kind of devotion in return. As she glanced around the space that allowed her to live her best life, she had an idea of exactly how to show him what he meant to her.

# CHAPTER EIGHT

STUART STOOD IN the back of the studio, plastered against the wall like it would give him the strength he needed to face the woman he loved. Strength he'd need if she didn't love him back.

He had no doubt Josie cared for him like a friend. But he'd changed the game for both of them with his declaration. He didn't regret it because his feelings were too strong to settle.

He knew what it was like to lose. His daughter's death had gutted him, and there were months after she was gone when he cursed each new morning he woke up. There had been nights of drinking and raging and praying to die because the pain was unbearable.

And in his selfish grieving, he'd added to his ex-wife's pain. Anna hadn't deserved a husband who turned away when things got hard, but Stuart found it impossible to do anything else.

Coming to Magnolia to take over his family's bookstore had been a blessing, and Josie was a big part of his healing, even if she didn't realize it.

But it was time for more or moving on.

Josie entered the studio along with her first class, a group of wee bumblebees ready to buzz through their program. She looked radiant in a floral-patterned dress in shades of lilac and peach with a tiered ruffled skirt. The bodice hugged her figure and the subtle V at the neck gave a tantalizing glimpse of her creamy skin. The graceful design looked perfect for dancing, and for a moment Stuart wondered if Josie herself might perform.

The students nearly shimmered with excitement as Josie welcomed the audience and introduced Jennifer Plowman, their special guest for the day.

From where he stood, Stuart searched her face to find any traces of tension or nerves. Any hint as to what answer she might give him. But she was fully focused on the recital. The dancers moved through the program without incident. Parents applauded and oohed and aahed at their children as they performed. With each new group, Josie seemed to relax more, especially since it was clear that Jennifer was enjoying every moment.

Unlike Josie, Stuart became more agitated as the program went on. Josie was purposely not making eye contact with him. He'd been to every one of her recitals and she'd always made a point of sharing a smile or raising a brow in silent communication about something they would discuss later.

Today she actively ignored him, and he couldn't help but think this hollow feeling in his chest was a harbinger for the future, empty and aching as he watched the woman he loved go about her life with him only on the periphery of it.

They hadn't spoken, but her body language seemed to communicate volumes. So much so that he stepped toward the exit as the final class took its bow.

He couldn't pretend to be happy for her at the moment. Then she called his name and he froze.

He turned to find her staring directly at him, her eyes wide and a tremulous smile tugging up the corners of her mouth.

Was she going to break his heart in front of half the town? Stuart gave a small shake of his head, but she beckoned to him and he found himself moving toward her.

She faced the crowd as he came to her side. "This is indeed a special day," she said. "Not just for our dancers but for me, personally. I've been blessed to be a part of the Magnolia community for a long time now."

She glanced at Jennifer Plowman in the front row. "I'm thrilled to share our local talent with the dance teacher who meant so much to me, but she isn't the only one I want to share something with today. Most of you know Stuart Madison, who owns Off The Shelf bookstore."

"He does good monster voices at story time," one of the younger kids shouted from where the students sat under the barre on one side of the studio.

Stuart was having trouble concentrating as it seemed all eyes were trained on him. "Wonderful monster voices," Josie agreed. "He is kind and gentle and the best man I know. The kind of man any woman would be lucky to spend her life with."

She took his hand and squeezed. "The man I want to spend the rest of my life with."

To Stuart's utter shock, Josie dropped to one knee in front of him.

JOSIE'S HEAD FELT LIGHT, and she wondered if she might actually faint from the nerves swirling through her. Suddenly, her plan for making a public declaration of love seemed like a horrible one, reckless and risky to both her heart and her pride.

She could feel the weight of his gaze on her but glanced toward the audience instead of looking up at him. What if this was too much? What if she'd gone too far?

Jennifer gave her an encouraging nod, as if her former teacher could read the doubts scrawled across her mind. She saw many of her friends smiling as if delighted to be witnessing this moment. Carrie and her sister, Avery, were there along with Mary Ellen and the town's mayor, Malcolm Grimes.

But as much as Josie knew these people would support her unconditionally, they weren't the ones who mattered at the moment.

Hand shaking, she met Stuart's gentle gaze.

"You don't have to do this," he whispered, and all of her doubts fled. She wanted to do this. She needed him to know how much he meant to her. How much…

"I love you," she said in a clear voice that belied her worries. "With everything I am and all that I have. You've been my best friend for years, Stuart, but I want more. Everything. I'm not a young girl anymore." She laughed softly. "I know this for sure based on how much my knee is protesting at the moment."

"Josie, stand up." He tugged on her hand.

She shook her head. "Not yet. I want you forever. I want to be your forever. To build the rest of our lives together, little moments and big ones. All of it, Stuart. I'm all in. Please say you are, too. Please tell me you'll marry me."

"Yes," he said, and pulled her up and into his arms. "Leave it to you to do this in your own unique way, my darling. I love you for it. For the independent, beautiful-on-the-inside-and-out woman you are. I love you, Josie."

He pressed his mouth to hers, and it felt like coming home. Josie wrapped her arms around his neck and hugged him tightly before stepping back. Her students rushed forward to surround them, and she nodded toward Mayor Mal, who hit the button to begin the song she'd cued for this moment.

"Can't Help Falling In Love" began to play and she slipped her hand into Stuart's. "May I have this dance?" she asked as she kissed the corner of his mouth.

"Every dance," he answered, resting his forehead against hers. "Every moment belongs to you."

As they swayed to the music while her students danced around them, Josie felt happiness wash through her like a refreshing spring rain, and with it, the contentment of finding her true home.

* * * * *

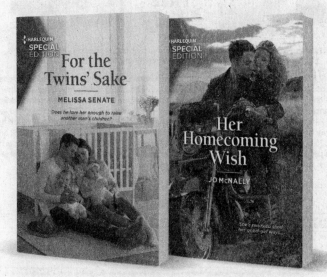

# Get 4 FREE REWARDS!

**We'll send you 2 FREE Books plus 2 FREE Mystery Gifts.**

FREE Value Over $20

Both the **Romance** and **Suspense** collections feature compelling novels written by many of today's bestselling authors.

**YES!** Please send me 2 FREE novels from the Essential Romance or Essential Suspense Collection and my 2 FREE gifts (gifts are worth about $10 retail). After receiving them, if I don't wish to receive any more books, I can return the shipping statement marked "cancel." If I don't cancel, I will receive 4 brand-new novels every month and be billed just $7.24 each in the U.S. or $7.49 each in Canada. That's a savings of up to 28% off the cover price. It's quite a bargain! Shipping and handling is just 50¢ per book in the U.S. and $1.25 per book in Canada.* I understand that accepting the 2 free books and gifts places me under no obligation to buy anything. I can always return a shipment and cancel at any time. The free books and gifts are mine to keep no matter what I decide.

Choose one: ☐ **Essential Romance**
(194/394 MDN GQ6M)

☐ **Essential Suspense**
(191/391 MDN GQ6M)

Name (please print)

Address                                                                                          Apt. #

City                                    State/Province                          Zip/Postal Code

**Email:** Please check this box ☐ if you would like to receive newsletters and promotional emails from Harlequin Enterprises ULC and its affiliates. You can unsubscribe anytime.

Mail to the **Harlequin Reader Service:**
**IN U.S.A.:** P.O. Box 1341, Buffalo, NY 14240-8531
**IN CANADA:** P.O. Box 603, Fort Erie, Ontario L2A 5X3

Want to try 2 free books from another series! Call 1-800-873-8635 or visit www.ReaderService.com.

*Terms and prices subject to change without notice. Prices do not include sales taxes, which will be charged (if applicable) based on your state or country of residence. Canadian residents will be charged applicable taxes. Offer not valid in Quebec. This offer is limited to one order per household. Books received may not be as shown. Not valid for current subscribers to the Essential Romance or Essential Suspense Collection. All orders subject to approval. Credit or debit balances in a customer's account(s) may be offset by any other outstanding balance owed by or to the customer. Please allow 4 to 6 weeks for delivery. Offer available while quantities last.

**Your Privacy**—Your information is being collected by Harlequin Enterprises ULC, operating as Harlequin Reader Service. For a complete summary of the information we collect, how we use this information and to whom it is disclosed, please visit our privacy notice located at corporate.harlequin.com/privacy-notice. From time to time we may also exchange your personal information with reputable third parties. If you wish to opt out of this sharing of your personal information, please visit readerservice.com/consumerschoice or call 1-800-873-8635. **Notice to California Residents**—Under California law, you have specific rights to control and access your data. For more information on these rights and how to exercise them, visit corporate.harlequin.com/california-privacy.

STRSMAX22